The Comfort of Strangers

"And just as Mother's four weeks in 1955 were four days to those waiting in Boston, my week in 1934 was one day to her. One very long day. Her face was etched with worry and relief and she looked as if she'd been waiting that whole week and I'd been far, far, away on a long and dangerous trip which ... I guess I was. All she said was *Welcome home*. We held each other in silence for a very long time."

Avra finished telling the story of the way things were and how the look of fear never left her mother's eyes.

"Grammy did say that my part in all of this is small." It was almost a question.

"Audrey asked only that I listen and make a record. I'll make my evaluation when we meet again, which will be when?"

"1996, after I return from 1955." Avra stood, but delayed her departure. "You still believe we latched onto a fairy tale and made up a whole story to go along with it." That wasn't a question.

"The very idea of Overlap being real is far-fetched at best. One simply cannot cause the outcome of events to change."

"Cause it! Is that why you think I'm here? To brag how I'll *cause* outcomes to change!"

Dr. Spector's silence spoke volumes.

"Grammy and I need a record of what is; because there's no way to *prevent* them from changing!" Avra was suddenly as certain as her grandmother that she would experience the second Overlap. "Time *will* take me," she insisted. "It *will* happen!"

Another moment of silence from Spector.

"What will it take to change your mind or at least open it up?"

"Proof." His tone was smug as he echoed her earlier word.

"What sort of proof?" Avra eyes narrowed.

"The kind you say you showed your Great-grandmother. Physical. Tangible."

Avra rested her eyes on the objects on Milton Spector's desk as she gave his request some thought then looked back up. He convinced himself that he imagined the quickest flash of light in her young eyes.

"You'll have your proof," Avra said

Praise for "The Comfort of Strangers" –the second novel in the Overlap Series and Debra Feldman's unique twist on time travel

"The Comfort of Strangers", with its dense and evocative language and its arcane and riveting insights, is a compelling book, full of power and insight. I recommend it entirely.
-- Robert B. Parker, author – Spenser and Jesse Stone Mysteries

Debra Feldman continues to challenge existing rules and devices regarding time travel in this daring new novel. Her very believable characters take amazing trips to the past, present and future, all of which makes for a fascinating read!
-- Jordan Rich, WBZ Talk Radio

Praise for "An Ordinary Hero"

Part sci-fi thriller, mystery, war saga and love story, "An Ordinary Hero" is an extraordinary novel that succeeds on many levels. Debra Feldman has weaved a fascinating story of time travel and the power of the human spirit in her debut novel that takes us from the 1930's to 2011 and back again with rich characters who never cease to surprise. Particularly engaging is her chronicling of the dedicated soldiers of Vietnam, five of whom play a pivotal role in the story.
-- Jordan Rich, WBZ Talk Radio

An Ordinary Hero is a well-crafted, cleverly plotted story [with] in-country scenes [that] work well in conveying the physical landscape of wartime Vietnam and [the] emotional landscapes of [Feldman's] characters.
-- The VVA Veteran, the Official Voice of Vietnam Veterans of America

Debra Feldman [sic] is an invigorated and talented writer, bringing a very different approach to science fiction.
-- Zebramag.com

Mysteries aren't my cup of tea -- but I loved this book! The way it mixed history and a gripping story just pulled me in from the beginning. Debra Feldman is a major talent and everyone should jump on the Overlap series bandwagon!
-- Anonymous (Barnes and Noble.com)

Looking for an historically-based novel that delved into the emotions felt by soldiers in Vietnam [sic] I found [something] much different, but I couldn't put it down. [Is it] a mystery; is it science fiction; or perhaps a mystical parable about the consequences of moral lapses? Don't worry about classifying this novel - just enjoy it.
-- Bill C.; Lexington, MA (Amazon.com)

The Comfort of Strangers

The Comfort of Strangers

Debra Feldman

To My Kat: I love you!
Debra Feldman
The one Kat I'm not allergic to!

The Comfort of Strangers

Copyright © 2002 by Debra Feldman

All rights reserved. No part of this book may be used or reproduced by any means, graphic, electronic, or mechanical, including photocopying, recording, taping or by any information storage retrieval system without the written permission of the publisher except in the case of brief quotations embodied in critical articles and reviews.

Studio Publishing books may be ordered through booksellers or by contacting:

Studio One Publishing
P.O. Box 2071
Salem, MA 01970
or
www.debrafeldman.com

ISBN: 978-0-9825778-0-6

Printed in the United States of America

This book is dedicated to my family and friends,
slivers of whose every-day lives line these pages
and brought the story to life.

And to Stephen Saltz and James Rabb,
this book never could have been possible without you.
Thanks.

Special acknowledgments to:
Lt. Richard J. Cashin – State Police, Boston Barracks
Trooper Stephen J. Walsh – Accident Reconstruction Section,
Massachusetts
State Police
Everett Plant
Trooper First Class Dennis Sullivan – Massachusetts State Police
Trooper First Class Gary Hodgdon – Motor Cycle Unit, Massachusetts
State Police
Trooper Geremiah Kelleher - Massachusetts State Police
Patrice and Mark – "Twisted" and "Untwisted"
Johanna Rothman
Mark Druy
Mr. Dave Frank - Local gun dealer, Salem, Massachusetts

Other books in the Overlap Series

An excerpt from:
The Book of Life – Dictionary of Time

Anti-Time (an•ti'•time), proper n. Any moment before a specific Reweaver's own time, or a time where it is possible for a Reweaver to overlap their own life.

Overlap (o•ver•lap'), proper n. Emotional Time travel. Naturally occurring phenomenon, long thought to be a myth or old wives tale, implemented by Time to correct outcomes of events. -- **See** UNLIVE, v.t. *1. to undo or annul (past life, etc.). 2. to live so as to undo the consequences of.*

Prior Memory (pri•or mem•or•y), proper n. Once Time and its Reweavers have cause outcomes to change, a memory from a previous outcome that no longer exists.

Red Tattoo (red tat•too), proper n. The pale red circular mark, placed by Time on the upper left arm (deltoid) of any Time-piece or other Reweaver.

Reweaver (re•weav'•er), proper n. Overlap missionary. Marked by Time with a pale red broken circle; also known as the Red Tattoo.

Second Memory (sec'•ond mem'•or•y), proper n. Though not personally experienced, a memory of a changed outcome.

Time-piece (time'•piece), proper n. First, or primary, Reweaver of any particular Overlap tale, transported to the very beginning. [**See also** REWEAVER, n.]

Unlive (un•live) v.t. 1. to undo or annul (past life, etc.). 2. to live so as to undo the consequences of.

Prologue

---------------------------- ▼ ----------------------------

Time's fragile fabric is an invisible weave of predetermined events, each written into *The Book of Life*, unable to be erased or altered. They literally construct the story of our lives. Where we will go. Who we will be. What we will become. Outcomes are left to make random twists and turns. Though Time always marches on, our choices are critiqued. For each outcome which sets any wrong wheels in motions, Time tears holes in the fabric which lead back to that outcome. Since Time immemorial, Time's only resolution was its travel process called Overlap; not the voluntary act it was long thought to be. Time conscripts travelers, Reweavers, leaving them stamped with a pale red broken circle known as "The Red Tattoo".

For each unsatisfactory outcome, there is born only one Reweaver; able to interfere without interfering, possessed of what is most closely identified as recurring dreams which come until it is time to travel. In that moment, the Reweaver's emotions slip into Anti-Time, a Time before the traveler's own, where the dreams are reality. Who are these Reweavers? Those with an unshakable sense of obligation to protect those around them and seek the truth though often times it is ugly. They bring the future into the past; preserving that which is meant to be and offer up answers to questions yet to be asked thereby interfering without actually interfering and *accidentally* correcting an outcome.

The conclusion of each Overlap story is just the beginning; an "opportunity" for all to be who they should have been in the first place. Overlap and the travelers are not the stuff of myth and legend. They are real. Reweavers live among us, tampering with the lives of people they never should have met; who they never should have loved, but do; because it is impossible to do otherwise. This is one such story of seemingly ordinary people performing extraordinary acts; because their emotions will allow nothing else; their hearts can accept nothing less.

Chapter 1

-------------------------------- ▼ --------------------------------

The Story
Miami 1994

And the pieces of paper; alone in the park, played leapfrog,
in place of the children who left the paper behind.

Avra reluctantly turned the doorknob and entered an outer office. The secretary gone for the day, she waited alone for the 3:00 appointment to which she had strenuously objected. Only her grandmother's persistence caused her to cave; grudgingly, and just when visiting Florida by herself was feeling like such fun. Avra knew the upcoming hour would be anything but. At exactly 3:00 PM Milton Spector emerged from the inner sanctum. He was not alone.

"Until next week." Spector said to his weary companion.

The man sheepishly acquiesced.

To Avra, the man looked as though he preferred to be almost anywhere else in the world. Sensing Avra as a kindred spirit; likewise preferring to be almost anywhere else in the world, he offered a feeble smile. Her poised nod of acknowledgment; which frankly was more interaction than she wanted, said she was not *kindred* at all.

Lucky kid, the young man thought, *not here for herself. What I wouldn't give to be in the same position.* He exited.

"I'm so glad you came," Spector said once the man was gone.

Avra thought Spector's tone a tad smug or superior or both. "Please," he swept a freshly manicured hand toward his inner office, "make yourself comfortable." He closed the door behind them.

Two leather chairs faced a mahogany desk. Avra chose the one closest to the window. Before Spector could take the chair on his own side of the desk, she spoke up. "Let's be perfectly clear from the start. I'm here only because Grammy insisted. I'll answer your questions, but that's pretty much it. This isn't an interrogation or a debate. Push me and I *will* leave."

Milton Spector was used to being the one in charge, the one issuing instructions; he was a respected psychiatrist with an alphabet soup of letters after his name. He did not take orders well. On the other hand, his old acquaintance, Audrey Spaulding, told an intriguing tale and asked for his help. For that, he needed details that only Avra could provide. He acquiesced and sat in the expensive chair behind the even more expensive desk. A recording device sat to his right, but he reached behind him withdrawing a yellow legal pad from a brief case.

Years earlier, a very young Milton Spector met Audrey when he was an Extern at the Biscayne Hospital Rehab and her mother was an in-patient. During the years since then, he occasionally ran into Audrey and her husband, Ted, at Hospital and other fund raising functions. Spector hadn't seen nor heard from either of them since mid-1966, that is, until ten days previous when Audrey claimed the urgent need for an appointment. Spector's 2:00 canceled. Audrey took their place.

Throughout their acquaintance, he never once considered Audrey might be a teller-of-tall-tales, but he didn't believe any of what she said. His attempts at tricking Avra into changing her rendition would fail miserably. The stories would match down to their smallest details.

Spector extracted a pen from the monogrammed holder in front of him and poised to write.

"Full name and age," he said.

"It's minutia, has nothing to do with anything," Avra protested.

"It's just for my records," Spector assured.

"Avra Jade August," her annoyance was clear. "I'm twelve."

Spector wrote the information and the date at the top of the pad. June 15, 1994.

"How many times do you believe you Overlapped?" Spector emphasized the word 'believe'.

"I Overlapped twice." Avra emphasized the word 'Overlapped'.

"Of course. To what locations and years did you go?" He pressed, as if Audrey hadn't already shared those bits of news.

"Michigan – 1934 and Miami – 1955."

"And when did you leave the present?" Spector asked.

"I traveled to Michigan on June 4 of this year."

"And Miami?" He prodded not understanding the hesitation.

"You'll just accept what I say?"

Spector silently agreed.

"May 17, 1996."

"That's nearly two years away!" He protested.

"I know perfectly well when it is," Avra's response was blasé.

"How can you know what will happen so far into the future?" Spector was bewildered.

"And know firsthand about the past," she added.

Spector shrugged.

"Because it is all meant to be and so it will be ... in the future as well as the 'future past' which already happened, but which hasn't happened yet," Avra said.

"And ... and you believe this mumbo-jumbo," Spector stammered. "Just like that?" He snapped his fingers.

"As a non-believer, for you it is mumbo-jumbo. That luxury is not extended to me ... and Grammy never lies. If she says it is so, then yes, I believe it. Just like that," Avra snapped her own fingers, "as I believe what is in *The Book of Matthew*."

"Which is?"

"*The last shall be first*," she quoted. "I don't need to have read those words myself to know that they are there."

"I see," Spector collected himself. "Do you have any recall of this second Overlap?"

"No, which is why Grammy insisted we speak now. Our intent is to document what 'is' so there will be some kind of record of what 'was' before certain outcomes are unlived. Altered. When next we meet only a few of us will remember both ways. Perhaps today's notes can somehow prove Overlap."

"It simply isn't possible to prove a myth." Spector was near exasperation.

"So you say now." Avra paused. "But suppose for a moment there was proof. Would you consider a conclusion that supports an answer other than myth? That perhaps Overlap is real."

"And if there is not? It is, after all, a pretty strong 'if'," Spector stated the obvious.

"Then you're off the hook with finding a way to go public and all you're out is an hour of your time."

Spector nodded. "Can you explain how Overlap works?"

"I saw the Time, and then Time took me there."

"Time *took* you?" Spector could hardly believe what he was hearing.

"Well, what did you expect happened? A giant hand came out of nowhere and snatched me? Of course Time took me."

"Of course," Spector's tone went sarcastic in an effort to conceal that he was in over his head.

"Listen here, Buddy. You asked to speak with me, not the other way around." Avra stood. "I may be a child, but I won't be patronized."

She was prepared to walk and Spector knew it.

"You're right and I'm sorry." Spector's apology rang as hollow as it actually was.

It irritated Avra no end; much as her *Buddy* reference had done to him. He suspected that her outburst of attitude and vocabulary belonged to someone older; maybe Audrey Spaulding, who handed off a well coached and well rehearsed story to her granddaughter. But with no appointments for the balance of the day he played along.

"How about we start over," Spector coaxed.

"Whatever." Avra sat, no happier to stay than to arrive.

"You speak of Time as if it were an entity," Spector continued.

"And what?" She answered his questioning look. "You think it isn't?

"So you see yourself as a time traveler."

"You make it sound so ... voluntary. If you're to help us, we need you to understand, not be a brick wall and make me endlessly repeat myself. I've Time's mark. The Red Tattoo." Avra exposed her left upper arm. "To be a Reweaver is not my choice. It's not anyone's choice. No one would choose this. We are conscripted! Time *takes* us!"

"Ah, yes." Spector pretended to reread the notes from his and Audrey's meeting. "To change past events."

"No one can do that," Avra corrected. "Events remain no matter what; travel or no travel."

"But to change them is what you want."

"Yeah, well, we don't always get what we want." Her words were little more than a whisper. "The best any of us can hope for is the slightest alteration in an outcome," Avra said.

In Spector giving Avra room to continue, her tone changed from self-assured to that of the very frightened child she really was.

"Considering the magnitude of the variables, much that we are counting on so heavily could simply *not* happen. What if Time doesn't take me again? Or worse, what if it does and I haven't managed to make the card for Gram to give to Grammy. It's the key linking the past to the present and exists intact, in all three Times, on just one day. Suppose I mess things up worse than they already are? I'm a child. Why can't Time just let me *be* a child? Grammy insists everything turns out as it should, keeps saying that it already happened, but if that's true why don't *I* remember the second time?"

Neither Avra nor Spector had the answer.

"Tell me what happened in 1934," he pressed.

"Far as I know? I told one person that another Reweaver would Overlap to insure the futures of others."

"Far as you know?"

"I'm one of several Reweavers and, in this life, everyone hasn't traveled yet. That means, until it's fully over, I know only what I did. Even so, I didn't operate in a vacuum. For those of the Time to which I traveled, I lived, I breathed, I interacted with them. No doubt, additional things whose outcomes are removed from my life happened simply because I was there."

"So, this person you told about the coming Reweaver, you warned them?" Spector was unclear.

"Not exactly. It was more like I," Avra groped for the proper word, "*prepared* her."

"And that was necessary?" Spector asked.

"It's what I did so it must have been. Perhaps she wouldn't have believed later if she hadn't seen proof before."

"What type of proof?"

"Physical. Tangible." Avra nervously fingered the thick gold necklace mostly hidden inside her shirt. Finally, she stood and extracted the three items hanging from it; her proof.

"This ring," Avra leaned toward Spector, "it belonged to my great-grandmother."

"It's an ordinary wedding band." He was less than impressed.

"Compared to the fancy-schmancy ones of today, but circa 1920 such a distinctive wedding band wasn't commonplace. Plus it's engraved, making it the only one of its kind in the world. Grand had it specially made of 18 karat gold, which is softer than 14 karat. Gram dropped it once and it dented." Avra turned the ring revealing its imperfection. "Being so identical to the one on her hand, Gram was persuaded to believe."

Dr. Spector reached across the desk. "These pieces of plastic," his fingers lightly touched them, "are they the card you mentioned?"

"Yes." Avra's answer gave nothing away.

"When does *that* figure in?"

"Later. Much later." She clutched the chain and its danglings and sat again.

"Why don't you start at the beginning," Spector suggested.

"Everything is a loop. Events and outcomes and Times all intertwined. My past. Their present. Makes it difficult to pin-point the beginning. We're only guessing at when the first tear formed."

"Well, do your best," Spector suggested, "and try not to leave out any details."

"In that case," Avra said, "maybe you'd better turn on your recorder."

"I came straight home from school feeling as if I had the flu; all feverish and kind of queasy with a whistling sound in my ears. I knew Mother was working with her dance company and, unless it was the ultimate 9-1-1, wouldn't want to be disturbed. My little fever seemed like no biggy, so I left a message with Aunt Lacey, took some Pepto, two aspirin, and crawled onto my bed shoes and all.

Lately I've been having kind of a recurring nightmare. I couldn't tell if I fell into the dream again or was having a fever induced hallucination. The whistle grew louder as I felt myself being pulled by my heart toward people and houses."

"What does that mean *pulled by your heart?*" Spector asked.

"As though something wrapped around it; squeezed it, to separate me from my emotions and took them to the place Time needed them."

"... to the place Time needed them." Spector repeated her words aloud as he wrote. "Needed them for what?" He looked up expectantly.

"To close the holes in Time."

*　　*　　*　　*

The whistle abruptly stopped and Avra was wandering a suburban tree lined street. It was a beautiful sunny day; the kind you get only in the mid-west in early June. A soft, gentle breeze greeted her and the sky was filled with light puffy clouds. In a park on the left, two groups of boys were having a noisy game of softball and a lone girl was sitting on a swing staring forlornly at the ground. Avra passed a street sign. 'Snowden'. It was a familiar name she couldn't quite place. The neighborhood, also familiar, was somehow different – brighter; cleaner; *something*. Avra's emotions transported quicker than her memory then there was a sudden flood of them together with family stories. They assured her that what she was experiencing was neither hallucination nor dream. It was very real.

Avra approached the girl unheard. "Okay if I swing with you?"

The girl looked up surprised, but delighted to have someone her own age with whom to share some fun. "Sure!" She said. "I was feeling kinda sorry for myself. The boys won't let me play." She looked at Avra curiously. "You from around here?"

"Not exactly," Avra said.

"I'm Audrey." She smiled.

"Aja," Avra introduced herself using the abbreviation her parents made from her initials. A.J.A.

The girls spent hours on the swings. They swung high, pretending to fly to the moon. They spun them, causing the chains to grow shorter and shorter until the metal links formed awkward knots and their toes only just reached the ground. Lifting their feet, the swings unspun and the girls pretended to be famous explorers being lowered into caves. They laughed in dizzy delight.

"Is there a bathroom?" Aja asked catching her breath. "I really gotta go."

"Not in the park, but I live nearby." Audrey checked the position of the sun. "And we could eat. It's lunch time."

Overlap still mostly a concept, Aja wondered *How can it be anywhere near noon when I spent a full day at school?* For the moment she didn't dwell; she needed to pee. "Sure, let's go."

They skipped the few blocks to the corner of Snowden and St. Lawrence where Audrey stopped. "This is my house," she said.

Not knowing the history of TV, the absence of antennas caused Aja to conclude everyone had cable. The girls entered thru a side door and went up three steps to the kitchen where a tallish woman with wavy auburn hair, exactly like Aja's, was in an apron washing a sink full of fruits and vegetables. But she wasn't exactly *at the sink.* An old-fashioned radio on a shelf above an old-fashioned stove was playing swing music and the woman sung and danced around the kitchen as if she were a professional entertainer. The woman caught a glimpse of the girls just as one song ended and another began. It was the instrumental to a song Aja recognized.

"Quick!" The woman said handing each girl a carrot. "Be my back-up singers."

"Come on," Audrey encouraged wagging her carrot. "Microphones. It's fun!"

The woman's melodious voice was already in the air as Audrey and Aja took places behind her. When the woman's performance was over, she collapsed into a chair out of breath.

"We should be on the stage," she said.

"And there's one leaving in 5 minutes," Audrey and the woman finished as a unit.

"You're my kid, all right!" The woman laughed then looked at Aja. "And who do we have here?"

"I brought a friend home for lunch," Audrey announced as if it didn't happen often. "This is Aja."

"I'm Audrey's mother, Mrs. Baum. Pleased to meet you."

"I'm glad to meet you as well," Aja said.

The woman's smile was warm as she extended her hand which Aja took. Each felt an unsettling jolt they both ignored.

"Any friend of Audrey's can be a back-up singer of mine. Plus you've got good pipes." Mrs. Baum paused. "Aja? That's unusual and pretty."

"Thanks," Aja said scoping the kitchen.

A large white porcelain sink and an old-fashioned refrigerator were on the opposite side of the room from the radio and the stove. *How inconvenient* she thought until she realized it was an actual ice box with actual ice. Grammy's stories of people having blocks of ice delivered to their homes to keep food cold were true. The thing was like a big camping cooler on legs. Heat from a lighted stove would have made the ice melt even quicker so stoves and ice boxes were always across the room from each other.

It was hard to believe, but everyone and everything was exactly where they belonged – right down to the kitchen's green linoleum and the park, complete with swings and baseball field. In that moment Avra knew she really was standing in Gram's kitchen and the girl to her right really was her own Grandmother. She laughed to herself. *These houses don't have cable TV. They don't have any TV. It's 1934 -- pre TV.* It was then Avra realized *she* was the one who spawned their family's Overlap legend and told Gram everything which was to come.

"I still really need that bathroom," she said to Audrey.

"Show your guest where it is, sweetheart, wash your hands then come help with lunch." Turning to the sink the woman spoke over her shoulder to Aja. "Don't forget to wash your hands too, dear."

Audrey rolled her eyes.

In Gram's own Time people called her the equivalent of a germ-a-phobe. In Aja's Time, Gram's rule was not only common practice but common sense and second nature. *The first thing you do when you come in the house or finish in the bathroom is wash your hands.* No wonder Grammy always said that Gram was ahead of her Time. Audrey escorted Aja back down the small set of stairs. There on the left and just before the bathroom door was a small door in the wall. It was the laundry chute of which Grammy so often spoke – just where Aja knew it would be.

She returned to the kitchen to find Audrey and Sylvia Baum seated at a well set table. In front of each place was a glass of milk and a turkey sandwich cut into triangles. Atop each triangle sat a piece of carrot that had been carved into a flower and the cloth napkins were folded into the shape of roses. Avra immediately thought of Grammy and her own mother making even ordinary meals seem special by making the presentation as important as the food. Aja recognized the dishes as well. Pink glass. Depression glass. Grammy still had a few pieces that survived the generations.

The trio talked mostly about school, favorite subjects and what the girls planned to be when they grew up. *Lucky I don't want to be an astronaut. Go ahead,* she teased herself. *Explain how astronauts walk on the moon to people who haven't seen a TV yet.* Aja was equally grateful Audrey and Gram didn't ask many questions about her family or where they lived. What would she say – that they didn't live anywhere because they weren't born yet.

Aja and Audrey spent the rest of the day at the park; because Aja convinced the boys to let them play softball. Someone hit the ball way out of the field for a home-run. It landed under a tree the girls were climbing. Aja jumped down to pick it up

"Toss it over!" A boy yelled.

"Only if you let us play!" Aja yelled back.

"We don't play with girls!" Came a chorus.

"Then I guess you don't want your ball," Aja said.

"Girls can't throw and they can't run," the first boy said.

"Then how is it you expect me to throw this to you?" Aja asked.

Meanwhile of waiting for a response, Audrey had climbed down and was standing next to her.

"You do still want to play?" Aja whispered the question.

"Well, sure, but they'll never let us," Audrey whispered in return.

"Ye of little faith." Aja smiled. "They will after they get their first lesson in *gentle persuasion*. My grandmother taught me. Aja winked conspiratorially.

Audrey noted a flash of light in Aja's eyes, but decided it was her imagination.

"Grammy says: *If you need someone to do what you want, offer them something they want then make it clear that the only way to seal the deal is to do what you want.* Run toward the swings," Aja instructed. "When I yell *heads up*, stop, turn around, and catch the ball. Don't worry," she answered Audrey's unasked question. "I'll make sure you get it."

"Will this work?" Audrey looked doubtful.

"I think the boy behind the back-stop is already on our side. He's been watching you all day."

"I didn't even notice him," Audrey admitted.

"Well he noticed you ... and he sure is cute," Aja said.

Aja was correct. The boy behind the back-stop was staring at Audrey and he was cute. Very cute. She smiled nervously. He smiled back.

"Gees, you're right," Audrey said amazed.

"They don't want us to play because they're afraid we'll louse up their game. We're going to prove that we won't. So ... you run as fast as you can. I'll throw as hard as I can. Then you catch this." Aja indicated the ball.

"And then?" Audrey asked.

"Then ..." Aja did a standing still version of Snoopy's *happy dance,* "we play softball."

Big nerves made the sound of blood pulse hard in Audrey's ears. She barely heard Aja when she yelled, but she did hear; she did stop; she did turn around and the ball landed right in her hands.

"Let us play?" Aja yelled the question.

"Anyone got another ball?" The first boy asked his friends.

No one did.

"Now what?" Another boy asked.

"Aw, let 'em play," the boy behind the backstop spoke up. "How bad can they be? One can throw the other can run and we can't exactly play without a ball." A few moments later the boys were in agreement.

"We'll take the catcher," the boy from behind the backstop quickly placed first dibs on Audrey.

The first boy accepted Aja for his team.

"We could use a good arm," he said, "even if you are a southpaw."

Backstop boy stepped forward and made introductions. "My parents insist on calling me Theodore, but I prefer Ted. That wise-guy over there is my cousin Billy," Ted indicated the boy who first yelled to Aja, "and this tag-along," he rested a hand on the head of a small boy who was almost his shadow, "is my brother, Mortimer. We're visiting Billy from Boston for the summer."

"Your parents named this cute little guy Mortimer?"

"Heck, no! I did," Ted said with pride. "Our parents named him Harry, but I think he looks more like a Mortimer."

"Hi." The younger boy raised his hand in a shy wave then elbowed Ted with a stage whisper. "Sonny, she thinks I'm cute."

"He certainly acts like a Mortimer." Ted covered his eyes with his hand, shaking his head in embarrassment.

The remaining introductions were made and the rest of the afternoon was spent in a raucous game of ball with both girl scoring runs for their team. When it neared dinner time, and everyone was preparing to leave, Evan Baum arrived to walk Audrey home. As he approached the ball field, he overheard Ted ask Audrey to return the next day.

"I'm afraid not, sweetheart," Evan answered for her. "Mother will be in rehearsal and I need to be at the bakery all afternoon to build a special wedding cake. I won't be able to come get you and I'd rather you didn't walk home alone."

"I'll walk her home, sir," Ted volunteered, "if that's okay?"

"It's very kind, young man, but, you see, I don't know you."

"Ted's okay, sir," Billy came to Ted's defense giving the thumbs-up. "A real straight arrow. Very responsible. His folks even trust him to watch the squirt." He jerked a thumb in the direction of his younger cousin. "If it carries any sway we'll all make sure she gets home. Won't we guys?"

"You bet," said one boy. "She's great for the team. She's a great catcher and, man, can she run."

"Please, Dad." Audrey looked at her father with adoring eyes.

"Seems you have quite the fan club." He smoothed his daughter's hair away from her dirt smudged face and reluctantly gave in. "I suppose it will be all right, but clear it with your mother." Evan looked at Ted. "Mrs. Baum has the last word on such matters," then added man-to-man, "you do understand."

"Of course, sir." Ted wiped his dirty hand on his t-shirt and extended it. "Put in a good word for me?"

"I will." Evan shook Ted's hand then Ted gathered their belongings, took his little brother by the hand and left the park.

"Mother said you made a new friend, but she didn't say it was a young man," Evan pressed Audrey for information.

"Dad!" She blushed. "Mom meant the girl tossing the ball with Billy, but--," she paused. "I don't think she's from our neighborhood. I think she ran away."

"Did she say that?" Evan asked concerned.

"Well, no. It's more what she didn't say. She hardly said a word about her mother or father or anyone and she acted kind of funny when mother and I asked about family and stuff. I've never seen her at school and no one came for her at noon or now. I don't think she has anywhere to go. And there's something else."

"Which is?" Evan pressed.

"She's the most beautiful girl I ever saw, but if you look at her long enough, even when she smiles or laughs, she looks kind of frightened and sad. Maybe there's trouble in her family."

"Do you think she'd want to come to dinner and spend the night?"

"Could she? Oh, Dad! You're the best!" Audrey hugged her father. "You know," Audrey continued, "she's the one that got the boys to let me ... I mean ... *let us* play ball. When I asked they just said *No*. She knew just how to get them to say yes. She's very smart."

"She chose you for a friend, didn't she?" Evan smiled.

Audrey beamed at the compliment and yelled over to her new friend. "Aja! Want to come for dinner?"

Evan and Audrey watched as Aja gave the ball a final toss then run over.

"Aja!" Billy yelled as he turned to leave the park. "Tomorrow?"

"We'll see," she called back.

Innocent enough words but, put together with Audrey's observation, Evan thought they sounded remarkably like an evasive answer. The threesome walked back to the house laughing and talking baseball. Evan silently agreed with Audrey. The girl had a special beauty. She tried to project a child's casual air with only marginal success. Her maturity didn't suit her, nor did it hide the fact she seemed frightened of her own shadow.

Evan updated Sylvia and asked that she speak with Aja to determine what was what. After dinner he conveniently excused himself to go over the bakery's books and Audrey disappeared to make up the spare bed in her room. Aja helped Sylvia with the dishes.

"Dinner was delicious. Thanks for inviting me," she said.

"We couldn't very well leave you in the park, now, could we?" Sylvia minced no words.

"Whatever do you mean?" Aja asked warily.

"We know that you ran away and had nowhere to eat or sleep."

"I did not!" Aja answered only part of Sylvia's accusation, but silently admitted that the rest was true. Where would she have eaten or slept if Audrey hadn't invited her.

"You needn't keep pretending." Sylvia knelt down to be eye-to-eye. "You can stay with us until you're ready to go home to your family."

"Mrs. Baum," Aja hesitated, but knew she didn't have Time to avoid an explanation, "I am with my family ... sort of. You and Mr.

Baum and Audrey ... you are my family. My mother is Audrey's daughter," Aja blurted. "Her name is Kendall. Kendall Layne Spaulding. Audrey named her for your brother, Kenneth, the one who died. And the boy she met in the park today, his name is Ted Spaulding. He's my Grandfather."

Sylvia thought of Ken and how she lost him in the Great War on some damn hill in France.

"I don't know how you know about my brother, but this is foolishness."

"It's not!" Aja defended then remembered her good luck charms received a few months earlier. "I have proof." Aja quickly removed the gold chain from around her neck and handed it to Sylvia. "That's *your* wedding band. You gave it to Grammy. I mean, Audrey, to give to me on my twelfth birthday. It was in a small box in a sealed envelope with a note to me from you. It read *Wear this, always. Xs and Os, Gram.* I wear everything on the chain because your ring doesn't fit me yet. You died before I was born, but you wanted *me* to have your ring. Not Grammy. Not mother. *Me.* You wanted to be sure I had proof that would make you believe me."

"I'm wearing my wedding band," Sylvia protested.

"I swear the one on the chain is yours. It even has the dent from when it landed on the cellar floor." Aja touched the imperfection.

"That happened only this morning." Sylvia checked Aja's ring. It looked identical in every way to the one on her left hand. "But Evan had my ring--"

"Specially made by the jeweler downtown on Woodward and engraved," Aja finished Sylvia's sentence. "Look inside," she prodded.

Amazed, Sylvia saw the two-word inscription in the ring on her hand. *Forever Evan.*

"In fact," Aja added, "I thought I knew everything about this family, except maybe that mine was the first Overlap not the last one."

"What do you mean *first*?"

"Uncle Terry Overlapped when he was little and years from now, when you're in the hospital having your hip replaced, my mother will come, only she'll be all grown up."

"There's nothing wrong with my hip," Sylvia tested.

"Except when it rains," Aja smiled knowing she passed with flying colors. "Dr. Cobb said it's becoming arthritic."

"My good god! How did you know about Dr. Cobb?"

"Because I am who I say. There's so much to tell you and I don't know how much Time we have. Do you believe me? Please believe me! You have to believe me!" Aja's eyes grew huge and pleading and welled with tears.

Sylvia searched Aja's face for even a trace of a lie. There was none.

"Yes," Sylvia admitted without wanting to. "I believe you."

Aja hugged Sylvia tightly and cried just a little with relief. Gram believed her and now everything would be all right.

"I was so afraid you'd send me away," Aja said.

"You can stay with us 'til we figure out all of this. We'll talk more later."

Audrey was in time only to witness the hug and hear their last exchange. She thought to herself *I knew she was a run-away.*

*   *   *   *

The next day and the next and every day for the rest of the week, Audrey and Aja played softball in the park. By mid-week, Billy stopped asking whether Aja would return by using his one word question of "Tomorrow". She had taught him a new word; *Mañana*.

The next night and the next and every night for the rest of the week, Aja and Sylvia talked in private until very late. Aja told of the people and events to come – the boy from the park who would become Audrey's husband; his little brother, Great-uncle Harry, who would save the Circus; the famous dancers her mother would accidentally teach; how Grampy would be shot; and the pieces of plastic that hung from her gold chain. Aja finished her story on the seventh night.

"My father breaks the card," she said, "and Mother comes home."

"You and your mother travel through Time. How do you do that?" Sylvia asked.

"We don't do it; Time makes it happen. I'll return home easily; because I'm ready, but Mother," Avra shook her head, "she won't want to leave. And Time won't be able to force her without your help."

"What can I do that an entity like Time cannot?"

"Time is strong, but love is stronger. Mother's love for you can keep her in the past, even after her mission is complete. Your love is the only thing stronger than Mother's, so only you can force her to leave. When you see a sort of light in her eyes you *must* push her ... just as hard as you can. Mother will pass into the holes in Time and they'll close behind her."

"What kind of light will it be?" Sylvia asked.

"Just a flash really. Kind of over before it happens, if you know what I mean," Aja said.

"Will I see that same light in your eyes?"

"I don't think so. It's seen only by people for whom the presence of a Reweaver changes the outcome of their life and only in the exact moment of change. I showed you the ring and card, but that doesn't exactly change your life." Aja thought for a moment. "That first day in the park, the boys wouldn't let Audrey play ball until I showed her how to *make* them let her. Maybe that was the very beginning where everything got started; Grammy ... I mean Audrey, meeting Grampy in the first place. You could ask if Audrey saw the flash," Aja suggested. "If she did, then you'll know the rest will happen. You see, I'm not a regular Reweaver," Aja admitted. "I'm a Time-piece, what's called *the beginning at the end*."

"A time-piece? Do you mean like a watch?" Sylvia asked.

"A watch, as a time piece, marks the passage of Time," Aja said. "A Reweaver, as a Time-piece, is literally marked by Time. See." She revealed her birth mark. "The circle will close and the 'T' will disappear after my second Overlap ... assuming I am successful."

"My grandchild, is she a Time-piece as well?"

"Each story has only one. For this story, I'm it. Mother's mark is just the broken circle."

"And she'll change the outcome of my life?

Aja nodded.

"Can you tell me in what way?"

"Only if you ask specifically," Aja advised.

"I'm already not liking this game," Sylvia said in all seriousness.

"It's no game," Aja said seriously. "Games have instructions and rules. This is the only rule I know and whatever instruction book there ever was, someone before me lost it."

Sylvia nodded. "In what specific way will your mother change the outcome of my life?"

"Grammy says that she was always closer to Grand than to you, but, after Mother Overlaps you and she are closer than Siamese Twins and Mother becomes afraid of you, even though she loves you."

"My grandchild ... afraid of me!"

Aja left Sylvia's look of shock unanswered.

"Fine. Why is she afraid?"

"I think it was something you said. Anyway, it's very important that you know how much Mother loves you. It will be difficult not hearing her say it, but tell her as often as you can that you know what's in her heart. Maybe she won't feel so guilty about not being able to tell you herself and maybe that will help her complete her own Overlap and come home, so I can be born, and come here, and meet you and Grand. By design, we ought to be blood strangers, but because of Overlap we're true blood."

"We have quite the family." Sylvia shook her head in amazement.

"They're wonderful!" Aja's eyes sparkled with pride then she hugged Sylvia. "You're wonderful!"

"Aja," Sylvia paused. "This card your father breaks, where does he get it?"

"Audrey gave it to him when she visited Boston in January of 1982."

"And where does Audrey get it?"

"Indirectly from you, after your hip surgery in 1955. You leave it with an attorney in Miami with instructions to deliver it to Grammy on January first, 1982. Smith is very young and never heard of Overlap, so he believes you're part of a prank and refuses to take your money. He plays along by delivering your manila envelope himself just to see what happens. Grammy opens it and somehow knows exactly what it is and that the contents are for me. Grammy tried to pay Smith too, but he refused. Said something like, *Explaining the fee to my accountant would only add to the weirdness.*" Aja chuckled.

Sylvia put the halves of the card together to examine them. "I wouldn't begin to know how to make this. Even Elite typeface is larger than these letters and I've never seen this material." Sylvia tapped it.

"The card is made of a brittle plastic called PVC; poly-vinyl-chloride, and the lettering was produced on a computer," Aja clarified.

"Poly-vinyl-chloride? Computer? I didn't make this." Sylvia looked to Aja.

She shook her head.

"Where do I get it?"

"Grammy says I'll give it to you the second time we see each other. Beyond my visit here and talking to you, my job is to make the card or find someone who can. Just look for me at the Rehab after your surgery. Grammy says I'll be there."

"And you believe this?"

"Grammy never lies," Aja said. "I'll be there."

Aja and Sylvia continued playing *Twenty Questions* until every detail of the story had been passed between them. The unsettling whistle and queasy feeling returned on the seventh night. Upon examination of Aja's arm, though the 'T' remained and the break in the circle was not closed it was definitely smaller. She and Sylvia decided it was a sign Aja would return to her own Time, likely the same way she arrived – without ceremony. Sylvia turned off the lamp in the den and they climbed the stairs. At the door to Audrey's room, Sylvia and Aja said their good-byes.

"I won't wake Audrey. There's a big game tomorrow and she needs her sleep. Besides, she and I will see each other again." They both chuckled. "Say thanks and good-bye for me?"

Sylvia assured Aja that she would.

"There's one more thing," she paused. "Aja isn't my name. It's my initials. My true name is Avra. Avra Jade. Mother named me for Grammy. But don't tell. It should be a surprise." Aja opened the door to Audrey's room then looked back at Sylvia. "Remember me?"

"I'll never forget you." Sylvia's look brimmed with pride.

"Me too, you. Not ever." Aja closed the door.

Audrey awoke the next day and the clock on her night table read 6:00 A.M. The spare bed in her room was made. She put on a robe and slippers and went to her parents' room. Their bed was made as well. Evan left for the bakery hours earlier and Sylvia was downstairs preparing breakfast. Audrey wandered into the kitchen and sleepily hugged her mother. "Morning. Where's Aja?"

"She went home," Sylvia said.

"But there's a game today and ... and she didn't even say goodbye." Audrey was visibly agitated.

"Aja asked me to thank you and say good-bye for her. She didn't think it was necessary to wake you last night."

"Not necessary! The boys will never let me play without her." Audrey pouted turning her back on her mother and stomped her foot.

"Audrey Joan, that sounds quite selfish. Aja belongs with the people who love her."

"But," Audrey spun back to Sylvia, "we love her. Don't we?"

"We love her enough to know that she belongs in her own home with her own mother and father." Sylvia brought a fresh linen handkerchief from her apron pocket to wipe away Audrey's tears. "You'll see her again." She took Audrey by the shoulders and smiled. "Just in case these tears are about something more than Aja not saying *goodbye,* Ted stopped by earlier to be sure you were coming to the park. He never even asked about Aja."

"Really?" Audrey brightened.

"Really. Now, how about some of my famous pancakes? You'll need a good breakfast. I hear there's an important game." Sylvia winked.

"Can I help?" Audrey asked.

"Don't you always help?" Sylvia asked.

As Aja's emotions returned to her, she vaguely heard Audrey and Sylvia's conversation and saw Audrey smile. The hold on her heart relaxed and she was back in her own bed, in her own time with the unsettling whistle gone. A hole in Time had closed.

*   *   *   *

"I woke up in Mother's arms. Apparently she walked into Aunt Lacey's office almost immediately after she and I hung up. When Aunt Lacey said I didn't feel well, mother canceled rehearsal, flew out the door and drove from Porter Square to our home in Arlington at warp speed. Turns out she'd been expecting my fever and knew it for what it was; the prelude to an Overlap. I thought I was alone, but Mother was with me every second. Time never forgets its Reweavers and apparently waited for her to get to me before I traveled." Aja shook her head. "No one should suffer an Overlap alone."

"And just as Mother's four weeks in 1955 were four days to those waiting in Boston, my week in 1934 was one day to her. One very long day. Her face was etched with worry and relief and she looked as if she'd been waiting that whole week and I'd been far, far, away on a long and dangerous trip which ... I guess I was. All she said was *Welcome home*. We held each other in silence for a very long time."

Avra finished telling the story of the way things were and how the look of fear never left her mother's eyes.

"Grammy did say that my part in all of this is small." It was almost a question.

"Audrey asked only that I listen and make a record. I'll make my evaluation when we meet again, which will be when?"

"1996, after I return from 1955." Avra stood, but delayed her departure. "You still believe we latched onto a fairy tale and made up a whole story to go along with it." That wasn't a question.

"The very idea of Overlap being real is far-fetched at best. One simply cannot cause the outcome of events to change."

"Cause it! Is that why you think I'm here? To brag how I'll *cause* outcomes to change!"

Dr. Spector's silence spoke volumes.

"Grammy and I need a record of what is; because there's no way to *prevent* them from changing!" Avra was suddenly as certain as her grandmother that she would experience the second Overlap. "Time *will* take me," she insisted. "It *will* happen!"

Another moment of silence from Spector.

"What will it take to change your mind or at least open it up?"

"Proof." His tone was smug as he echoed her earlier word.

"What sort of proof?" Avra eyes narrowed.

"The kind you say you showed your Great-grandmother. Physical. Tangible."

Avra rested her eyes on the objects on Milton Spector's desk as she gave his request some thought then looked back up. He convinced himself that he imagined the quickest flash of light in her young eyes.

"You'll have your proof," Avra said

Chapter 2

-------------------------------- ▼ --------------------------------

In the Beginning
Beantown – 1920-1950

Jack August and medicine were like a hand in a glove; a doctor's size
11 rubber glove. He never wanted to be anything besides a doctor.
And as a doctor, he led a rewarding life filled with hard work,
accomplishments and honors. He also had the love of a good woman;
Dorothy Ginsberg.

Adam August was Jack's younger brother by four years. He was a
playboy, ran with a fast crowd and had an equally fast girlfriend
named Sarah Cohen. He didn't love her but she knew how to have a
good time and how to please him in bed. He got her pregnant their
sophomore year of college. Adam arranged for an abortion by a third
year medical student but Sarah was in love, or so she told herself, and
believed that with Time and the birth of their child Adam would
realize how much he loved her. They married early in the spring of
that year and with Time Adam grew only to resent Sarah, their
daughter Susan and his life with them.

His father, Gerald, assured Adam that even married his tuition
would continue to be paid so long as he maintained a decent average.
Failing that, his tuition was terminated at the end of the school year.
He was no longer a playboy living the care free life of a student; going
where he wished, when he wished. He was married with a pregnant
wife and no longer traveled light. He had baggage and it weighed him
down. Gerald requested a meeting about the future. Adam went like a
child pleading not to be grounded.

"What will I do if I can't go to school?"

"You'll get a job," Gerald said.

"What about my degree?" Adam whined.

"You aren't seriously expecting a degree. You don't attend class."

"I go!" Adam lied.

"Adam, please! Take responsibility! Showing up once in a while is not the same as learning the material and passing tests. Perhaps you don't belong in school. You were never such a wonderful student."

"You mean like Jack, the book worm!"

"Do not put words in my mouth. I have never compared you to your brother. Jack was blessed with scholastic ability, but you have people skills which are every bit as valuable."

"They never did me any good," Adam complained.

"They earned you a beautiful wife who will soon give you the greatest blessing of all, a child."

Adam hadn't shared his thoughts on the subject of children; *Better seen and heard in someone else's house.* His child was ending the college career he expected to last for many years. His child was forcing him to go to work. His child was a curse and it was just Adam's kind of luck to be presented with this curse precisely when Jack was doing so remarkably well in Medical School.

Jack was smart, made pleasant conversation; even with people he didn't especially like … and he had Dorothy. Adam was convinced those facts turned him into 'The Invisible Man' when Jack was around.

The brothers met Dorothy the summer Jack earned his undergraduate and Adam graduated High School. All of them were boating on the Charles. Dorothy's sail caught too much air causing her boat to pitch sideways. The sail landed in the water. Adam dove into the murky, stinky Charles, righted Dorothy's boat and pulled her back aboard, leaving Jack to sail his and Adam's boat to shore. Adam safely returned Dorothy to the Boat House certain she would be appropriately grateful and reward him in the *'appropriate'* manner. Even before reaching dry land, however, Dorothy was shivering and her nail beds were blue. Adam immediately lost his patience. Jack, on the other hand, found towels, hot coffee and something dry for her to wear.

Adam was the more handsome brother, but he was shallow and cruel; a fact which did not escape Dorothy. For her part, Jack's kindness and concern made him the more attractive brother. From that day forward, Dorothy and Jack were an item. Adam saw it as yet another instance his big brother one-upped him.

Admittedly, Jack's interest in Dorothy was real and Adam's merely fleeting, but she had everything he wanted – a beautiful face, a body that wouldn't quit and a rich father. Adam became obsessed, almost desperate, to get Dorothy out of Jack's life and into his. That was before Sarah was stupid enough to get pregnant. The reality that he'd never have Dorothy, not even temporarily, was a bitter pill. Adam vowed that someday he'd *'get'* Jack and show everyone. Until that day he'd make Jack's life as miserable as possible. To his mind Jack was doing the same to him, it was only fair.

Adam drifted from one dead end job to another, never liking his work, never liking his life. One evening, Gerald invited Adam, Sarah and his only grandchild, to dinner at his favorite upscale restaurant. Adam and Sarah argued bitterly over going. *He terminated my education,* Adam said. *There aren't many opportunities for us to have meals in nice restaurants. We're going!* Sarah insisted. Guess who won that round.

"My friend, Mort Spear, is opening a second real estate office in Newton," Gerald began awkwardly.

"How nice for Mort that he's so successful," Adam's voice dripped sarcasm.

"He's looking to hire five agents for that office," Gerald continued seemingly unphased. "I asked if he'd grant you an interview."

"I can get my own job!" Adam snapped.

"I didn't get you the job. I secured only the interview."

"What did you say to make Mort think I could sell real estate? I have no experience."

"I told him what I keep trying to tell you; you have good people skills. Use them wisely and you could be great at it ... once you get your license."

"A license means classes and tests. Not interested!"

"Would you be interested if I pay for the classes?" Gerald asked.

"Now you're willing to pay for more school?"

"Not more school. This school. Real estate school," Gerald said.

"Oh, I see. I have to be what you want or I'm on my own," Adam protested.

"That isn't exactly fair, Adam. You were floundering in college and had no idea which direction to aim your life. You have no more idea today than you did two years ago. This is a terrific opportunity. You'd be there in the beginning to help shape the business. For you, college was not only a waste of time but money."

"Yeah, well, it was my time."

"Yes," Gerald agreed gently. "But it was my money. It may be made of paper but it doesn't grow on trees. You didn't seriously think I would indefinitely finance you as a professional student."

"Why not? Jack's been at it seven years and he's nowhere near done."

"Adam, please don't twist things. Jack is earning a degree. He pays half of his tuition, attends class and passes his exams. But this dinner and conversation are not about Jack. They're about you and what, if anything, you're going to do with your life."

"Swell. So are you saying you have a higher opinion of me now than you did two years ago?"

"I was hoping you had a higher opinion of you now than you did two years ago. I was hoping you matured to the point of seeing your responsibilities to your wife and daughter. I thought a good word from the old man might get you an interview instead of someone else's son. I thought you might be glad for the opportunity. If I was wrong just say so. We won't say another word about it."

Sarah, who had been sitting quietly at Adam's side, piped up. "It's so great of you to help Adam this way, Dad."

Adam glared at her, but she ignored him and smiled sweetly for Gerald.

"It's a very generous offer, but it's so much to digest all at once and such a big decision. Adam would need to give notice and possibly train his replacement. May we take this evening to discuss it and let you know in the morning?" Sarah asked.

"Of course! Of course!" Gerald's tone sounded much less parental. "I didn't mean to imply that I needed an answer right this minute. Let's just enjoy the rest of our dinner." Gerald turned to Susan, the proverbial apple of his eye. "So, what marvelous things has my beautiful granddaughter been doing ..."

For Adam, the rest of the conversation melted into white noise that drifted into the background. Sarah had bought him time to consider the job and school. More school. No matter how much Adam blustered, his father was correct; he was a poor student and could not face Gerald or himself with another failure.

The next day Adam had Sarah call on the pretense of saying *Thanks* for dinner. Sarah gushed adequately and stroked Gerald's ego by emphasizing the importance to Susan of seeing her grandfather.

"Adam's standing right here," she said, "and I know you men have a lot to discuss."

"Dad!" Adam was a bit over-enthusiastic. "Listen, thanks again for last night and the good word. Sarah and I talked until the wee hours and decided I'd be a fool to let an opportunity like this slip away simply because I didn't get the interview myself."

The truth was that Adam and Sarah fought until the wee hours with Sarah ultimately throwing in Adam's face that he had been fired yet again. Sans the chance of working with Mort Spear, he hadn't even the prospect of a job; on top of which, though they had not mentioned it to anyone, Sarah was nonetheless pregnant.

"Oh, Adam! I'm so pleased!"

Gerald hoped the decision to at least speak to Mort meant that his son really was maturing and wanted his life to have some direction.

Surprisingly to Adam, his interview went like a charm. He immediately started working part-time and spent every spare moment studying for his license. Mort offered all the tutoring Adam needed and when his license came through, he began working full time in the new office. One year later Adam was the office manager, with more property sales under his belt than he thought possible. Gerald was right. Adam's people skills could be used to his advantage. He used them often and not just for sales. The seemingly endless bevy of young women receptionists was too tempting not to invite for a drink and a little something extra on the side.

By the time Jack finished the first year of his internship, Adam was helping Mort Spear open yet another office in Weston. By the time Jack completed his residency, Adam was living in the finest house the Weston office ever represented; fifteen rooms that required the services of two maids. As Jack's shadow covered only Philadelphia, Adam was the star and his life was going in a good direction for a change. His relationship with Sarah, however, did not change, except that three years earlier she gave him something that changed how much he resented her. A son. They named him Peter.

*   *   *   *

The minute Jack completed his residency he and Dorothy married. They opted for a quiet ceremony in the chapel of his alma mater, the Pennsylvania College of Medicine. Dorothy's parents, Saul and Sofie, went to Philly early to spend some quality time with Dorothy, but they couldn't have been more proud of Jack had he been their son by blood. He and Dorothy were together for so long that the Ginsbergs already thought of Jack that way; their son.

Gerald was of course every inch the proud father and he and Saul spent the better part of Jack's Exit-day celebration congratulating each other on what a great job they did shaping such a fine young man. Adam's jealousy caused him, Sarah and the children to miss the pre-wedding festivities.

"I feel really awful about it," Adam lied. "But we won't miss the wedding!"

What he meant was they *couldn't* miss the wedding. Since the group was so small, Saul Ginsberg paid for everyone's round-trip to Philadelphia. How could Adam and family not show up when the weather was perfect and they had tickets in hand.

"I know you have your hands full," Jack said. "Besides, I couldn't get married without you. You're my brother, my best man. Have a safe trip and we'll see you in a few days."

Dorothy knew better and, over the years, she'd seen the jealousy in Adam's eyes whenever she and Jack visited Boston. She didn't understand the origins, but it was unmistakably there. Actually, the origins were irrelevant when Adam's jealousy made him so pompous he'd surely end up in trouble if he weren't careful. Jack asked Dorothy to cut Adam some slack explaining how difficult it was for his brother to grow up in his shadow.

"Your shadow is not Adam's problem," she corrected.

"He's really a great guy. He turned his life completely around. Look how much he's accomplished. When we're all family and you get to know him, you'll see."

"I just wish you saw him as a person instead of your brother," Dorothy insisted, "then you'd see that you're the great guy."

"Are all women so protective of their men?" Jack kissed her cheek.

"Don't patronize me when I'm right, Jack," she scolded.

"Can we talk about this another time?" Jack asked.

"Any time." Dorothy smiled, knowing there would never be a time to discuss Adam the way he needed to be discussed.

Adam and family attended the brief ceremony, Susan and Peter endlessly fidgeting. After the *I do-s* Jack made an announcement.

"I wanted everyone here before I said anything. I've been offered a position at Boston Memorial, effective immediately after the honeymoon. I said yes. We're coming home!"

Dorothy was so excited she missed the fleeting expression on the faces of both Adam and Sarah.

"Baby!" Saul Ginsberg hugged his only child. "We get to have you close by." Tears welled in his eyes as he hugged Jack.

"Son, this is great news. You're bringing the biggest part of our world home to us." Saul retrieved a rolled parchment, tied with a ribbon, from his inside jacket pocket. "This is Sofie's and my wedding present. We never dared to dream you'd use it in Boston." He handed the parchment to Dorothy and quickly swiped at his joyful tears with the back of his hand.

Dorothy slipped off the ribbon and unrolled the paper. "Mom, Dad, I don't know what to say!" She turned to Jack. "Look!" She displayed the beautiful scroll with calligraphy in Saul's own hand. "It says *This is a deposit on a house. Any house!*"

Jack looked to Adam. "When you make the biggest purchase of your life, you go to an expert. Baby brother, you have a new client. Find us a house!"

Sofie, too emotional to speak, at last chimed in. "Now remember, we love children and your father doesn't mind changing diapers." Everyone laughed except Adam and Sarah.

Two years later Dorothy and Jack had a son. They named him Gordon.

Chapter 3

---------------------------------- ▼ ----------------------------------

Ski Accident
Weston, MA – 1960

It seemed to Gordon he'd been looking for her forever. The woman, whose face haunted his sleep and drew him toward her in the night. She appeared naïve, with giant blue eyes and seductive lips that always seemed to be smiling at him. Her hair was short and brown, neither one his preference. Though small boned and fine featured, she had broad shoulders and long tapered hands which trembled ever so slightly, as if she were nervous ... or cold ... or both.

Gordon's inner coldness had been his life's partner for as long as he could remember, though there was a time before memory when he knew warmth and safety and contentment. Up to the point of actually meeting *dream woman*, he wondered whether she had the power to return him to that old place of warmth, the one his parents shared with each other and him as a child ... if only *dream woman* were real.

*   *   *   *

Jack and Dorothy August died so many years earlier it was as if they never lived at all ... or did so in another life. Someone else's life. For Gordon, at thirty-one, his parents lived only in a dream where he was still a small boy of six standing between them, each of his tiny hands in one of theirs.

In the decades since their deaths he closed off the world, semi-disenfranchised except from the nameless *dream woman*. A stranger. No one else in his life provided any comfort. And so, he searched for her face in the face of every stranger, hoping one day to find her yet fearing that very thing. Now that he had, he was scared shitless.

Dream woman first invaded his sleep when he went to live in the home of his aunt and uncle. With children of their own, Susan and Peter, ages 14 and 12 respectively, Gordon's Uncle Adam and Aunt Sarah were less than eager for the responsibility of yet another child. Someone else's child. Susan and Peter didn't much care for Gordon's either. From the moment he arrived they considered him *The little intruder* and treated him accordingly. His once happy life morphed into one containing no kindness of any variety.

Adam became Gordon's guardian because there simply wasn't anyone else. Grandma Ruth, Jack and Adam's mother, died the summer before Jack entered college. At least she'd seen Jack graduate high school ... with honors.

Gordon lost his three remaining grandparents in fairly short succession. Grandpa Saul died four years after Gordon was born; Grandma Sofie, only six months later. Grandpa Gerald passed eighteen months after that. During their lifetimes, each was doting and inclined to make Gordon feel special. Even in absentia, somewhere in the compartments at the back of Gordon's head, he could still see and hear them. In one compartment was Grandpa Saul calling to Grandma Sofie as he entered the front door. *Where's my Sofala?* Gordon's grandmother would appear from the kitchen responding *Right here, Doll.* Grandma Sofie called everyone *Doll.* Gordon loved that memory. In another compartment was the distant sound of Grandpa Gerald saying *A buck for the pig if you sing a song.* Gordon always sung to great applause and *a buck for his pig.* Dorothy would gently scold Gerald calling him Dad, though he was Jack's father. *Dad, you're either bribing him or spoiling him. I'm not sure which, but I don't like either one.*

I like to think of it as bribing him not to be spoiled Grandpa Gerald would say. *Singing is hard work. You work, you deserve to be paid.* Then he'd whisper in Gordon's ear *Let's go stick your buck in the pig we bought. Save it for the future.* The pair would run hand-in-hand to Gordon's room. At nearly five, he hadn't the slightest idea what a future was, but if Grandpa Gerald thought it was a good thing, Gordon wanted one. They slipped each hard earned dollar into the fat bellied ceramic piggy-bank which sat on Gordon's dresser. Their dollar-pig routine brought such a glow to Gerald's face that it was difficult for Dorothy to complain too loud.

Gerald did his best to shower love and praise on Susan and Peter as well. Neither child knew such love from Adam, or Sarah for that matter. With the loss of Grandpa Gerald, so went all form of warmth for them. The only emotion Susan and Peter garnered from their parents was resentment. Once Gordon was living in their house, they passed the resentment along, as if Adam and Sarah's behavior were somehow Gordon's fault.

Saul and Sofie passed their love and affection to Gordon's mother who, in turn, passed it to him. But with the loss of all three grandparents and then his own parents there was no one left to continue the passing of love and affection. Ultimately, Gordon's remembered experience of love and support was more than Susan or Peter ever knew from parents who, it turned out, outlived them both.

Except that it was neither love nor warmth, it was impossible for Gordon to say exactly what kept Adam and Sarah together after the deaths of their children. Gordon suspected each would have walked away years before except maybe they had nowhere else to go. He was certain that their polite exterior was a sham and the only thing keeping them together was him ... and maybe that they had nowhere else to go.

When Jack said the prophetic words *You never know* and *just in case,* he never anticipated Gordon actually living with Adam, yet there he was. For Gordon, there was literally nowhere else either.

* * * *

It wasn't just Gordon that Susan and Peter detested. They had no great love for each other, however, they took every opportunity to mutually exclude Gordon from anything and everything. The cousins each enjoyed down-hill skiing, but one day they refused to let *The little intruder* tag along.

It was the first of March, during school break. There were several large snow storms, even considering how close it was to actual spring. Inches of powder piled on top of earlier inches of powder. In the final storm of the season, Mt. Upton got dumped – an irresistible twenty inches. Susan and Peter were out the door at 5:00 A.M. headed for the White Mountains of New Hampshire. Claiming Gordon was too young to go without an adult along Uncle Adam didn't press the issue. Aunt Sarah would have been just as happy to have him out of her house, if only for the day, but she didn't seem to care one way or the other. Too distracted. Too much on her mind. Too much to do. She wouldn't be around that day to mind Gordon's presence or see the sad longing in his eyes. With him out of sight she easily put him out of her mind.

The air on the mountain was clear and crisp and held a snap that turned noses and ears bright red. Susan and Peter were first to the summit taking the first, longest powder-run all to themselves. Areas of greatest accumulation were roped off and marked **DANGER**. Peter paid no attention to people, let alone a sign no one was around to enforce, and could usually solicit Susan into being a party to his schemes. The powder looked safe enough to him and Peter convinced them both that the Ski Patrol roped off the area for their own night skiing after the mountain closed. They unlatched their skies and walked around the barriers.

"Race you to the bottom!" Peter challenged as he snapped his right and left boots into their bindings. He was younger but the better skier by far.

"Petie, wait up!" Susan called him Petie only when they broke the rules.

"No friends on a powder day!" Peter said and took off.

He was half-way down a trail as Susan struggled to latch her skis.

"Petie!" She yelled.

"Suzie!" He yelled over his shoulder.

The skiing was marvelous and the sound of their echoing voices bounced off the mountain as they continued calling back and forth to each other. With the day so clear, neither of them anticipated a low lying mist; the remnants of a very soupy fog from the night before.

Suddenly the mountain started to move. The sound of Susan's cry for her brother evaporated into the rumble headed toward them. She vanished from Peter's radar and one of her poles sped past him. Cold bit his face as panic propelled him to the bottom in front of the on-coming avalanche. Faster. Faster. Peter and Susan started out racing each other. Suddenly Peter was racing the snow.

The Ski Patrol and several early arrivals heard the echoing voices followed by the terrible rumble. They saw Susan get caught up in it. And Peter, poor Peter, almost made it. But the snow was faster than skis; faster than a foolish, cocky young boy racing for his life. When the Ski Patrol reached him just ten minutes later his neck was broken. At least it was quick.

Others went to the place on the mountain where they saw Susan go down. Digging fast, Andrew Long, captain of the Ski Patrol and his crew, Janie Tremont and Ben Larsen, hoped against hope that she was alive. They found her in the small pocket of air she created during her descent. Hers was a relatively short slide into a stand of trees. She hit her head against a low burrled knot and lost a lot of blood. Working against time, they bandaged her head and ferried her down the mountain. By the time they reached the bottom she was dead. Two lives gone in a blink, all for a cheap thrill. Or maybe it wasn't so cheap. What price for a life? For two lives? Selfish, cold, and sad lives, yes, but still, lives with possibilities.

Even Gordon, only ten when they died and no love for either of them, saw their potential. At just eighteen, Susan was an accomplished pianist accepted to Juilliard. Peter, only fifteen and a mathematical wizard, was planning a summer at B.U. to earn early college credits. Now the piano in the library would be silent and Peter's ham radio wouldn't crackle to life in the middle of the night. There would be only two more foot stones in the family plot at Mt. Sinai Cemetery in Sharon.

All the way back to Gordon's Great-Great-grandparents, generations of Augusts and Augusteins were buried along side each other. His own parents were on one side of Grandma Ruth with Grandpa Gerald on the other. Marching forward from that fateful spring day, nearby, were Susan and Peter. Gordon didn't miss them;

they could be so cruel, but with them gone Uncle Adam was no longer even civil. He spent increasingly more time at his office, began going in weekends and holidays, anything to keep from being with Sarah, whom he did not love, and Gordon – the permanent reminder that the best part of Adam was gone forever.

Adam and Sarah each found themselves silently asking why Susan and Peter left Gordon behind. If they'd had taken him along, perhaps they could be alone in their individual sorrows. But they didn't take him. He remained as living testimony to their selfish pettiness and Adam and Sarah's unvarying evidence of how unfair life could be. Unfair for Gordon; he was alone. Unfair for Adam and Sarah; he was alone in their house.

Chapter 4

-------------------------------- ▼ --------------------------------

The Meeting
Cambridge, MA – 1980

Kendall Spaulding. Gordon August. They were destined to meet (or maybe it was doomed). It seemed to Kendall he had always been a part of her life without actually being in it. Something of him hovered just outside her line of vision, seen only from the corner of her eye, as if he were peeking at her from around corners like a teenage boy afraid of being caught snooping on his girlfriend. He just watched; never approached; never came too close. The instant she sensed his presence and looked up he disappeared. Like a ghost. Sometimes she thought she made him up. Then, she'd feel him watching again, almost catch a look and knew that, somewhere in the world, her *ghost* was quite real.

On a night when Kendall was about 14, she and Lacey spent a Friday night sleep-over at Kendall's house. They pushed her twin beds together for more room to practice dance moves, but neglected to return them to their proper place before spending Saturday night at Lacey's. Late Sunday evening, too tired to do the task herself, Kendall crawled into her own bed leaving it butted up against its mate. She figured Lacey would be coming over that Monday anyway and together they would return the room to its proper configuration.

In the defused morning light that came through Kendall's bedroom window, during the time that lies between dawn and day light, she awoke to see him lying next to her on top of the covers of her spare bed. He was older than her, about 17, and wearing the clothes she was certain she'd seen countless times; red plaid flannel shirt, dark blue jeans with a belt, socks, and shoes that were some sort of loafer.

His ankles were crossed and his left arm, at the far side of the spare bed, was lifted and tucked under his head. He behaved as if he didn't know she were there. When she got up to use the bathroom he got up as well. While she was gone, he stood at the left side of the window and appeared to be looking out of it. Sleepy as Kendall was, she still noted he seemed to be waiting … for something ... or someone, his impatience so raw and thick she could feel it.

When she climbed back in bed, the ghostly figure lay back down beside her. He re-crossed his ankles and placed his bent left arm back under his head; still giving no note of her presence. In that moment, half asleep and groggy, she didn't speak to the figure. She simply fell back to sleep next to him memorizing every detail of his face: his worried brow, his deep-set eyes and the small bump at the bridge of his nose. Each contour of his lean body and wavy brown hair etched themselves into her mind.

In the full light of morning, with the sun beaming through her window, her *ghost* was gone and never got that close again, that is, until last week. Only, this time, he was flesh and blood.

Kendall was in the Boston Public Library looking through old newspaper ads for ideas to promote her dance company. *He* was pouring over stacks of old newspapers. The sleeves of his recognizable flannel shirt were rolled up revealing tightly muscled forearms. Though *He* was older than the night she'd seen him on her bed, she'd have known him anywhere.

Shocked, Kendall dropped her open clutch purse sending everything everywhere and created an echo of chaos that bounced off the hard surfaced silence of the library. Several people helped gather her belongings. *He* wasn't one of them. The old newspaper in his large strong hands held his full concentration. This time, *He* was obviously searching for someone … or something. Again, Kendall felt his impatience and an odd connection to a total stranger which left her with a most unsettled feeling.

Shaken at the sight of a flesh and blood *ghost*, Kendall bolted from the library, she hoped unnoticed, and doubted ever seeing him again.

* * * *

As everything in Kendall's life was dependent on the shape she was in, staying in shape was more important than almost anything. Gordon felt the same about his own body. It was his temple. Once he met Kendall, her body became his temple and he came to love her more than life. To the point of their meeting, however, Gordon spent decades absent any form of that feeling, to the point that on the day they met he claimed he had no heart. To Kendall, the thought of it actually being true seemed a tragedy. Such a beautiful man. Such sad, wonderful eyes. Crystal blue and never looked away once he got that first good look at her face.

After the fiasco at the library, Kendall headed for Celebrity Gym, in Cambridge, to do resistance training on her own for a change. Gordon sauntered into the weight room and began his own session with forty pound free-weights. He never broke a sweat. Not immediately realizing who he was, Kendall made a mental comparison of his workout to hers and laughed at herself for feeling so buff hefting tiny two-pounders.

Even from the back it was hard to ignore the way Gordon's black bike shorts fit his rear and the way his sweaty t-shirt stuck to his broad back. More noticeable, however, was the way he completed each set.

"Pardon," she volunteered, "but you're hurting your hands."

"The compressions relax them," he said, with something less than conviction. "Don't they?"

Kendall gave a disapproving look but said nothing.

"This isn't helping one bit," he said with disgust.

"'Fraid not, but I know what will," Kendall offered.

That personal trainer I'm paying a small fortune hasn't a clue, Gordon thought.

Kendall stepped behind him and demonstrated the correct neutral posture for his hands so they remained relaxed even as he worked-out. Doubtful, Gordon accepted her instruction. Though rather general in nature, the information was spot-on. His hands felt better. He was amazed, even intrigued, that anyone interrupted their own workout to advise him. In his experience strangers didn't do that. Then, the timbre of her voice set off the rerun of a whisper *Body and soul you will be mine.*

Mental case he chided himself and shoed away the thought. Gordon would have blown-off the woman's familiarity to her being 'a type', except that her voice was one he knew. It was the voice in the whisper came to him in dreams and woke him in the night.

Facing Gordon by that point, Kendall recognized him again but forced herself to stay, forbid herself to panic and run. Before she could stop herself the words *It's you* left her lips.

"I should certainly hope I'm me," Gordon responded.

"I mean, I've seen you before; earlier, at Boston Public." *And years ago lying on my bed in the middle of the night*, she mentally centered on the unspoken thought.

"Someone caused a commotion. Would you be that someone?" He acknowledged the half remembered moment.

"Guilty," she admitted.

"How did someone so small make such a big racket?"

"Years of practice." Kendall's cheeks colored with embarrassment.

"What made you offer the advice?" Gordon changed subjects. "None of the so-called professionals in this place notice if you hang yourself, let alone that you might hurt yourself."

"Unless you have a spare in the closet, you were about to damage the only body you're likely to get." Kendall smiled. "It's obvious you take care of yourself and I respect the hard work. I'm also familiar with the struggle of coming back from an injury when all I needed to prevent it was more information. Now you have your information. To sit idly by while you hurt yourself when I know better is nearly as bad as me hurting you. That brand of foolishness would break my heart. I prefer not to live with a broken heart."

"Wouldn't know." Gordon tapped the left side of his chest. "I'm like the Tin Man in *The Wizard of Oz*. No heart." He didn't miss a beat. "So, you care so much about me?"

"Let's just say I care so much. We are, after all, strangers." Kendall verbalized his earlier thought about her being a stranger. "But you have a nice face." She put her hand to his cheek sending a vaguely familiar electric charge through his body. "I'm sorry about your heart. Hopefully it is simply misplaced and someone will turn it in at the Lost and Found."

Kendall left the weight room and Gordon watched her go.

The next day, Kendall arrived late as usual for her regular evening workout with her friends and partners, Lacey Hart and Dana Phillips. She described her encounter.

"It isn't that he's heartless, like Stuart," she shuddering at the name. "This guy's just without."

Potayto, potahto Lacey thought. She knew Stuart and what he'd done. For her, Stuart's name was unspeakable. She thought of him only as *Asshole*.

"Calm down, honey, or you'll explode," she recommended then glanced at Dana. Their eyes locked in mutual concern. "You can't save the world."

"Most don't want saving," Dana offered her show of support.

"Right," Lacey agreed. "This guy is probably another *worse case scenario* like Asshole, not one of your Dad's endless lot of wayward interns in need of a home cooked meal and a few hours as part of a family."

"Guess I did inherit Dad's rescue gene," Kendall said looking from Dana to Lacey. "Can't save every wounded animal. Shouldn't want to," she repeated the words her mother said from time to time. "So, why can't I get him out of my head?"

"You want one of us to explain what goes on inside of that head," Dana attempted to play it light as she assumed a push-up position.

"Say! You can't talk to me like that. I'm your boss," Kendall pretended to pull rank.

"First of all, we're off-hours. Off-hours, I have no boss and you have no clout." Dana squeezed out the words between reps. "Second, since I made partner, I have no boss and you have no clout. All ways 'round, my friend; I have no boss and you have no clout."

"But I did have clout when I was your boss."

"Not really, since Lacey was my boss.

"Hmm, that's right," Kendall mused, tapping her lips with her index finger. "Just the same, don't I deserve even this much respect?" Kendall made a half-inch space between index finger and thumb.

Dana pretended to look then returned to her reps. "In your dreams," she confirmed.

Kendall made a small harrumphing noise, mostly to herself, then placed her sneakered foot on Dana's butt and pressed her flat to the mat.

"How about now?" Kendall asked.

The three friends laughed, two of them knowing Kendall was hopeless when it came to lost causes. As Stuart Cosgrove before him, Lacey and Dana feared any association Kendall had with Gordon August would end up a crusade to find a heart that probably was never there in the first place.

Gordon stopped short, just outside the entrance to aerobics, when he heard Kendall's exchange with her friends. He felt like a voyeur eavesdropping on their private conversation, but Kendall's voice had a soothing quality, though it commingled with an unsettling familiarity. There was also the matter of the body jolt she shot through him simply by touching his cheek. It was all quite captivating, which made him wonder exactly what Kendall thought of him. Now he knew. The lovely jury of one had delivered its verdict; *wounded animal*. An animal who associated her face and voice with the root of his wound – the horrible sound of crushing metal and breaking glass.

Kendall's was the face and voice that haunted Gordon's sleep never revealing whether she was friend or foe. He centered on her laugh. God, it was a real woman's laugh – warm, infectious, caring, and somehow reassuring; not an imbecilic twitter meant to demonstrate fake fragility. For the time being, as Gordon was the subject of her inclination to save, he labeled Kendall as *friend* and had a sudden yearning to tell her about his dream and learn what she thought of the whole thing, but couldn't. Most probably, he never would tell anyone. Certainly not on that day, not when the end of the day included dinner with his Aunt and Uncle. Gordon always considered such occasions a trip down the River Styx in a leaky boat that disembarked its lone passenger at the foyer to Hell. The three of them had dinner together only at holiday or the anniversary of his parents' death, Aunt Sarah insisting that Gordon needed them on those nights. On those of all nights, Adam and Sarah were the very last people he needed or wanted. Upon his return home that night, he would light three yahrzeit candles; the candles of remembrance, one for each of his parents and a third for the life he lost when he lost both of them. How much better it would be to share this night with Kendall, to be cared for by her the way she cared for her friends or the "lonely lot" her father brought home to dinner.

The meal Gordon would share with his Aunt and Uncle was sure to be civilized and cordial despite their dislike of each other, which Gordon suspected would always be the case. Even after so many years, they struggled to maintain any level of conversation. No matter how he felt when he arrived at whichever restaurant Sarah chose, Gordon always left feeling like *The little intruder*. All things between them remained exactly as they were in the beginning; the day he went to live in their house.

Gordon never went into the aerobics room that day and, without even learning her name, expected he had seen the last of Kendall.

Chapter 5

----------------------------- ▼ -----------------------------

The Second Meeting
Cambridge, MA – 1980

Backing her way out of the gym, saying *goodbye* to Lacey, Kendall literally ran into Gordon as she exited the building.

"Gee, I'm awfully sorry!" Kendall apologized, turning to face her victim. "Oh, it's you! How are your hands?"

"Fine." Gordon's reply was curt.

"I meant to give you my card." Kendall grabbed one from her bag and pressed it into his hand. "In case you change your mind." She continued backing her way into the parking lot. "I mean about not having a heart."

"Heart. Me? Never happen!"

"The name's Spaulding. Kendall Spaulding," she pretended to ignore his remark as she retreated further away. "Ice cream. My treat." Then she disappeared into the lamp-lit darkness.

Gordon was shocked at her nerve and more shocked at himself. Since their first meeting, the touch of her hand and her kind words, he did change his mind, though his flip remark of a response remained. He used the answer for so long it was knee-jerk. though it was no longer exactly true.

Headed home after a particularly grueling day, he realized that he hadn't so much change his mind as it had been changed for him. However ridiculous, Kendall's simple touch touched-off electric sparks that pulled at his heart; the one he was no long so positive wasn't there. Since she was correct about his hands, what if she were equally correct that he tucked his heart so far away he simply couldn't find it. Yes. Kendall Spaulding changed his mind.

Though she was no longer visible, Gordon hadn't heard Kendall's car door slam or engine fire-up. He felt certain she was within earshot.

Frustrated, Kendall angrily threw her gear in the back seat. She stood at her open driver's side door mumbling to herself. *No heart. Why does he keep saying that?*

"Hey Spaulding!" Gordon called out, taking a chance she would hear him speak into the night. "When you said to give you a call did you mean I had to use a phone or will this do?"

No response.

Gordon ventured into the expansive lot and found her muttering with her head bowed. He approached and placed a hand at the small of her back. She jumped then turned and saw it was him. He saw anger in her face, but kindness to mediate the volatility. Embarrassed, she looked away and dropped her gaze toward the pavement. He lifted her chin and looked into a face he knew too well. Acting unchecked, he leaned in and kissed her cheek.

It was as if a remembered bolt of lightening coursed through her body. She placed a hand over his kiss.

"I think your missing heart just touched me," she said.

After nearly a life-time of waiting for the other to show up, there they were, together, in the flesh. This time, when Kendall looked, her ghost didn't disappear. This time, when Gordon reached for her he didn't jerk awake only to discover he was alone. All either of them could do was smile. Whether destiny or doom, they were meant to meet; meant to be together. So it was written at the beginning of Time. As with everything which is meant to be; one day it would be.

*   *   *   *

Days passed with Gordon still wondering how Kendall managed to touch his heart. It was impossible. Well ... nearly impossible. Why had she even tried? He hadn't allowed his heart to feel anything in ages. How long since he'd received a warm welcoming touch? Too long. Then Kendall put her hand on his cheek and said he had a nice face. He stared at himself a long while after their first encounter. His eyes kept drifting to the rear view mirror nearly the entire way home.

What had she seen that he no longer could, that he was certain wasn't there ... except that, for her, it was. Gordon allowed the touch only because it wouldn't matter, wouldn't make any difference. But it did matter and it did make a difference and nothing would ever be the same without Kendall's hand on his cheek or at least her hand in his hand.

Chapter 6

------------------------------- ▼ -------------------------------

At Gordon's – 1980

Gordon halted the progress of their relationship at somewhere just past platonic and kept his true feelings under wraps. It wasn't what Kendall ultimately wanted but, post Stewart Cosgrove, just past platonic was about all she could handle.

Some of their shared days lasted well into late evening. In an effort to spare Kendall a late drive, Gordon offered free reign over his apartment as long as she slept in another room in bed other than his.

Fearing sleep that nearly always ended in a nightmare, adult life found Kendall functioning on very little sleep. Still, there were nights she suffered a degree of crash. Some of those nights she was at Gordon's place. Barely able to keep her eyes open, he found it remarkable that it was necessary to chase her off to bed in order to avoid 'crash and burn'.

She'd borrow a t-shirt and, as Gordon would do for a child, he placed a glass of water on the bedside table then lay beside her on top of the covers until she was warm and dreamy. They'd kiss. *Stay*, she'd say. *Another night* he'd answer getting up and shut the door behind him. But there never was another night. And Gordon made sure such a night was well out of Kendall's reach. Each night the most Kendall took to bed was the lingering aroma of his cologne.

Most nights Gordon suffered his own nightmare, the climax of which was always a flash of Kendall's face as he reached for her, the sensation of imminent tragedy very nearly a presence. Next came a semi-distant audio replay of crushing metal and breaking glass followed by a blinding pain at the back of his head. Dream's-end consisted of a ground shaking tremor and whispered words in Kendall's voice *Body and soul you will be mine.* The words always jerked him awake only to return him to a life where heart-breaking loss was his daily reality.

Those nights he awakened with Kendall in his home, he had an inexplicable need to confirm she was there, an actual part of his life. He felt like a spy as he opened the door to what he thought of as her room, her small form looking even smaller in the big pull out bed and simply listened to the quiet rhythm of her breathing. One particular night Gordon awakened reaching for Kendall, the usual; physically aching for her, not so usual. His ritual of looking in on her complete he spotted his t-shirt at the foot of her bed. That wasn't so usual either. *What the Hell* he figured, *why should her night be usual? Mine isn't.* He stood wondering if he haunted her sleep the way she did his. Secretly he wished it was so and became lost in that thought. The sound of covers being shoved away brought him back to the moment and Kendall *al fresco.* Of course he'd seen her at the gym in an assortment of what she referred to as 'very serious leotards'. But they were layered-over by bulky leg warmers and pieces of knit this-and-that camouflaging her true shape. Naked, he saw how toned and defined each and every muscle was. Naked, she was more tempting than he imagined.

Mesmerized, he imagined himself next to her. Unable to continue simply imagining, he climbed onto the bed and lie next to her. Somehow Kendall's complaint of always being cold was negated by a radiant heat coming from within her. Gordon, almost always warm, felt the chill air of the winter night even in his sweats. Kendall's warmth was comfortable to be near – maybe too warm, maybe too comfortable. Praying she wouldn't awaken, he allowed himself to touch her. Her long legs, narrow hips, tiny waist, her breasts – small and firm, the fragile curve of her long neck. Lying behind her, he slid closer until they were nestled together like spoons.

Clearly she was under his skin. *No!* He promised himself. *I will not become attached.* But, attached or not, there he was, in what he thought of as her bed, her naked body folded into him.

Feeling very much the pervert, or at least a Peeping Tom, he risked waking her to caress her flesh; to kiss her bare shoulder. Kendall never moved. He wondered if she even knew he was there.

Her silence and heat emboldened him to kiss the familiar back of her neck. She moved backward totally wrapping herself in the cradling curve of his body. He draped his arm around her to rest his hand on her tummy, the very flat tummy of which she was so proud. Her sleepy warmth and the remnants of her perfume intoxicated him.

"I love your body," he whispered into the darkness not really wanting her to hear.

"I love *you*", was Kendall's mumbled response.

Gordon was struck by instant jealousy of the *who* that inhabited her dream. He shook it off. His jealously was replaced by the fear that he was the *who* in question. Considering he was in no position to do anything about it; considering that he was terrified of what a connection to anyone would mean, especially someone like Kendall, still he found it impossible to leave her side.

She wasn't answering me! He told himself. He convinced himself her words were part of some fast-asleep dream populated by a person or persons unknown. In other words, someone not him.

But it must be me he thought. *Who else would she be loving, even in a dream?*

Who indeed?

Kendall never spoke of the dream which caused her frequent nocturnal awakenings; the dreams which left her upset and afraid. Instead, she feigned immediately forgetting them; silence reigning over everything to do with them, including that they were recurring, much as Gordon's … only not. His was a scrambled memory. Hers felt like the harbinger of doom.

When next Gordon looked at the digital clock across the room, fifteen minutes had ticked by. He realized he must have dosed. Reluctantly, he slid off the bed. Much to his surprise, Kendall, who had been so warm, began to shiver and whimper then cry. Had the *I love you* dream turned on her? Would this be one of the many nights she awakened drenched in sweat? She groped for the covers and pulled them to her chin. The shivering stopped. The cascade of tears subsided as quickly as it began and, whatever the nightmare had been, it was over.

Attachment to Kendall was scarier than the fiery death Gordon knew accompanied the real-life version of his dream; the one which claimed his parents' lives. Something soft and soothing and classical always chased away that fear. Feeling dazed and more than a little confused by his growing feelings, Gordon headed for the living room. He turned to WCRB; on the air whenever needed – 24/7. Robert Schuman floated from the speakers in the form of a waltz, the name of which Gordon failed to recall. He lay on the sofa under an afghan hoping for dreamless slumber. No such luck. He slipped into the music and entered his dream. The woman with short brown hair, pale skin and a face which was little more than a blur appeared in his arms. Light as a feather, and without conversation, she followed every nuance of his dance. Left, right, left, turn, pause. Right, left, right, turn, pause. The music in the dream ended. Gordon stepped back to bow in a formal thank you to his partner. The woman began backing away and Gordon attempted to reduce the distance between himself and *dream woman*. He failed. A voice from behind called his name. He stopped and turned toward it. It was the brown-haired woman. As she headed toward him, her face came into focus.

Gordon began having the dream when he was a child, but that was as much as he remembered. Today *dream woman* had a name – Kendall. For reasons unknown, Kendall felt as if it were the wrong name. When Gordon reached for the Kendall in his dream, she disappeared as always. In her place were the sounds he hoped to drown out in the first place. He jerked awake only to find a living, breathing Kendall sitting next to him, back in his t-shirt. The Schuman piece still playing, Gordon realized his trance seemed longer than it actually was.

"That must have been some dream." Almost in a whisper she added, "Was I in it?"

"No." He lied, forcing annoyance.

"Something woke me." Kendall confessed but revealed nothing of her nightmare; especially not that for the past year it was coming more and more often. "I ... I guess I heard the radio. Is that Schuman?" She yawned.

Gordon didn't come clean either, not about having been in her room; not about having been in her bed; not about practically wishing her awake; and certainly not that he was the culprit who woke her.

"I'm cold. May I crawl in?" She asked.

"I already said no sleeping together," he rebuffed.

"I'm not asking for sex. I'm asking for heat."

For the moment Kendall was happy just to be near Gordon and have him know that she was willing to wait, though his aversion to commitment ran deep and came with constant assurances that it always would. Kendall believed that time and patience on her part would bring him around; that someday he'd feel differently; that over time he'd come to love her, want her. Little did she know, that ship had sailed.

"You're always cold," Gordon tried to sound exasperated. "Can't you make your own heat?"

"I can, but only when I'm asleep. The Catch 22 is that I can't get to sleep to make heat if I'm too cold to fall asleep in the first place," she declared in her own most exasperated voice.

"Fine, but no conversation and keep your cold feet to yourself."

"Yes boss." Kendall offered a small salute then slipped in beside him. She cuddled up, her head on his shoulder, her right arm draped across his chest.

Gordon pulled her close, wrapping his right arm around her. He hated to admit it, even to himself, but he enjoyed the feel of her sleeping next to him.

"Comfortable," he asked.

Kendall remained silent.

"I said no talking but you can answer a question."

Still no answer.

"Kendall? Yes, well, I suppose you could have answered if you'd been awake long enough to hear the question." Gordon blustered trying and failing to convince himself that he was irritated. The reality was that he was delighted to have Kendall next to him and pulled her even closer. Though he said otherwise, he was aching to make love to her, be inside her, fall asleep next to her. His past wouldn't let him.

Kendall didn't know the gory details of Gordon's past, just the parts of which he was not ashamed. The rest kept him from loving her out loud. He questioned whether that would always be the case and what would be if and when Kendall knew everything? The unanswered question was like a vice around his heart, keeping him silent ... even while Kendall slept in his arms.

Chapter 7

------------------------------ ▼ ------------------------------

Go Away Little Girl
I'm Not Supposed to be Alone With You

Boston – 1980

Gordon grew to need Kendall and care for her more by the day. She often said he was perfect for her. He hated when she said that, couldn't have it. He didn't understand that her idea of perfect meant slightly imperfect. Maybe more than slightly.

Gordon knew he could never measure up to any sort of perfection, real or imagined, and if Kendall saw him as some paragon of virtue he couldn't be what she saw. When she eventually discovered his degree of imperfection, he envisioned her running toward the nearest exit, leaving him alone. Again.

*   *   *   *

Gordon wanted things to be casual with Kendall the same way he thought they were casual with Babette. Right up until the day she casually announced that she was pregnant and Gordon casually told her to get rid of it. He told her to choose, the baby or him. She hit the roof. Said she wanted both.

Gordon was with Babette only because she was convenient and asked little of him. He didn't love her and could never be or become a real husband to her or a father to her child. He simply walked away; from Babette, the baby, The Big Apple, and his partnership at Conrad and Wilkins, high powered legal council to the entertainment industry.

He moved to Boston and started his own practice with a friend from law school; spending his days in the State Street offices of August and Mendelson, Attorneys-at-Law.

Babette sent weekly letters updating the progress of her pregnancy. After a month or so, she confirmed the slightest hint of movement. Three months later, while in New York finishing up business for Anthony Conrad, Gordon silently chastised himself for not even considering seeing Babette or checking in on her. Instead he had dinner with Leonard Perkins, a former associate at Conrad & Wilkins, only to accidentally learn the truth.

Not only was Babette not pregnant then but she never had been and probably never would be. Word was, Babette spent so many years literally starving for her craft that her protracted boarder-line anorexic condition insured conception had not been an option for years. All the same she desperately wanted the man she'd been seeing to believe her story and take responsibility for her make-believe pregnancy.

Babette's life as a principal dancer with The Ballet Center of New York had its rewards, but they were significantly less than the luxurious, glamorous and expensive life she wanted or could acquire as the wife of a successful New York lawyer. The best way for Babette to become *Mrs.* Successful-New-York-Lawyer was to convince her man that she was already pregnant. He would, of course, be overcome with guilt and marry her immediately. Later she could say the baby spontaneously aborted and her man would be none the wiser. Babette would retain her station in life as Mrs. Successful-New-York-Lawyer sorrowfully unable to conceive a 'second' time.

"As it turns out," Len concluded his story, "the guy, whoever he was, dumped her and left town. Guess she wasn't as clever as she thought."

Gordon represented the Ballet Center in all legal matters and was careful to keep his physical relationship with their principal dancer under wraps. Len had no idea Gordon was the very man in question, tremendously relieved that he hadn't really deserted Babette. Still, his conscience reiterated that he did or certainly would have, had the baby been real. Gordon was certain that should a similar situation present itself he would do it again, even if the woman were Kendall.

*   *   *   *

Gordon decided it would be foolhardy to partake of another physical relationship until he was certain he wouldn't run from its product; commitment and family, that which could be taken away in an instant. Just like that. Just like before. His parents were the people he cared for and counted on. In the blink of an eye, they were gone. He simply could not re-experience the awful feeling of abandonment.

Gordon never dreamt things would go so far with Kendall; that they'd become so close or be so serious. That she'd be so serious. Each day that passed drew them closer. It was a closeness that came with fear and destructive thoughts that disappeared only when they were together but ritually returned when Gordon was alone.

I don't need anyone he'd assure himself. *She deserves a family; a committed husband and kids who love her. I can't be that or offer that. She's better off without me. I'm better off on my own. I'll be fine. I'll survive when she goes ... and she should.*

His feelings about family and commitment unchanged, it was an enormous mistake to let her into his life. And a worse mistake to think that Kendall, always so serious about everything, would acquiesce to a casual relationship of any kind, with anyone, in deference to a life with a husband and children.

If she stays, it'll turn out the same as with Babette. She'll trap me thinking I'm something I'm not; that I can be something I can't. She wants something I can't give. Better she leaves now than when she finds out what I've done, he told himself.

Gordon knew that for Kendall, it was 'all or nothing' and the fact of it made him panic. He saw himself as the *nothing* option and wanted her to have at least the option of *all*. Time to choose – fight or flight. Gordon opted for flight by picking a terrible fight. He chose for Kendall to go, all the while silently acknowledging that he was the one leaving.

Kendall had her last appointment for the day then met Gordon at his office. They took the 'T' to Haymarket, had dinner at one of her favorite restaurants – The American Oyster House, then returned.

Gordon sat at his desk unseeing, flipping through briefs in the manila folders in front of him. He decided that moment was as good as any to have the conversation he'd been dreading for the last week. Unfortunately, Kendall chose the same moment to step behind him, wrap her arms around his neck, put her cheek to his and steal a hug. Even enjoying the experience Gordon unhooked her arms.

"Don't do that," his voice was cold.

"What did I do? It was just a hug."

She waited for him to respond. He didn't.

"Lately, it seems everything I do is wrong. You can't keep shutting me out and expect me to just keep taking it. I'm willing to wait, but not forever and certainly not if there's nothing to wait for."

Again Kendall gave Gordon the chance to respond. Again he did not.

"Is that what you're saying? There's nothing to wait for?"

"Please, just go. It will be better if you do. This isn't what I want. You ... aren't what I want." It was the worse lie he ever told. "I want a different kind of woman, a different kind of relationship."

"A different kind or just a different one?" Kendall demanded, unable to believe Gordon was actually sending her away.

"It's the same difference," he said.

"Not to me."

"Well it is to me," Gordon said with a sigh.

The strain of what he was trying to do showed on his face. Kendall wanted to soothe it away, persuade him down a different path. She tried to touch his cheek. He turned away; afraid to let her, afraid to look at her. If he couldn't get her to leave right then he might lose his resolve, pull her to him and never let go. But he was determined to do the right thing, even if he hurt her by doing it the wrong way.

"I need someone career minded with a serious career, not this paid recreation you and Lacey pass off as a profession." Gordon saw his words bite into her very soul.

"Is that what you think of my business?"

"More or less," he lied again.

"Have you no idea how hard we all work? I get that it isn't brain surgery or rocket science, but it isn't exactly a day at the sand box. It's

not as if we all have nothing better to do than rise at the crack of dawn
to operate Hott Jazz like it was a ... a hobby. We're good at what we
do. And Hott Jazz holds an extremely important place in the dance
community, in the art community as a whole. You can't be serious!"

Gordon only hoped that his face said he was.

"I can't keep this up." Gordon meant the boldfaced lies; wishing
Kendall out of his office before his mind understood that he was losing
the one person who might save him from his life. "There's nothing
here for you. Do us both a favor and find someone else. Get married.
Have a pack of kids."

"It's over." Kendall couldn't believe what was happening. "I
thought you cared about me. I thought we had something special that
comes along once in a lifetime." Tears welled in her eyes that she
refused to cry. "You want me to walk away?"

"Yes. Just go." He tried to think of what would make her want to
leave. "How do I make you understand?" He took her by the
shoulders, looked into her eyes and chose his words carefully. "I
neither want nor need the hassle of another person permanently
attached to my hip. I'm simply not interested in being interested." He
turned her away and gave her a little push toward the door.

She whirled back around with fire in her eyes.

"You want alone? I'll give you alone! In fact, I'll go you one
better. You never met me. I never heard of you." Kendall poked
Gordon's chest with her index finger punctuating each 'never'.
"You're dead! You got it!" She didn't wait for a response.

She stormed out slamming the door. Gordon wanted to go after
her but stopped himself. He pressed his hand to the spot her finger
stuck him like a sword and winced. Her final words resounded in his
head. *You're dead! You got it?*

"Dead," he responded to her in absentia. "That would be my
parents. Fate says that I must remain here in emotional limbo, unable
to properly care for another living soul."

Kendall ran past the secretary's unoccupied desk, down the hall to
the elevator and out the lobby door onto State Street. She ran to the
Green line's Government Center entrance, down the flight of stairs
and rode the 'T' to Porter Square. She ran until she reached the relative

safety provided by the locked front door of Hott Jazz and the door to her own office.

Alone and livid, she paced and voiced her thoughts to reinforce them. "Why lead me on? Does he think I'm a toy, a stone without feelings? Has he no concept of how much I love him, how much we need each other? Can't he see how important we are to each other? Is he blind?" Kendall thought perhaps he was and decided to open his eyes. She composed and typed a letter then did as Gordon asked. She left. Her letter arrived by special messenger the next day. Three days later found Gordon, once again, rereading her parting words.

.... *It always felt so good just to be with you and talk and maybe make you laugh. I'm sorry it wasn't as good for you to be with me. I cared so much because it's the only thing I know how to do, the only way I know how to be. I started things by reaching out, but you encouraged me by reaching back. You had me believe there was such a thing as you and me together in the same breath. I wanted to believe it – that things were as they seemed, that you were changing or at least changing your mind. I was wrong on both counts. Everything was a lie.*

You have now made yourself abundantly clear. I was an entertaining inconvenience that you prefer left you alone because for every day of the rest of your life you don't want you and me to be an 'us' together in the same breath. You want me to be an 'us' with someone else.

Perhaps you think I want something from you, something you don't have. All I want is what we already had, except that I wanted you to want it as well. I wanted to know that at the end of every day I could cuddle up next to you and fall asleep to the feel of you breathing in my hair, to the smell of bodies that made love to each other, to sometimes have a shower with you or touch you awake from a dream. I want so much to sleep naked next to you for the rest of my life ... my very long life.

It sounded so nice, I convinced myself you wanted it, but you don't. I offered you everything I have, everything that I am, so that we could share it. I didn't know it was too much of all the wrong things ...

Gordon's head throbbed as the words bit into his heart, the one he was no longer so sure he didn't have. He refolded the half read letter and returned it to its envelope.

While Kendall was in his life, he didn't realize how important she'd become or how he looked forward to being with her, talking with her, touching her, or how he counted on her being there. Without Kendall everything was upside down and sleep had become the torture of the damned. His recurring nightmare came every time he closed his eyes. Each time he opened them it was Kendall's face he wanted to see; needed to see, but she was gone. Fully realizing the mistake of banishing her, Gordon made every effort to win her back. He called her home only to get her answering machine three days in a row. He left the same message three days in a row.

"It's Gordon. Please call."

He phoned her office only to be informed for the third day in a row that Kendall was unavailable, but he could leave a message. He didn't. What message would alter the fact he'd been a complete horse's ass. No insult meant to the horse.

Chapter 8

-------------------------------- ▼ --------------------------------

Baby, Come Back
Porter Square – 1980

Lacey arrived at the office the next day to find Kendall's car in the lot. *What's going on* she thought. *How is the 'Queen of Late' in before me?* But when she tried the lobby door it was locked. *What the ...?* Lacey unlocked it and called to Kendall from where she stood in the still dark office.

"Spaulding, where are you?"

"What's left of me is in here." The muffled voice came from Kendall's office.

Lacey walked to the ribbon of light just barely visible under the closed door. She opened it and casually asked, "Okay, who are you and what have you done with my partner? She's never in this early."

"I'm not in this early. I'm in this late. I never went home."

"Why not?" Lacey looked around the office and saw a pillow and afghan on the sofa. "Did you sleep here?"

"I wouldn't exactly call what I did sleeping, but yeah. Now, I've got to get out of here."

"So go home. Get some real sleep."

"No. Not just out of here." Kendall waved her arms to indicate her office. "I mean out of Boston."

"What about our bookings?"

"Send Andi or cancel," Kendall said.

"Honey, you can't just leave!"

"Yes, I can." Kendall's voice was expressionless. "I spent most of last night rearranging our confirmed bookings as well as those pending. Here are my Client Contact Sheets." Kendall handed a bewildered Lacey two folders full of dog-eared paper. "I got hold of some of the Bookers last night. Those marked in pencil are willing to reschedule with Andi. I said you'd call to reconfirm. The one in red pen understands, but is cancelling just the same."

"Can we afford to lose the business?" Lacey asked.

"I know only that I can't afford to stay. I need to get away from ... everyone."

"Does 'everyone' go by the name of Gordon August?"

"I thought we were good together," Kendall said. "That we could offer each other something more and better than either of us could have on our own."

"Did you tell him that?" Lacey asked.

"I tried. But when I went to touch him he turned away. It almost killed me. I saw us as helping each other be happy. Turns out he wasn't even interested in being interested. He doesn't want the responsibility of another person in his life. Personally, I think he's afraid of having kids."

"Even if you're right about the kids part, it's not reason enough to cut you out of his life," Lacey said.

"Enough reason. Not enough reason. It no longer matters. He said be with someone else; anyone else, as long as it isn't him. Then, he suggested I settle down and have a bunch of kids." Kendall looked up at Lacey from where she sat on the floor. "How come you're not laughing? This is funny stuff."

"No it isn't. Honey, didn't you tell him you--"

"No!" Kendall interrupted. "And don't you tell him either. If he stays it's because he believes he'd have a better life with me than without me. I want me to be the one and only reason he stays regardless of whether there's a next generation with little pieces of our DNA. Either he understands that I want to be his partner for life because I love him or he doesn't. Brood mare and warden are not titles I seek to hold. It's all mute anyway. It's over," Kendall added.

"It's not over if you need to leave town," Lacey said.

"Well, it's over enough so it amounts to the same thing."

"Are you going home?" Lacey asked.

"To Lindsey's. He's been pestering me to meet an agent friend of Kenneth's. The way things stand, now is as good a day as any. Ken's agent friend thinks we could be the next 'Bob Fosse show on wheels'. Gordon sees our business as a hobby. 'Paid recreation' is the way he put it."

"What about new business?"

"Do whatever you like." Kendall rose and patted Lacey's shoulder. "You're the business manager."

"But you *are* the business," Lacey protested.

"Not for the next few weeks I'm not," Kendall said wearily. "You be the business. I'm a crumpled old dish rag."

"Is there anything I can do?" Lacey asked.

"You'll be doing it soon enough. Those papers," Kendall indicated the folders. "They're the equivalent of me leaving you holding the proverbial bag. I have no idea how long it will take to clean up the rest of my own paper work, so if you could find out what flights leave for L.A. later, with some choices, that would be great."

Lacey left Kendall's office closing the door behind her. She silently worried; for her friend and partner, for their business. She went to her own office to call airlines. In usual organized fashion Lacey compiled a list of available flights, placed it in a folder and stuck it in the bottom drawer of her desk. Mission accomplished. When Dana arrived she and Lacey sorted through the dozens of pages Kendall handed-off. They divided the work and began calling clients.

Number one on Lacey hit parade was the chairperson for the up-coming Esplanade Summer Concert Series. As it was only the preliminary meeting, she hoped it nonessential for Kendall to make a personal appearance. Perhaps a 'representative' of the Hott Jazz Organization could stay the committee and provide some damage control. Yes, a representative was an excellent idea.

Kendall always described Gordon as 'The Incredibly Hunky Hulky', but as Stewart before him, Lacey could think of Gordon as nothing more than *The Incredible Ass!* with no idea the value of what he'd thrown away.

The phone on the other end rang. A pleasant voice answered and Lacey pasted on her brightest smile hoping it would come across in her voice as real. "Good morning," she said. "This is Lacey Hart, of Hott Jazz. Is Mr. Clements available?"

*   *   *   *

Two hours later a defeated Kendall shuffled into Lacey's office, took the chair facing the desk, leaned against the back cushion and closed her eyes. "What did you find?" Her voice betrayed how tired and beaten she was.

"When do you want to leave?" Lacey retrieved the folder from her desk drawer.

"Right away. I'll just run home and pack a few things. I probably won't need much and if I end up needing anything I didn't take I'll buy it there. Besides, considering the size of Lindsey's place he always says I bring too much crap. You know his motto."

"Think trailer!" They simultaneously echoed his catch phrase.

"National Airlines flight 436 lands at LAX, 4:30 their time," Lacey suggested.

"Fine," Kendall sighed. "Book me one-way."

"One-way!" Concern colored Lacey's voice.

"Don't panic. I'm coming back, I'm just not sure which day. It'll unfortunately cost more, but in the long run the better part of valor is to just buy the return ticket in L.A. I'm out of here." Kendall stood to leave. "I'll call when I get to Lindsey's."

"Does he know you're coming or do you need for me to call ahead?"

"We talked last night. He's running lines at home so he can pick me up any time. I said someone would call with my flight details. Would you mind?"

"Sure thing."

Kendall stopped at the door as she opened it. "Lacey?"

"Yeah?"

"I know he can be a great big jerk sometimes but from the first time I laid eyes on Gordon I saw us together ... as if it already happened. I know it's stupid, but it was so clear and real like I was seeing ..."

~ 65 ~

"The future," Lacey finished Kendall's thought.

"I didn't want to say that out loud and have you think me more insane than usual, but yes. Everything about him was so familiar, it was as if I recognized him and not just as the ghost on my bed that time." Lacey was the only person Kendall dared tell that story. "And in spite of everything," she looked at her oldest and dearest friend, "I really do love him."

"I know. Do you want Andi to drive you? She's in the building but doesn't have a class until 2:00.

"Yeah. In my condition it would be unwise to allow me behind the wheel of a moving vehicle."

"I'll take care of things here. Kiss Lindsey for me."

"I will and thanks for everything you're about to do."

Kendall returned to her own office and waited for Andi to bring around the van. Soon she would be with Lindsey and everything would be okay. Well, everything would be better.

*   *   *   *

Gordon stormed past Dana sitting at her desk on the phone.

"I need to see Lacey," he said breezing by.

"But she's on the phone," Dana said, exasperated. "Please hold," she said into the receiver then depressed the orange button.

Lacey was sitting against the corner of her desk facing the door when Gordon burst into her office.

"Where's Kendall?" He demanded.

"I'm so sorry, Ms. Hart!" Dana apologized following him. "He got past me when I was on the phone."

Lacey covered the mouthpiece of her phone with her hand. "It's okay," she assured.

Dana left to continue making calls.

Lacey uncovered the mouthpiece and spoke into the receiver. "Can I call you back in ten? Something ... unexpected just came up." She returned the phone to its cradle. "Fine, and you?" She answered Gordon without bothering to stand.

"I said *Where's Kendall?*"

"I heard you the first time," Lacey said calmly. "She isn't here."

"Then where is she? She hasn't been home for at least 3 days and no one will tell me anything."

"Really!" Lacey feigned surprise.

"Yes and I'm worried about her."

"Really, again. Funny, I heard you weren't interested in being interested."

"She told you that?" Gordon asked.

"She tells me everything," Lacey confessed.

"Oh ... I see."

"No, I don't think you do," Lacey remained calm as her anger expanded, "otherwise you'd know better than to storm in here with demands of any kind."

"But ... you have to tell me." He was bewildered at her refusal.

"I have some late breaking news fella. You're not my boss. You don't scare me. And ..." she paused slowly walking behind the desk to take a seat in her cream colored leather chair, "... I don't have to *anything* – neither do nor say. You're on your own." Lacey waved him off with her hand as if he were a pesky fly.

"But she could be hurt or in trouble," Gordon complained.

"She certainly was when she left," Lacey confirmed.

"I deserve that," Gordon said embarrassed.

"You deserve worse!"

"But I need to talk to her," Gordon made a second demand.

"I think you've said quite enough," Lacey said. From Gordon's disheveled appearance and his frantic look, Lacey was unable to simply turn him away without saying his piece. She glanced at her watch. "Okay. You have five minutes. Convince me."

"I can't," Gordon objected.

"I suggest you try; because frankly, Gordon, I don't like you right now. There's no reason for me to do anything that would make it even slightly possible for you to do more damage."

"I'm not sure I can make you understand."

"Give it our best shot," Lacey refused to give another inch.

Gordon took the chair facing Lacey's desk, put his head in his hands and stared at the floor wondering how he could possibly persuade her to help him.

Lacey buzzed Dana on the intercom while she waited.

"How are you doing on your lists?"

"Almost done," Dana's voice came back. "You want me to work on yours while you're tied up?"

"Please. We need to figure out who's still in and who's out and we don't have a lot of time to work out a new schedule."

A moment later Dana was in Lacey's office collecting the stack of papers that lay on the desk.

"Thanks." Lacey handed them off. "Call every gig not marked in red, then caucus with Andi and work out a datebook everyone can live with, even if it means hiring another person. It's time we brought another full-service performer or two on board. Kendall's working too hard. If Andi can recommend someone, and that *someone* can sing as well as dance, so much the better. You probably won't be able to finish today but do your best and when you tell them about Andi be sure to say how 'great' she is."

"No problem. You okay with this?" Dana motioned toward Gordon still staring at the floor.

"I'll let you know."

Dana slipped from Lacey's office to complete the task at hand. Meantime, Lacey took Gordon's silence as an opportunity to speak her own mind and let him have it with both barrels.

"You listen to me, Gordon August. As much as we all do our parts around here, Kendall is this business. It may only be temporary but it remains that, right now, she's gone. That means the rest of us are scrambling to reschedule bookings or cancel them. By tampering with Kendall's life you put all of us in a very tough spot, possibly put this business in jeopardy." Lacey made certain Gordon knew his damage was not localized to Kendall. "And while we're on the subject, let me assure you that this is very much a business. I get that your precious law practice does more important work than we do, but this is the work we do and our clients think we're good enough at it to pay us. Hott Jazz is no one's toy, nor anyone's charity. It pays its own way

and provides lives ... correction, very nice lives for all of us. To use
Kendall's words *people actually pay us to have a good time.* How
many people can say that about their work? These last few days I did
not have a very good time. Have I made myself clear?" Lacey walked
around to the front side of her desk, sat against the edge of it and
looked down at Gordon, arms akimbo. "I'm waiting."

Gordon returned her gaze with eyes shiny from held back tears that
his voice did not betray.

"I can't lose her."

"Lose her? You threw her away. You didn't expect her to just sit
around pining away. Life goes on oh-center-of-your-own-universe,
with or without you."

"You couldn't possibly understand. You didn't lead my life,"
Gordon said.

"That's it? That's your excuse? You had a rough life! Mister,
everyone had a rough life!"

"It's not an excuse," he said flatly. "It's just the best explanation I
have. The rest is a long, boring and ugly story."

"Kendall's likely the best thing ever to happen to you and all
you've got for tossing her out like an old shoe is a rough life!
Kendall's life hasn't been Renoir's *Luncheon of the Boating Party*,
everyone sitting around sipping wine or cooing to their dog. She's
never said so, but it's as if she believes someone is out to do god only
knows what to her. Why, I can't imagine. I don't think even she
knows, but whoever it is, why ever it is, the fear is real. I expect the
'who' in question is equally real. I've caught her any number of times
looking over her shoulder for who or what isn't there. She has dreams
that scare the crap out of her but won't talk about them. Don't even
say you don't know this or never saw that scared look in her eyes. Just
don't even."

Gordon neither confirmed nor denied.

"Just so you and I are clear, you need to get through me to get to
her, so you'll need to do better than a rough life. You really are a
piece of work!"

"Did she say that?" Gordon asked.

"She didn't have to!"

Gordon knew he deserved the rest of Lacey's assault, but couldn't bear it. He returned to his original question asking more gently. "Where did she go?"

This time Lacey confessed. "She's with her best friend."

"But ... you run this business together. You're so protective of each other and close. Like you said, she tells you everything. I thought you were her best friend."

"Kendall and I trust each other with our futures and our lives. We are each other's oldest and dearest friends. She was Maid of Honor at my wedding, but her best friend ... that would be Lindsey. They hear the same distant thunder; tell each other what to do and what to wear; take vacations and, when necessary, give each other a good swift kick. They do everything but chew each other's food."

"Do you think Lindsey would help me?" Gordon asked.

"I doubt Lindsey would plead your case. He wants Kendall to forget you and move Hott Jazz to the left coast."

"He? Lindsey's a man!"

"I thought surely after all of this time Kendall would have told you about Lindsey. Well, it's not exactly Lindsey. It's Seth. Seth Lindsey."

"If they're lovers just say so. Don't give me euphemistic crap like *best friend*!"

"Hold up! Lindsey and Kendall have known each other since we were all kids. Are you saying that simply because we grew up they can't stay friends. Platonic friends. What's the matter? You don't think it's possible for men and women to be friends without sex."

"That's for kids!" Gordon snapped.

"Well, someone forgot to tell Kendall!"

"Who do you think you're kidding? She takes vacations with this Lindsey character and you expect me to believe they aren't intimate. All this time Lindsey was a ... a ... a man," Gordon stammered.

"Yes," Lacey said calmly, "and all this time you were a jerk. She's been your friend. She often stays at your place. Is she having sex with you as well?" Lacey asked, knowing full well that Kendall and Gordon had never been intimate. "Perhaps you think she sleeps with all of her friends. I'm her friend. What is it you think she and I do when it's just the two of us?"

Though Gordon's thoughts on Lindsey reflected the knowledge that any normal man-woman relationship not only involves but often revolves around sex, inwardly he knew Lacey was right. It would be wholly unlike Kendall to sleep around. He knew, too, that his relationship with Kendall was something less than normal. He couldn't bring himself to allow a truly intimate moment, while at the same time he barely kept his hands to himself when they were alone. He allowed himself to cross the line of strictly platonic, but just over the line was as far as things ever went.

"Lindsey believes in Kendall," Lacey continued, "and loves her out loud. Their friendship is something so rare that they're more like pieces of each other's souls than friends. It's been that way since the moment they met. I should ever be so lucky! You should ever be so lucky! Lindsey thinks she could have a career choreographing for the film industry, has an agent chomping at the bit to represent her, represent us while you, on the other hand, think she's ordinary. So, why the big concern?"

"Is she all right?"

"She will be after some time with Lindsey, away from here and you."

"I have to see her. Please!" Gordon begged. "Help me."

"Your five minutes are about up and I've heard nothing to persuade me."

It was the first time since Gordon was a child that he admitted needing help, that he was willing to accept help. It was the first time since he was a child that he thought someone would actually help him if he asked. Lacey would either believe him or not. He told her everything including the story of the night that changed his life and the recurring dream of the dancing woman just outside his grasp; the woman with Kendall's face.

"It's as though I met her a long time ago. I know it's impossible, but when I think of her it's in the same breath with ..." Gordon stopped himself, looked back at the floor and went silent.

"Continue."

"In the same breath with my parents' death. My father was a prominent physician working on some hush-hush research. His death made all the headlines and news reels. His office was sealed immediately, the night my folks died in fact. Their attorney personally boxed the contents as part of the estate, but never found Dad's notes and research material. To this day no one knows what happened to it. Everything just disappeared.

"All I have is a police report and a pile of newspaper clippings; none of which provide any useful information. Each of them say it had been raining and we'd been to Wonderland. It was the night Benny Goodman's Orchestra appeared. That much I remember myself; that and arguing with my mother over wearing my school slicker over my winter coat. Seeing Benny Goodman was a fancy event and the slicker was, well, a dumb yellow slicker.

"Way back, when I originally received the police report, I tried contacting the responding officer, but he died in the line of duty that same night. I hired two private-eyes to locate the only witness, but it seems she fell off the earth. Neither was able to find her meaning there's literally no one to ask. I even tried hypnosis hoping for something, anything, to spark more of my own memory, but it's useless. The police report is sketchy at best and no one can remember what they didn't see." All expression was gone from Gordon's voice. "And there's something wrong with the report; it says we were on our way home ... which can't be right."

"Why not?" Lacey probed.

"We were on Storrow Drive in-bound; that means east. We lived in Brookline at the time. East is the wrong direction to be heading home. I was only six and it was late when we left the Ballroom. I expect I was installed in the back seat to sleep my way home. I can't be sure of anything beyond the cold and the heavy rain and that history says Storrow nearly always floods in such conditions. Our car probably skidded or hydroplaned or both which is maybe what caused our car to roll. I was thrown clear, through an open back window, but my parents," Gordon's voice trailed, "they were trapped in the front seat. The car ... there was an explosion.

"The funeral was two days later. Five days after that I regained consciousness at Boston Memorial with a concussion and a broken arm. It was over ... and I didn't even know it happened. I went to live with my aunt and uncle. To this day neither of them will speak of that night."

"Where does Kendall fit in the mix?" Lacey asked.

"She was there."

"You and I both know that's not possible."

"As I said, you can't remember what you didn't see, so if she wasn't there, why do I *remember* her?"

Neither of them had an answer.

"It's as if I blocked out everything other than Kendall, Benny Goodman, the cold, and the rain. From the time I was a kid I've been plagued by a recurring dream of a woman. I've been afraid of meeting the woman in it; because I knew that when I did I would care for her like no other woman in my life. I feared that caring for her would enable her to hurt me. As a child, my solution was to shove all women away, care about none of them; which created Hell of an emotional armor," Gordon said almost sadly and brushed the awful thought away with his hand. "When I was no longer a child, I finally caught the clue that no matter how much we think they are dreams, and the stuff in them, aren't real which meant *dream woman* wasn't real either. Then Kendall walked into my life. Dream woman was real. The day we met at the gym she touched my cheek." Gordon put his hand to the spot still feeling the back of Kendall's hand against it. "Did she tell you that?"

Lacey shook her head.

"It was so familiar. The smell of her sweat mixed with the scent of her perfume and created waves of memory; memory of Kendall. Intellectually, there's no way she could have been there, except that I know she was. I know it! Nothing has been the same since that day at the gym. It's like a train wreck. You know you shouldn't look but you simply can't help yourself. I finally just had to get away, but couldn't be the one to leave. I did whatever was necessary to maker her leave; to make her want to leave. Don't tell me how sick and twisted it is. I know and ... I know.

"Tell me about this dream," Lacey said.

Gordon did.

"I bow, the way I learned at cotillion a hundred years ago. The woman's face comes into focus and it's Kendall. I dream her there. I wake up reaching for her and smelling her perfume," Gordon finished.

"Carmen," Lacey said.

"I know what it is," Gordon said flatly. "I checked out every new fragrance the moment it was advertised. I think I sniffed every perfume ever made. In the spring of '78, there it was. I recognized it immediately."

"You recognized a perfume that wasn't introduced until 1978. You must be mistaken."

"Do you imagine I don't know how crazy this sounds?" Gordon leaned back. His head fell against the soft cushion of the chair. His gaze landed on the ceiling. "My parents died nearly twenty-five years ago. Kendall was a young child living in Miami. My life's tragedy took place in Boston; 1500 miles away."

"If it's a dream perhaps you're seeing the future."

Gordon shook his head. "I researched dreams to help unravel this. All studies say they are the leftovers of reality. Existing reality. If that's true then somehow Kendall was there that night."

Gordon searched Lacey's face for some indication as to whether she believed him. She gave nothing away. Having left nothing unsaid Lacey understood why Gordon kept everyone at arm's length, especially Kendall. She even understood why he was so afraid of losing her, even if he, himself, did not. If Kendall really was the key to Gordon's past, maybe she was the missing link to both of their futures; the one in which Kendall said she saw him so clearly.

"Is that it?" Lacey asked with some sympathy.

"It's everything I know."

"There must be more."

"What kind of more?"

"The kind that explains you being thrown through the car's window."

"It was before mandatory seat belts for kids." Gordon sat up.

"Yes, but who opened the window?"

"Maybe I did or my dad," Gordon offered.

"You, sir, were asleep. You just said so. And I have kids, so I'm here to tell you that, even in The Fifties, no right-minded parent opened a rear window on a night that was cold enough for a coat and wet enough to need a slicker on top of that coat."

"Okay. Fine." He looked at Lacey bewildered. "You tell me. Whodunit?"

Gordon was spent and with no answer to that or any other question. He and Lacey stared at each other in silence then he rested his head against the soft cushion of the chair again. With his eyes closed he silently prayed Lacey would ask no more of him, prayed that Lacey would help him.

"Dana." Lacey buzzed the intercom and pulled a manila folder from the bottom drawer of her desk. "Get Security in here on the double. Mr. August won't be staying."

Gordon went wild. He leapt from the chair sending it toppling over backwards.

"I trusted you and, for five seconds, I actually thought you'd help me. I told you everything. What more do you want?" He demanded, banging his fists on the desk. "I never discussed that night or that dream with anyone. I'm a lawyer and you out-maneuvered me." He leaned forward over Lacey's desk and his hands gripped the edge of it. There was a menacing look in his eyes as his broad shoulders cast an ominous shadow across her face. His face crimson with anger.

Dana appeared at Lacey's door, but before she could say a word Lacey demanded, "Where's Security!"

"Just getting off the elevator."

A slight young woman, obviously one of Kendall's dancers, took Dana's place in the doorway. She was dressed in sweats and her long blond hair was tied up in a pony-tail pulled through the back of a Red Sox cap.

"You sent for me," she said.

Gordon glanced at the blond then back at Lacey, his stance unaltered.

"This is your great security?"

Before Gordon knew what hit him, the left side of his face made contact with the floor and one of his arms was pinned behind him. The blond had her knee in his back and the bill of her cap in his face.

"As a tenth degree black belt, I am obliged to inform you that I am a weapon. Resist and I'll be only too happy to do you bodily harm. Do you understand?"

"Great!" Gordon gasped for breath. "What next? Will you have her throw me out of the building?"

Lacey peaked over the edge of her desk at a prostrate Gordon and a smile crossed her lips.

"Actually I was going to have her take you to the airport."

"Some business woman! You pay a security guard to run errands."

"Security guard!" Both women exclaimed in unison.

"Who said anything about a security guard?" Lacey asked.

"You said *get security*," Gordon struggled to speak, what with Andi's knee still in his back.

"Andi isn't a security guard but, what with her expertise in Shodokan Karate, we call her Security. Actually, she's Andrea Securitas. One of our performers slash teachers. Kendall was forever late or getting lost on the way to gigs, so Andi fills in as driver. That's why I asked Dana to page her. Perhaps you're familiar with her family's businesses. Security Armored Cars. Security Burglar Alarms. Security Self Defense Schools. Security–"

"I'm familiar," Gordon said from the floor interrupting the long list of Securitas owned companies. "I represent them."

"Oh, crap," Andi said. "You're Daddy's attorney?" Once again she put the bill of her cap in Gordon's face still pinning him to the floor. "Um, nice to meet you." Her embarrassment made the words form a question.

"I'd say the feeling's mutual but from this position–"

"I think you can let him up," Lacey said. "I'm sure there will be no more threatening outbursts, will there Gordon?"

He got to his feet.

"Against my better judgment, I'm going to help you. Don't make me sorry," she said, opening the folder on her desk and repeated the information she gave to Kendall four days earlier. Shall I see if they have room for one more?"

He nodded.

"You can't go looking like ... that." Lacey indicated is overall appearance. "Leave your car and Andi will take you home to shower and throw some things in a suitcase. Here's Lindsey's address and phone." Lacey handed him a slip of paper. "I'll call ahead and let him know you're coming."

"Why are you helping me?" He was almost afraid to ask. "Do you believe me?"

"I don't want to but, frankly, your imagination isn't good enough to come up with a whopper like that on such short notice. What I believe is that you believe it. Kendall loves you and, heaven help me, I'm finding it hard to hate you myself. There will be hell to pay when she finds out what I've done so, I repeat, don't make me sorry."

*   *   *   *

Andi and Gordon drove to his apartment in virtual silence. Her only thought was explaining to her father that she literally floored his attorney. His thoughts revolved around what he'd say to Kendall and Lacey's idea that perhaps he had not cheated death unaided.

Andi waited in the lobby of Gordon's building while he went upstairs to quickly pack. In the process, he got a look at himself in the bathroom mirror. Lacey was right. He couldn't face Kendall in his disheveled condition. He stripped out of his clothes, had a quick shower, shaved to rejuvenate himself then quickly dressed. He and Andi arrived at Logan forty-five minutes later. While they waited in a line of traffic for passenger drop-off, her eyes trained on the road, she broke their silence.

"So you're what all the hub-bub is about."

"Yeah," Gordon answered flatly.

"Do you think you can fix it?

"If she's taken lessons from you, she may pin me to the floor before I get the chance." A slight smile passed his lips.

"Apologies for that, but I thought someone might get hurt."

"I could never really hurt Lacey."

"I didn't mean Lacey," Andi said as she inched their vehicle forward, never taking her eyes from the road.

Gordon understood Andi's thought that he might hurt himself wasn't an accusation just concern. That's when he took his first good look at Andi. He noted her soft even features and the warmth that fairly spilled from her eyes. Everything about her said poise and self confidence. Though she was certainly dancer-lean, she was in no way a replica of The Ballet Center's corps of tattered ballerinas; each one anorexic thin like refugees just off the boat and high on some pain killer or other to camouflage an endless series of injuries. Unlike Babette and the others, Andi was substantial as were Kendall's other dancers. Now that Gordon considered it, none of them vaguely resembled the tired rag-a-muffins he met during his time at Conrad and Wilkins.

"Will you be okay on your own?" Andi interrupted his thoughts. "Another teacher is filling-in my class so I needn't rush back. I can park and wait with you."

Gordon turned her down.

"L.A.'s too long a flight for nothing but your own thoughts. Maybe a book or there's a mag on the back seat if you don't mind GQ."

"GQ?"

"As you well know I have a father and four brothers, each one a fashion plate. A girl's got to keep up," Andi offered with a smile.

"Thanks, but I think I'll sleep. It'll be a treat considering I haven't had much lately."

It was finally their turn. Andi pulled up to the curb and Gordon opened the door. She rested her hand on his arm delaying his exit.

"Don't go with your mind already made up about Lindsey. He's a decent guy and a good friend. Give both of you a break and yourself a chance to like him."

"You know Lindsey?" Gordon asked.

"He's the one hooked me up with Kendall. If not for Lindsey, I'd still be just another spoiled rich kid partying on my Daddy's money."

Gordon nodded and exited the van.

"Everything will work out," Andi added. "It always does."
"I hope you're right."
With Lacey's help and Andi's kind words Gordon entered the terminal to begin the journey he prayed would bring Kendall home.

*   *   *   *

Gordon checked in, got his ticket and took his one carry-on to the gate. The flight began boarding within fifteen minutes and he was grateful for no delays. He handed his boarding pass and hanging suitcase to the first class steward.

"I'm sorry, sir, but your seat is in coach," the steward said.

Embarrassed, Gordon took back his luggage and boarding pass, found his seat and stashed his bag in an overhead bin. He was so grateful for Lacey's help that he allowed her to make his travel arrangements totally forgetting that she and Kendall ran Hott Jazz on a tight budget. *Coach!* Gordon sighed in exasperation. He never traveled coach. The seats were too small and there was always at least one screaming baby sitting entirely too close. At worst that would end up being the scenario. At best it would be an uncomfortable way to spend five very long hours. At least his seat was by a window.

A mother with a small baby in tow took the seat next to his. *Just great!* Gordon thought. The baby was sleeping, but he would likely wake up crying from the change in cabin pressure or throw up from motion sickness. The woman carried so much paraphernalia she couldn't get herself organized and hold her baby as well. She placed the sleeping infant in Gordon's arms, asking if he wouldn't mind holding the child for a minute. Gordon started to object, but she spoke over him.

"If he starts to squirm, just pop him up on your shoulder. He'll go right back to sleep."

The woman dropped her belongings onto her seat and the floor in front of it. She leaned over the baby, put her hand on the side of his head and whispered, "Please be good for the nice man, Timothy." She gently kissed the baby's head and left to find a flight attendant.

Out of ear-shot by the time Gordon understood she was leaving him alone with her baby, the infant began to stir. Not knowing what else to do, Gordon followed the woman's instructions certain they would be absolutely useless. The infant continued to squirm and began to whimper.

"There, there, Timothy," Gordon said uneasily, picturing himself holding a squirming mass of diaper and tears. "Your mother will be back soon. I hope."

The baby settled down.

What do you know, Gordon thought smugly, *handling babies isn't so hard.* What he failed to realize was that the baby was handling him. Little Timothy nuzzled his face into Gordon's shoulder and neck and literally made himself at home. Gordon had no clue babies as young as Timothy could hold on so tightly and even less idea that he would like it. Gordon needed to remind himself that he was uncomfortable around babies. He certainly had no desire to hold them, but this young life clinging to him was changing that.

The mother returned with a stewardess who helped arrange all of the baby gear in the remaining cabinets and, as the infant was sleeping quietly, never inquired how Gordon was managing. She took her seat, turned toward Gordon and reached out her hands.

"I'll take him now." When she placed the baby flat on her lap, the little boy awoke offering his mother a toothless smile. "Were you a good boy for the nice man? He wasn't any trouble?" She asked Gordon. "He's been so fussy lately. Won't let anyone but me or his father anywhere near him and cries near strangers. It's been a nightmare. We're relocating so my husband, Art, is already in L.A. to find us a house, which leaves just me. I think Tim misses him.

"Your Daddy is the center of your universe," the woman spoke to her son. Timothy looked at Gordon, smiled, reached out his arm and shook it up and down as if pointing. "He seems to like you. Maybe there's something familiar, perhaps your cologne."

"After shave. It's called Spectrum."

"Oh, Timothy," the woman admonished sweetly, "what am I going to with you and your Daddy? Such expensive taste!" She then propped him up on her shoulder where he snuggled down and fell back to sleep.

A stewardess walked up and down the isles making sure everyone's seat and tray-tables were in their fully upright and locked position. When she stopped at their row, Gordon informed her he intended to sleep the entire way and did not wish to be awakened for anything short of a full-on emergency.

"If you don't eat, you'll be hungry by the time we land."

"In that case I'll eat when we land. Plane food has too much salt and fat and everything else I don't eat."

"I'll tell the others," the stewardess said. "For next time, you can order special food when you make your reservations."

"I would have done so this time only *I* didn't make these reservations. I never travel coach. Is it possible to move to first class now and have the airline charge my account when we land?"

"Sorry. I'm afraid we're full. There isn't an empty seat on the plane." The flight attendant continued down the isle.

"Was it something I said?" The young mother parried with Gordon.

"What?" Gordon returned, not really listening.

"I should have asked someone else to hold Tim. It's just that, as I said, he's been so fussy and when he didn't cry when we came near you, I took a chance that you wouldn't mind. It was a terrible imposition." The woman looked completely embarrassed.

"I'm sure your son's a great little guy," Gordon reassured. "It's just that I was planning to sleep and I won't be able to with a baby crying in my ear the whole way. Besides, I never held a baby before."

"Really! You did it like an old pro." The woman pulled a *Snuggle Baby* from her bag and strapped her sleeping son inside it, then fastened the contraption to herself in preparation for take-off. "Even when Tim isn't being fussy," the mother confessed, "he's very particular about who can hold him."

"I guess I'm flattered," Gordon said.

The pilot's voice came over the intercom. "Ladies and gentlemen, we are next in line. Will the crew please take their seats in preparation for take-off."

Once the plane reached cruising altitude and the seat belt sign went out, Gordon put his seat back, stuck a pillow behind his head and fell asleep. The woman next to him did likewise. Gordon, Timothy and his mother slept the whole way and never woke up once.

The stewardess came back down the aisle asking that seats be returned to their upright position as the plane made its final approach to LAX.

"I never asked your name or what you do," Timothy's mother said.

"Gordon August. Attorney-at-Law."

"Are you in town on business?"

"Not exactly."

"Not that it's any of my business, but you look as though you've been through the wringer."

"I guess I have," Gordon admitted.

"Life sure can be stink-o sometimes. You may quote me. It may be a bit presumptuous but, if you don't already have plans, would you care to join my husband and me for a casual dinner? Thai food up in Malibu. We're meeting a prospective client and I'm sure no one will object to some intelligent conversation. Plus, I don't think the client has legal representation, so it could be a nice business connection."

"I couldn't effectively represent a west coast client when my practice is in Boston."

"I guess I forgot to mention, the client is from Boston."

"I couldn't promise. I'm here to find someone and I don't know how long it will take or if I'll be successful."

"But I do see," the woman said. "This someone, is she the reason you look as though you were run over by a tank?"

"I'm afraid that's my own fault," Gordon admitted. "How did you know the person is a she? A touch of the clairvoyant?"

"Just been on the planet a while is all," the woman quipped. "Anne Page," the woman extended her hand, then extracted a business card from her purse. The card labeled her as a Talent Representative and listed numbers for offices in New York, L.A. and Boston.

"Tim and I are headed straight to the hotel so, unless someone is picking you up, our driver can drop you wherever."

"That isn't necessary."

"Yes it is," Anne insisted. "You helped me. The very least I can do is return the favor."

"I can get a cab. I'm fine on my own, really."

"Sorry to be such a Mom and contradict, but no you're not, really," Anne said matter-of-factly. "You look as though you haven't slept in days. You haven't eaten in at least six hours I know about. You're trying to find someone who probably doesn't want to be found. Frankly, you could use a friend."

Gordon had no rebuttal. He was beaten for the second time that day.

"In that case," he said, "I accept. I guess I could use a friend."

"Good!" Anne said, cupping the head of her sleeping son. "Timothy, sweetheart, your new friend is going to join us."

The little boy woke to the sound of his mother's voice and his face lit up when he looked at Gordon. Having thought Anne meant herself, Gordon was surprised to learn his new friend was a baby, not quite one year old.

The other passengers disembarked leaving only Anne, Timothy and Gordon to collect their belongings. The threesome stopped to pick up Ann's suitcases from the luggage carrousel and exited the terminal to find Anne's driver. Gordon helped load the trunk of the waiting limo. Gordon climbed in back with Anne and Tim.

"Where would you like to go?" Anne asked.

"I have an address." Gordon reached into his shirt pocket and retrieved the paper Lacey gave him.

"This is on the way to the hotel," Anne said, lowering the window between them and the driver. "Mitch, we'll be going to the Hollyweird Hills first. 2145 East Canyon Road."

"Holly-weird." A smile touched Gordon's lips.

"You'll understand once you're here a while."

The ride passed quickly with Anne talking about the great new client she and her husband hoped to represent. Gordon listened with only half an ear and they were at Lindsey's before he knew it. Mitch retrieved Gordon's bag from the trunk while Gordon, still in the back seat, made his goodbyes.

"We *will* see you later," Anne encouraged.

"I'll try, but–"

"I know. This is more important than food."

"I'm only now learning just how important." Gordon felt the need to unburden. "I shoved her away and I guess, at the back of my head, I thought she would always be waiting in case I changed my mind. Now, I'm afraid that she's out of my life forever and I had to follow her here just to talk. I put her on hold while I took my Time. I realize now I wasn't taking it, I was wasting it." A little embarrassed he added, "Tim showed me that."

"Was he spouting Kirkegaard again?" Anne smiled.

Gordon laughed for the first time in a week. "He's a baby. No ulterior motives; no agenda. On the plane, he fidgeted and whimpered when you stepped away–"

"Sorry," Anne interrupted. Her cheeks colored.

"It's fine. I just did what you said and he calmed right down. It was then I realized it wasn't just me holding him; he was holding me, just like her. I didn't know such little babies could do that. He didn't want anything other than to be held."

"Just like her. And all this time you've kept her at arm's length because you thought everyone has ulterior motives and agendas."

This time he blushed as Anne finished his thought.

"I've been on my own a long time and it's always been my experience that they do. I haven't given anyone the benefit of the doubt, until Tim, even though any reasonable person would have given it to her." He looked away from Anne continuing. "Worse, her partner accused me of being the center of my own universe and–"

"And she was right. You're mortally afraid that if you let anyone enter your world you'd no longer be the center of attention, not even your own, and you're embarrassed that you were so transparent," Anne finished his thought again.

"How did you know that?"

"Are you kidding? I'm married to the author of those thoughts."

"Not to be personal but how did you get Tim?" Gordon asked.

"I told Arthur he wouldn't be giving up anything he wouldn't get back if he made the investment in me and, during a moment of temporary insanity, he drove us to New Jersey to get married that

night. A few years later, when we were discussing a family, I assured
him that having a child and being a child weren't mutually exclusive
activities. He said he'd think about it. So happens, that night the
condom box was empty. Nine months later Arthur was in the delivery
room ... under duress. When the nurse handed him his son, and he
held that new life, one would have been hard-pressed to convince Art
that having Tim wasn't his idea.

"Tim would rather be with him than anyone in the world including
me and, Hell, I'm the food source," she laughed. "Art is no longer the
center of his own universe but he's still the center of mine and Tim's,
so it all came out in the wash. Is that the problem? Your lady wants
babies and you don't?"

"She never said so, but she's a woman. I assumed it was a given."

"I suppose you're mostly right, but a friendly word of advice ...
assume nothing. Ask what she wants. You may be surprised. When
you assume, you make an ASS of U and ME. Get it?"

Gordon nodded.

"Give us a call at the hotel, either way," Anne said. "Sleep on a
plane is worthless, so I'm headed for a nap, but speak to Art. I'll tell
him to expect your call. We're at the Bon Aire, Bungalow 4, under the
name Collins. We use my maiden name," she explained, "because, in
this town, even the bell-hops are actors and we're far too recognizable
using Page."

Gordon got out of the limo, thanked Anne for the lift and took his
bag from the trunk manned by the patiently waiting driver.

"Good luck at the Lost and Found," Anne called to him, leaning
out the window, as the limo drove away. The vehicle rounded the
corner and was out of sight by the Time Gordon remembered that
Lacey had named her new baby Paige and that she was just about
Tim's age. Inwardly he asked himself whether he might not be the
only one who thought Page and Paige wasn't just some sort of weird
coincidence, but a sign of something, or of something yet to come.

Kendall and Lindsey's dog, Astro, returned from their hike to the
sound of an open door conversation. Hearing only Lindsey's voice,
she naturally assumed that he and Kenneth had enough *alone time* and

now had company. Kendall unclipped Astro's leash and he bounded down the steps into the apartment ahead of her. She descended the stairs to the sound of an angry male voice, the back of his aggressive form looming large and foreign in the open doorway. Taking advantage of the ever energetic Astro throwing the man off balance, and not waiting to ask questions or to realize who the man was, Kendall used one of the take-down moves Andi showed her in case of emergencies. Kendall dropped the man to the floor, her knee in his back, the left side of his face pinned to the cool tile floor.

"Not twice in one day!" Gordon gasped.

"How did you find me?" She asked then answered her own question. "Lacey!"

"Yes," he answered simply and got up from the floor brushing off his clothes.

Seeing Lindsey and Kenneth still in bed and in a snuggle Kendall quickly stood and turned to face the door.

"Lindsey, honey, I am so sorry!

What's wrong with you?" She angrily demanded of Gordon. "You went to college. You know that a neck tie on the door knob means **KEEP OUT**, even when you find the door unlocked. For god sake, turn around! Kenneth, Lindsey, we're out of here. In fact, we were never here."

Kendall took Gordon by the elbow and escorted him outside continuing her verbal spanking as they exited. She closed the door firmly behind them to the sound of Kenneth's and Lindsey's laughter. Out of earshot, Kendall turned on Gordon.

"Exactly what did you think you were doing back there?"

"I thought you and Lindsey were ... you know."

"No, I don't know. I'm a bit dense in that department. Why don't you explain it to me."

"What with the tie and hearing someone call you; I mean the other guy, *Kenny, honey.* I thought you and Lindsey were–" Gordon didn't finish the sentence. "I just lost it and–"

"And you thought you'd save me from my best friend in the world?" Kendall didn't wait for a response. "For the record, I don't need saving, especially not from Lindsey. And I don't sleep around.

I'm with one man or no man. Get it?" She poked him hard in the chest with her index finger.

"Ow! I get it."

"And you no longer have the right to lose it, since you're not interested," poke, "in being interested," poke again.

Gordon winced not only from Kendall's physical attack but at his own words come back to bite him for the second time in the same day.

"Besides," Kendall said," is *my* name Kenny?"

"Well, no, but it was a natural assumption."

"Natural for whom? You know better, as does someone who's known me as long as Lindsey. Think about it! Does anyone call me Kenny, ever?"

"I didn't think. I just reacted," Gordon defended.

"Yes, and poorly!" Hurt still laced Kendall's voice. "What do you want now? I already granted your wish."

"I ... I missed you," Gordon confessed.

"I think not! You made it abundantly clear that the only place you want me is out of your life. I obliged you."

"I changed my mind," he said sheepishly. "I tried calling to say so, but I could never reach you; not at the office or home. When I got your machine for the third day in a row, without so much as a *Go to hell* I got worried. I convinced Lacey to help me.

"How? Blackmail?"

"Don't be angry. I just showed her my heart was in the right place."

"You mean the heart you don't have," Kendall reminded him.

"I decided you were right. I want you to be right. It's that I forgot where I put it. It took you being gone to realize I'd never find it without you. I need you."

"That's rich coming from someone who finds me so repulsive."

"I never said any such thing."

"Actions, Gordon. They speak louder than any words. That night, when I tried to touch you, you turned away. There's nothing left to say after that. I'm not some yo-yo you can send away and pull back as it suits. I need a real relationship with someone who's my friend and understands the importance of touching all night and breakfast together the next day. I can't come back knowing you don't want those things. I'm done being your sister!"

"I don't want you for my sister," he insisted. "But it's difficult to trust anyone enough to let them get close." Still seeing her as the woman who disappears from his dream; leaving him to wake up alone in the night, Gordon asked, "How do I know you won't leave me again?"

"I didn't leave you this time," she answered not understanding there was more to know. "I mean, obviously I left town because I'm here; but only because you shoved me away. Have you any idea what you put me through? You don't suppose I'd choose being this mess. I know it's hard for you to hear and harder for you to believe; because you're such a jerk, but I love you. I've always loved you."

Gordon took her in his arms, held her close and repeated her words. "Even though I'm such a jerk?"

The sound of his voice stirred something in Kendall's heart.

"Even then." She pressed her face against his chest and was sure that she was finally home.

"Is there somewhere we can go?' Gordon changed the subject. "As you recall, there's a neck tie on the door knob."

"How about a tour of Griffith Park," she suggested. "Astro just showed me all of his favorite trees."

"I assume you mean that small pony."

"He's just a puppy." Kendall laughed. "Part Shepherd, part sled dog."

"And part horse," Gordon added laughing as they headed for the entrance to Griffith Park. "Doesn't it bother you Lindsey's with that guy? Lacey never said he was gay."

"He's Bi," she corrected. "And there's no reason for Lacey to explain Lindsey's private life. It's why they call it a 'private life'. If he tells you, that's his deal, but it's neither Lacey's place nor her job to explain him. I would never use Lindsey's sexual orientation to explain our relationship or make it easier to trust us. You either do or you don't; simple as that. As to anything else about Lindsey; he's my best friend, nothing he does bothers me. And 'that guy', as you so delicately put it, happens to be a very successful film maker and a wonderful friend to both Lindsey and me. Kenneth accepts Lindsey's and my relationship without jealousy or fear of Lindsey being unfaithful. He trusts us. Can you could do the same?"

"I can try," Gordon offered.

"See that you succeed!" Kendall punctuated each word by poking his chest again.

"Ow!" Gordon's hand massaged the now tender spot. "You know, that hurts!"

"Good!" Kendall said. "Then you'll be sure to remember it won't you."

When they returned to the apartment the doorknob was still unlocked, but necktie free.

"Can we have dinner?" Gordon asked.

"Kenneth arranged a dinner meeting with an agent friend. It will be casual but not so casual it wouldn't be awkward to just bring you along. How about after?"

"After is okay," Gordon tried to sound as if it didn't matter that he spent five hours on a plane, in coach, and now had to take a number. "I met someone on the plane who extended an invitation to join their party this evening. They're hosting a business dinner for a prospective client without legal council. I said I'd let them know. All right if I use the phone?" Gordon looked to Lindsey.

"Help yourself, old man," Lindsey said. "I'm going to hop in the shower, luv," he said to Kendall. "Won't take a moment." With a sly smile he looked over his shoulder on his way to the bathroom. "I went through your things and selected an outfit. Wear it."

"Hey!" She ran after him like a kid sister, but he was too quick and locked the door behind him. "Hey, Boss Boy!" She banged a fist on the bathroom door. It remained shut.

"Yes, luv," Lindsey's unflustered voice floated out, smooth as glass.

"Come out of there and face me like a man!"

"When I'm clean and gorgeous."

"If I have to wait 'til then we'll miss dinner."

"Stop being difficult," Lindsey admonished. "Wear the outfit!"

"You're on thin ice, Boss Boy. Don't tell me what to do!" She banged her fist against the wood one last time before walking away.

"That's right break down my door," the pretend hurt in Lindsey's voice followed her, "and after everything we've been through together."

"In your ear, Boss Boy," Kendall called back over her shoulder.

"Kids!" Kenneth jerked a thumb in the direction of the bathroom.

Gordon dialed. Arthur Page answered. Gordon took a taxi to the Bon Aire and the same limo that dropped him off earlier took everyone to the restaurant, the ever silent Mitch behind the wheel.

Upon arrival, Gordon offered to hold Tim while Anne went inside to see whether their prospective client had arrived which left Arthur to handle the assorted 'baby crap'.

"In some families the man is considered the bread-winner. In this family," he joked, "I'm the designated schlepper."

Through the front window of the restaurant, Gordon saw Anne in animated conversation with someone just outside his line of vision. He entered to find her with none other than Kendall and Lindsey.

"What are you doing here?" Kendall was visibly annoyed that he followed her when she specifically said he should not join them.

"Anne is the 'someone' I told you about." He chuckled at the coincidence, wondering for the second time that day if it were one. "I expect that makes you the client without legal representation. Can I recommend a good lawyer?"

Everyone appreciated the humor of the situation, that all their lives should have been so intertwined. Even Timothy seemed to laugh at Gordon's joke. Kendall wondered to herself whether 'The Pages' being in the same place with her and Gordon was a fluke or some force was in charge of their lives. 'The Pages' combined with Lacey's baby, Paige; nick-named 'Paiges', didn't feel like very much of a coincidence to Kendall.

The maitre d' sat their party in the restaurant's private dining room. Gordon hooked Timothy's baby seat securely to the table between himself and Anne. It was clear to a blind man Tim and Gordon were smitten with each other. Gordon talked to Tim through almost the entire dinner and it seemed that the baby hung on his every word.

Watching Gordon, Kendall worried. *He changed his mind about me, but what about a childless life.* She shoed the thought away while Anne and Arthur made their sales pitch.

"We handle some hot young recording talent," Art began. "They need a hot young choreographer to stage their music videos."

"Not that I don't want the work but what about someone like Fosse or Paula Abdul? Their work is amazing and well known. You've never seen mine."

"Not exactly true," Arthur corrected. "We lived in Boston until just recently and my family dragged Anne and me to a special Dance Umbrella performance by guest choreographer Kendall Spaulding of Hott Jazz."

"Big Sky," Kendall said, remembering how well the performance was received and reviewed.

"Exactly," Art said. "So we're not entirely ignorant of your work. Bob and Paula are big name talents, but we'd mostly be getting just Bob or Paula. And they're so booked they're probably unavailable until Y2K. Our need is immediate.

"Working with Hott Jazz also opens up whole new possibilities; because you, Miss Spaulding, are a package; a *dance company* – the choreographers *and* the dancers. No more time wasted on auditions and worrying over where we'll get the next group of dancers or whether they'll work well as a team or if they can handle the choreography. You took out all of the guess work. You turned a great idea into a well run organization. We'd like to take your great idea and move it to the next level; rock and music videos. It's the next wave. I see us all hopping on and taking a nice long ride." Arthur used his hand to demonstrate the path of a wave. "What do you say?"

Trying to control her excitement Kendall looked at Gordon. He said nothing but gave her a quick wink and his sly smile. Kendall looked from Anne to Arthur.

"My lawyer seems to think it's a good idea so, barring any objections from my partners," she extended her hand to Anne then to Arthur, "I say we're in the rock video business."

Dinner concluded and everyone made their farewells. The Pages collected their load of baby crap and returned to the hotel in the Limo which brought them to Malibu. Lindsey hailed a cab, but when Kendall made moves to join him he shoed her away. "You and the lawyer have important things to discuss. The Ass may be gone, but the Ass taste lingers on and on."

"You saw him with the Pages' son. How do I tell him?"

"Gently," Lindsey stroked her cheek, "very gently."

Lindsey got into the cab, closed the door and it pulled away, headed for Kenneth's Bel Air home.

Kendall and Gordon entered Lindsey's apartment. It was silent except for the sounds of Astro sleeping on his Land's End doggy bed. He dragged it to the foot of Kendall's bed, apparently to protect her.

"Would you like something to drink?" She offered. "There's regular tea and herbal or there's–"

Gordon interrupted her with a kiss. Holding her, he felt the tension in her back.

"What's up dancer?" He smiled. "Not planning to poke me again?"

Kendall pulled away. "We need to talk."

"I'm not going to like this, am I?"

"No." Kendall turned to face him. "It's about my past."

"I don't care about anything that happened before you and me," Gordon protested.

"You'll care about this." Kendall looked at the floor and began. "When we met I couldn't believe my luck; a man who actually didn't want children. It seemed too good to be true. Tonight, I see that it either wasn't or you changed your mind, after all you can." She looked up at him with tears in her eyes she struggled not to shed. "I can't."

"I don't understand," Gordon said.

"I was engaged once. I wanted to believe that the guy loved me and was faithful, so I convinced myself it was true. The reality was, he was a good-looking slime-ball; binge alcoholic who occasionally partook of his secret professional sideline; cocaine. Apparently he also slept around. I was so naive I didn't see any of it.

"I woke up one morning with unbearable pressure in my pelvis. I could hardly sit. I've always had problems in the reproductive department. I assumed my discomfort was just a new wrinkle. Bottom line? Stewart gave me a raging case of P-I-D. For those of us in the room not familiar, that's Pelvic Inflammatory Disease for which one needs antibiotics, and after which Dr. Petry suggested a laparoscopy to determine the extent of the damage."

"Damage?" Gordon looked at her with concern.

"Scarring ... in my fallopian tubes. We caught it early and that's good. But the situation with P-I-D is that a little can go a long way. And that's bad."

"How bad?"

"From the way you were with the Pages' little boy, I'd say it's pretty bad."

"But you're all right now." Gordon started to go to her, but Kendall held up her hand like a stop sign.

"Depends on your definition. I guess I'm healthy enough, but children ... that would take a minor miracle and I'm fresh out of those. Given my medical history, there was only ever a tiny chance that I could conceive. Now there isn't even that. You see, last week when you were still so sure you didn't want a wife or family and told *me* to have a pack of kids, it was almost funny. Almost."

"We'll work it out," Gordon said.

"There's nothing to work out. Dr. Petry's advice was to adopt." Kendall turned away and stared sightlessly out the sliding glass door behind her and into the Hollywood hills. "Are you still so sure *I'm* the one you want?"

Gordon walked up behind her, wrapped his arms around her shoulders and held her to him. Kendall's hands went up to hold on to his forearms. Her head fell into the natural cradle that formed at his shoulder.

"You're the one." He kissed the exposed back of her neck. "The only one."

They were married six months later.

Chapter 9

----------------------------- ▼ -----------------------------

In Bed – 1981

Once upon a time, in a land far, far away, Gordon pictured living a solitary life. Today he couldn't picture a life without Kendall. Beautiful Kendall; with skin like alabaster and shining blue eyes. She was the center of his every thought. He missed her when they were apart; wanted only to hold her when they were together.

Often times, she stared out their porch door and seemed to become lost. Gordon never understood the fascination of grass and trees, but in deference to her mood he'd stand behind her, wrap his arms around her shoulders and wonder what she saw. Her hands always took hold of his folded arms and her head drifted into the natural cradle that formed at his shoulder, exactly as happened that night at Lindsey's. Kendall's short hair left her neck exposed. Gordon said it just begged to be kissed. He always obliged and she always seemed surprised. He loved that about her. No surprise was ever too small. Nothing ever got old.

Knowing his Kendall was *dream woman*, Gordon no longer minded the dream. Now, when he reached for her from his slumber, he awakened reaching for her for real. She was always right next to him, so warm, so loving. She was the woman in his bed, the woman he loved, his wife.

As on a night which seemed a lifetime in the past, he slid closer causing their bodies to nestle like spoons. The intoxicating remnants of the day's perfume thrilled his senses. What was it called? Mmm, yes. Carmen. Again, his hand reached around to her flat tummy, always crushingly aware that its inability to be anything other than flat was a heart-break for her. Still in her reverie, Kendall grabbed Gordon's hand and pulled his arm more tightly around her and lifted his hand up to her chin as if he were a blanket in which she was wrapping herself. She moved backward enveloping her body in the cradling curve of his. Gordon drifted back to sleep holding her and she awoke in his arms. His breath on her neck provided the sensation of home.

Gordon's *dream hold* became purposefully confining, but regardless of his *dream purpose* Kendall never wished to escape. He began to rock then jerked awake surprised to be holding her.

"Hey, Spaulding," his morning greeting was soft in her ear; his voice still husky with sleep.

"Hay is for horses," her usual response.

"I'll give you horses." Gordon nuzzled the back of her neck pretending to nip like a horse and whinnying for effect. Kendall began to squirm trying to get her ticklish neck away from his ardent mouth. The pair wrestled until they faced each other, staring into each other's eyes, wondering how either of them existed before the other showed up. They kissed gingerly at first, then found passion and heat. They ravished each other, each tantalizing the other in only a slightly sadistic way.

Half on top, he pinned both arms and one of her legs to the bed. "Open!" Gordon said. With pretend fear Kendall looked deeply into his eyes but didn't move. "Open!" He commanded again and she wordlessly spread her legs. Gordon reached between them. His hand moved up and down the length of her body touching her, caressing her. He stopped at her breasts licking and kissing until the nipples were rosy and hard. His hand moved to her inner thighs to tease Kendall into the wetness for which he could barely wait. Finally his touch was inside her.

"You're torturing me," she moaned.

"I can stop," Gordon offered.

"No! Torture me some more. Mmm," she purred. Kendall loved the way he made love.

Gordon on top, his body between her legs, they were nose to nose.

"How about staying in this morning," he suggested.

"In where? Kendall knew she was asking the wrong question. "That's in whom?"

"Ohhh ..." she sighed accepting the force of his passion inside her. "I hope you have no plans for the next 3 or 4 hours."

"My plan is the gym. Abs and legs," Kendall tried, and failed, to sound as though it were more important than her present activity.

"Change of plan." Gordon grinned pinning her more firmly. "I'll give you a workout that includes every single muscle, including my favorites. To make it an official work-out, I'll make sure you sweat."

"Sweat? Me? Never happen!"

"That sounded a great deal like a challenge," Gordon said pressing his lips to hers preventing a response.

He began moving slowly inside her. Torturously slow. Grasping both of her hands in one of his they remained pinned over her head. With his other hand he touched and stroked the places that drove her closer to the ecstasy that always came at the end of their love making. Kendall road the waves of pleasure with climax just out of reach.

"Not yet," Gordon sensed her heightened desire.

"I ... I can't wait," she said breathlessly.

"But you must. I'm not done with you," he assured.

"I ... I ... oh, Gordon."

Their lips met. Tongues darted in and out of each other's mouths. Kendall tried to release herself from his grasp, but he let go of only one hand. She used it to hold him tightly to her.

"Please ..."

"Please what, Spaulding? You want a 'happy ending'?" Gordon's voice was thick with his own desire.

"Oh, God yes!"

"Just a little longer ... deeper ... harder," he said, making the most of their pleasure. "How about right ... now?"

Wonderful electric shocks ran all through Kendall's body making her explode inside. It was always that way. Gordon was never in a hurry and made love so that it lasted for hours and they climaxed together, spent. They lay still a moment, then Gordon slid off, moved to be behind her, until once again they nestled like spoons. He kissed the back of her neck then lay breathing in her hair exactly as when he slept.

The minutes passed in silence. Kendall broke it whispering, "Again, please."

"Again," Gordon feigned disbelief. "Right now!"

"On your back, mister." Kendall nudged Gordon away with her elbow and shoulder. He complied, pretending to be completely at her mercy. She sat on his belly straddling him. When they were nose to nose they stared into each others' eyes and Kendall demanded a repeat performance.

"Lady, give a guy a break," he pretended to plead.

"No breaks! When I say again, I mean again," she used her most commanding voice. Reaching between Gordon's legs she found him ready for her.

"Yes ma'am. Anything you say, ma'am. But please," the slave pretended to beg of his mistress, "be gentle with me."

Chapter 10

------------------------------ ▼ ------------------------------

The Baby
Brookline, MA – 1981-1982

They were married for six months before Gordon broached the subject of trying for a baby, knowing that Kendall's infertility, and the circumstances surrounding it, could never not be a sore subject. He sought counsel from her brother, Terry, a physician whose practice consisted exclusively of overcoming female infertility. Sometimes Gordon and Terry would grab a beer and a laugh as Terry proudly reported the latest results of his work. *I got three women pregnant last week.*

Terry Evan Spaulding. Kendall's baby brother. Gordon had heard their parents rehash the story of the day they brought Terry home from the hospital many times. *Please,* Kendall pleaded dragging them by the hands into his room. *I need to talk to Terry. It's 'portant.* Being so earnest, Audrey gathered her new born son from his crib then she and Ted and Kendall sat together on the bed that would one day be Terry's.

Kendall touched his cheek to make him turn toward her. Practically a baby herself, she sounded very grown up. *'Member me, Terry? I'm your big sister. I was angry you took so long to get here, but you're home now and I never have to be angry at you ever again.* And she never was. Kendall and Terry were true friends from day-one. Never fought. Never even had a cross word. When he was so sick with measles, she insisted on being with him over Ted and Audrey's strenuous objections.

"I already had measles and Daddy said I can't get them again," she said. "Terry needs me. I know he does."

Ted and Audrey finally caved. The moment Kendall climbed onto Terry's bed he clung to her as if she were his salvation. She stayed until his fever broke and, in the end, sister and brother were closer than ever.

When Kendall went away to school they wrote each other nearly every day. The University of South Florida, U.S.F., was an eight hour bus ride from Miami, but Terry made a quarterly *Tampa run* to watch Kendall perform in on-campus dance productions and for some kid time.

The spring before Terry's fifteenth birthday, and pretty much out of the blue, he began attending the not so nearby Dade Junior College. He transformed himself from the casual kid he'd been into a serious student, his nose forever in a text book. His days were filled with high school life, his evenings with 'for-credit' courses in math and the sciences. His every moment was filled with study and his Junior year found him in a series of A-P science and math classes as a straight 'A' student.

At his counselor's urging, or so Terry claimed, he applied for early acceptance to University of Florida. With a nod from The Gators' admittance committee, Terry began his college career Pre-Med one full year ahead of schedule. He installed himself in a quiet off-campus Gainesville apartment two days after graduation. He wangled assorted syllabi from a secretary who took a shine to him, then purchased used books from an exiting student who discovered a life in medicine was not his cup of tea. Terry bought the books on the cheap, as the boy wished never to see the volumes again, and spent the summer getting a leg up on his studies.

He also took a job at the local pizza joint for extra cash, as their summer delivery guy. Summer deliveries being comparatively slow, he had time to pour over his texts and be well ahead of the game come September. The end of the fall quarter found Terry on the Dean's List where he remained, even continuing his course overload and accelerated course of action. For unexplained reasons, he seemed in a tremendous hurry to get in and get out. Attending year round, all four quarters, meant he completed his undergraduate in just over two years.

The year before Terry graduated, Kendall and her friend Lacey transplanted themselves to New England and took up residence in the home of their Uncle Harry and Aunt Beverly. Soon enough, they found a place of their own in the college town of Cambridge, in the bustling area known as Porter Square. It was there they started a business in a second floor walk-up loft that sported a small office area, lots of windows and a fine wooden floor. On a shoe-string budget, provided by Lacey's family, the girls provided the rest – a great deal of talent and enthusiasm. They divided the work into what they only hoped were equal shares of burden.

Lacey, having been a business major, took on the role of *CEO-alike* and Kendall that of instructor. All decisions beyond *how to run* and *how to teach* came from the committee of two. Brain-storming a nom de company, they finally settled on *'Hott Jazz'*. Lacey designed flyers which they had professional printed by the nearby copy place. Kendall dispersed them when visiting local Junior and Senior Highs to motivate potential students into their studio instead of someone else's. Even with stiff competition from other and better known facilities, like The Joy of Movement Center, Hott Jazz gave everyone a run for their money.

Their two person organization quickly expanded to include three additional teachers. At that point they had four working dance studios which filled the balance of loft space on the second floor of the building. Beyond standard Tap, Ballet, Jazz and Modern, Hott Jazz offered classes in club dancing, which became de rigueur. Each was virtually SRO and forced a rotating room schedule. They expanded their lease and existing space to include the entire third floor. Life was good.

At graduation from U. of F., Terry announced his acceptance to Harvard Medical. Too happy and busy to be fraught by jealousy, Kendall invited him to be third roommate in Lacey's and her apartment, saying it was near enough to The Yard to be an easy commute and far enough away to be a quite place for study without too much distraction. Having additionally accelerated his medical education, Kendall noted the toll the non-stop study was taking on her brother. She suggested Terry dial it back a notch.

"You're killing yourself and to what end?" She asked without reply. "Med School is a four year program for a reason," her tone was stern and parental.

"I appreciate your concern and I love you more than anything," Terry hugged her, "but you're my sister not my boss."

In well established fast-forward mode Terry finished his Juris Doctorate in three years rather than four and his career in medical research began three and a half years ahead of schedule. Half way thru Terry's Med. School Kendall began dating Stuart Cosgrove. Both Audrey and Terry took an immediate and unexplained disliked to him, to the point of hostility. Unfortunately, nothing either of them said dissuaded Kendall. When she announced their engagement, Terry hit the roof.

"I won't let you marry that slim-ball," Terry objected. "He's poison, I tell you and a bum. Not that I want you to be alone, but I swear you're better off alone."

Kendall's response came back to bite Terry in the ass. She hugged him and whispered in his ear, "I appreciate your concern and I love you more than anything, but you're my brother not my boss." Any and all other words from Terry fell on deaf ears. Shortly after Kendall's announcement, Terry didn't need to say another thing; it was no longer necessary.

*   *   *   *

Gordon approached Terry to discuss his and Kendall's chances for conception.

"It's a crap shoot for anyone," Terry said. "But in Kendall's case those chances are remote. There's a lot of scaring from the P-I-D and additional complications from a bad reaction to the Tetracycline which cured it. It scorched her esophagus. Swallowing brought mind numbing pain, so she mostly didn't. Not solid food anyway. She consumed only fluids she could guzzle; like milk, juice and water which provided few vitamins and nearly zero protein. Her system became more delicate than we expected and it was pretty scary. By the time she could swallow solid food again she was pretty frail and pounds lighter. She didn't have so many pounds to start with. She and I have talked at length about how she feels and functions on a daily basis, which is damned good by any standards, and her status finally upgraded from frail to fragile. But, that may be all the improvement there is.

"Physically she claims to be able to kick down doors with those dancer legs. Her internal system is a separate story. We may have already seen critical max in that department. The kid's had a tough time and modern medicine can do only so much. The up-side is, since recovery, she hasn't canceled or handed-off a single class and, as fit as you and I are, she leaves us both in the dust. I swear, it's god-damned embarrassing when your big sister's belly is flatter and harder than yours and the rest of her is like rock. Have you ever seen her in rehearsal?"

Gordon indicated he had not made the time.

"Really, you should go," Terry suggested. "She leaps. She lands." Terry did a clumsy dance parody. "Damn, nothing moves." He shook his head in amazement. "I took her class, only once. There are no breaks. Man, it wasn't pretty." They chuckled.

Terry returned them to the matter at hand. "We can try the standard clomid and some other fertility drugs, but they'd be awfully harsh on an already compromised system. There's another process we've been developing which I believe could be a 'best chance'. It's a new drug designed to allow us to harvest more eggs at one time, combined with a manual process for literally injecting the sperm into the egg. When it works, bingo-bango, you're pregnant. It's a Petri-dish pregnancy, but pregnant is pregnant."

"And you think this will work?"

"'Will' is sort of strong. It's really more like 'can', if you are able to live with 'can'. There are no guarantees and there are drawbacks.

"Which are?" Gordon prodded.

"We've only just begun clinical trial and the drugs haven't been thoroughly tested on humans nor are they FDA approved. There could be side effects we can't anticipate and–" Terry stopped.

"And," Gordon pressed.

"The procedure isn't approved either. Testing on lab animals went remarkably well and we're ready to turn human subjects into lab rats, but I hesitate to include Kendall. I'd kill myself if anything happened to her."

"What *are* the risks?"

"Unknown. Of course she would be very closely monitored but, right now, it'd be a gamble."

"Giving birth, a DNA baby, is major important to her so I'll ask again, you really believe it can work?"

"There's no reason to believe our success rate will be less with humans, but think long and hard. Discuss it and let me know. Word of warning, tread lightly. If Kendall says 'No', leave it at no."

Gordon found the moment to approach his wife. Back and forth they went.

"What if it doesn't work? It would be because of me. I couldn't take it if you blamed me."

"Sweetheart, I knew going in. I swear there won't be blame. I just want us to try before we throw in the towel. If it doesn't work we'll adopt. Swear." Gordon crossed his heart. "If we're successful maybe we'll luck-out and she'll look like you."

"No pressure here! You're already counting on a daughter. Have you picked out a name as well?"

"I'm not counting on anything just looking forward is all. If we're lucky enough to get pregnant, son or daughter, you name our baby. Any name you like."

"You realize we're setting ourselves up for almost certain failure, not to mention bombarding my body with god-knows-what. Anne and Art are sending a ton of work to Hott Jazz. In this business we need to strike while the iron is hot and deliver on time. If I agree, will I be able to do that?"

"Terry feels you can continue to work as long as you don't over-exert. You may need to take it easy for a spell, but it should be of short duration."

It all sounded so unpleasant, but Kendall wanted at least to try for a biological child. Gordon's child.

"All right! All right!" She caved. "We'll try. But when I say enough I'm holding you to your promise. We go with adoption."

Three months later enough was enough. This would be their fourth and final try. Kendall simply could not continue to feel as she had for the past three months. If she became pregnant this time 'round, fine. If not, they would simply have to accept that it was not meant to be.

*   *   *   *

Gordon picked up Kendall at the splashy new Mass. Avenue diggs of Hott Jazz. They drove to Terry's office on Beacon Street in a pensive silence. Gordon found a space a short distance from their destination, parked and slipped some quarters into the meter. Early for their appointment they strolled hand-in-hand, passing a store-front window that announced the grand opening of a dessert store called The Pie Lady II. The aroma of freshly baked pastry slipped under the narrow slit at the bottom of the door, wafted into the air and enveloped them like a warm blanket. It was too much to resist, so they didn't.

Gordon grasped the lovely brass handle on the old fashioned door and they stepped across the threshold into what could only be described as a blast from the past. The Fifties to be exact. Each fixture in the establishment was deliberately chosen for its decades' earlier charm, fairly screaming that it either came from another time or was a damn good replica. For Kendall, the fifties were a time when her life was still simple and the fragrant bouquet of homemade baked goods constantly flowed from her mother's kitchen. They slipped off their coats. Suddenly feeling over-warm and a little queasy, Kendall stripped down to her dancers' uniform of a spaghetti strap leotard. She and Gordon stepped toward the cases and she allowed herself to absorb the enchantment of culinary childhood memories.

A petite blond woman behind the counter and the woman filling the refrigerated case beside her each wore old fashioned, but well fitting, pink waitress uniforms. The blond, whose name tag read *Connie,* greeted her new patrons with a warm smile. As they approached, she noted Time's mark on Kendall's exposed upper arm.

"Good afternoon," Connie said.

"This bakery is brand new but the sign says 'II'. Is there a 'I' somewhere?" Kendall asked.

"Up north, in Keene," Connie proudly admitted. "This place is my idea of an expansion program."

"You're *that* Pie Lady? I mean, you're *The* Pie Lady," Kendall said.

"In the flesh. Connie Craig, at your service." She took a tiny curtsy and offered a bright smile mixed with a degree of humble. A plate of fresh cookies in her right hand, Connie extended her left across the counter to Gordon in an awkward left-handed shake. Thrilled at meeting such a famed celebrity he hardly noticed the ineptitude of their grasp. As they clasped hands, the short sleeve of Connie's uniform rode up her arm revealing Time's pale red circular mark; the sign of a Reweaver; a mark Kendall knew all too well; a mark Gordon had not seen.

"Gordon and Kendall August," Gordon made their introductions then stepped away to examine the cased pastries.

Kendall and Connie locked eyes and shared a silent moment. But for Kendall being warm and Connie's otherwise occupied right hand neither woman would have known about the other's unspoken life.

Kendall eyed Connie carefully.

"I can help you," Connie said seriously, in double entendre she hoped only Kendall caught.

"What smells so good?" Gordon asked, missing Connie's look and tone.

"That'd be Pecan pie," she said. "Just came out fifteen minutes ago. Not allergic to nuts?"

"Naah," Gordon answered absently for both of them.

"For here?" Connie asked.

"Definitely for here. How swell is this place!"

"Since when do you say swell?" Kendall asked.

"An old-fashioned place requires an old-fashioned word. Tell me this place isn't swell."

Kendall had to agree.

"What *is* that heaven that smells like coffee?" Gordon asked.

"Coffee," Connie teased. "It's my son's special blend; coffee and hazelnut."

"Two of those," Kendall added to their order.

"One of those," Gordon corrected. "Terry says you're a caffeine free zone until he says otherwise."

"Spoil-sport," Kendall teased.

"There's a decaf version," Connie offered a compromise.

Kendall stuck her tongue out at Gordon in triumph.

"Best put that thing away unless you mean to use it," he warned as if making a real threat.

The three of them shared a laugh.

"The blind for the table by the window is stuck in the up position and the sun is too strong at this hour," Connie warned. "Have a seat anywhere else and Matthew will bring your order right over."

The tables were beautifully set with actual silverware and cloth napkins. No plastic. No paper. Connie stepped into the kitchen and Kendall heard the muffled sound of a conversation. Immediately afterward, a very tall man with exceptionally broad shoulders and a fresh crew cut appeared at their table. An apron was tied around his middle and a light dusting of flour decorated his close-cropped blond hair. His short sleeved O-D t-shirt fit so close it was practically painted onto his body. On the back was printed the single word *ARMY*. Their order was on a fancy serving tray.

"On the house," the man said.

"Oh, we just couldn't!" Kendall objected.

"Speak for yourself," Gordon said. "My conscience is okay with free pie."

"I'm with him." The man jerked his thumb at Gordon, as a smile played at the corners of his mouth. "Give your conscience the day off. It's easier than saying 'No' to my mother," the man suggested. He balanced the tray on his right hand and served Gordon with his left, the sleeve of his t-shirt shrinking up against the strain of his back muscles. Seated to the man's left, Kendall caught sight of his left upper arm getting the distinct impression it wasn't a coincidence.

"Connie's your mom?" Gordon asked conversationally.

"That she is," the man said.

"But she's so ..." Gordon placed a hand low, "and you're ..." Gordon placed his hand high. "I'm no slouch, but you're incredibly ..." Gordon spread his arms to indicate the man's shoulders.

"Noticed that, did you. Genetics. Go figure. Hard to believe this broad side of a barn is the product of that tiny little mommy." The man shook his head and chuckled at the obvious physical difference between himself and his mother. "Of course, one must take into account my early farm life and a career in the military."

"Thank you for serving." Gordon offered his hand.

"You're welcome." The man accepted the handshake. "I don't get much of that. The first war the others and I fought didn't exactly have the support of WWII, but you fight the war of your generation, go where they send you and say, *Yes, Sir* ... a lot. Being home on leave, I thought it would be fun to help mom with the new store." He offered his hand again in introduction. "Tre."

"Gordon and Kendall," Gordon made the introductions again. "Not that it matters but Connie said "Matthew" would be our waiter."

"In a distorted way, Tre is Matthew."

"The last shall be first," Kendall mumbled, mentally drifting.

"According to *The Book of Matthew*," Tre said, "they always are. And it all works out," he placed his huge hand on Kendall's shoulder and gave it a gentle squeeze. "It always does." The man named Tre strode away.

"*What* was that?" Gordon asked when they were once again alone, feeling he'd heard Tre's words before from a source he could not place and wondering at Kendall's espousing of biblical knowledge he did not know she possessed.

"I'm sure I don't know," Kendall said out of her daze. It was the first and only lie of her life, but somehow she couldn't 'out' people she hardly knew. Still, she centered on their marks – Tre's matched her own, its one inch break saying that travel had not yet happened for him, but would one day. The full circle on Connie's arm said her travel was completed and she looked remarkably whole for her effort. Neither of them seemed worried about Tre's mission. Apparently, they didn't want Kendall to be either. In that moment she was certain the blind for the table by the window worked just fine and Connie's suggestion was only to make sure their table was one over which Tre could control her view of his left arm. It was the first time in a long time Kendall didn't feel afraid; but hopeful for the future.

Their dessert finished, Gordon and Kendall redressed for the temperature awaiting them outside.

"Please come again," Connie offered in farewell.

Tre stood beside his mother, an arm draped protectively around her shoulders. The Pie Lady II's old fashioned door with the lovely brass handle swung closed behind them. Kendall turned back for a parting glance and to wave goodbye. The petite blond woman named Connie waved back. Tre shot Kendall two thumbs-up; a faint look of trepidation mixed with hope crossed his face.

*   *   *   *

"I was going to wait until we were at Terry's but you might as well know now; this is our last try. I'm sick and tired of being sick and tired. It's time to face the fact that the drugs are stronger than I am. The side effects are worse each time and it's gotten progressively difficult to work this last month."

"Terry is certain we'll be successful if we're patient. What if you took a short leave of absence?"

"I'm done. We're done. If it doesn't take this time we go the adoption route and start putting our book together. You already agreed."

They reached Terry's building.

"Can't we discuss this?"

"What's to discuss? The jury is in, as is the verdict. You and I will pass the August name and the Augustein legacy to a baby we buy instead of a baby we make."

Kendall's earlier nausea suddenly worsened and an eerie whistle blew in her ears. She attempted to block out the weird sound with her hands and failed miserably. Though the air was brisk, Kendall was overcome by a flash of inner heat. The world began to spin and she saw what she believed to be an hallucination.

"The Augustein legacy ..." Kendall tried to continue. "Gads, I'm so hot. I–" She collapsed awkwardly to the sidewalk. Gordon caught her, but not before she lightly bumped her head.

"Kendall! Oh God! Please, no! Baby, wake up!"

Gordon scooped up his wife and rushed into Terry's office.

Terry immediately called for an ambulance. Meantime of its arrival, he called Hott Jazz and spoke to Lacey. From what she said, he inwardly acknowledged that this moment of this day was the start of a future predicted decades before and there was nothing he or anyone else could do but wait for the outcome. Terry promised to keep Lacey informed all the while praying his sister, his very soul, would be okay. He continued to examine Kendall still offering part of his attention to a visibly agitated Gordon who was pacing the length of his office.

"What happened? One minute we were holding hands, talking. The next she's out cold, but I wasn't quick enough," Gordon explained. "She bumped her head. It's a good size goose-egg for such a light tap. Is it serious?"

"The bump is small compared to everything else."

"Which 'everything else'?" Gordon instantly knew his concern was well-founded.

Realizing his dangerous slip and, for the time being, keeping his information to himself, Terry gave Gordon a plausible and more easily accepted explanation.

"As I said in the beginning, everything we're doing for you guys is experimental. We don't know the side-effects from physical exertion like Kendall's work. Lacey said she's been pushing herself and these last few weeks nauseous all the time."

"The drugs?" Gordon asked.

Terry shrugged noncommittally.

EMTs arrived and Gordon watched, helpless, as they lifted his wife onto a gurney.

"Isn't there something you can do?" Gordon practically begged. "I waited my whole life to find her and I already screwed it up once. I can't lose her again. Tell me what to do. Whatever you say, whatever it takes. If you think it will help, I'll sit with her day and night so she's never alone."

"Actually, that's probably the best course of action. Ride with her, let her hear your voice so she knows you're there. I'll call the folks then meet you at the hospital. It could be days. Mom and I can spell you."

"No. It should be me. After all, I'm the smart genius that got her into this. I won't leave her side."

Before the EMTs exited with their patient, Terry leaned in pretending to retake a pulse from Kendall's left hand. He whispered things Gordon did not hear, the last of which was, "Don't forget to come back to us Candy-cane." Terry only hoped she could still hear him, knowing there was naught he could do if she couldn't.

Gordon climbed in back of the ambulance with his wife.

"I'll call Kevin Gruenwald," Terry offered. "He's a neurologist; the best." Terry hesitated then added, "If you know any prayers, I'd say them."

The ambulance screamed down Beacon Street racing Kendall to Boston Memorial Hospital.

Chapter 11

------------------------------ ▼ ------------------------------

Home
Miami – 1955

Time wrapped itself around Kendall's emotions pulling them from the Time she knew. The sound of Terry's voice swirled in her head, *Don't forget to come back to us Candy-cane.* When she regained consciousness, there was an ice bag under her head. The hot flash, queasiness and whistle were gone and a doctor was applying damp cloths and smelling salts.

"You gave us quite a scare," the doctor said from behind a surgical mask, his eyes more than a little familiar. "It appears you fainted. That ever happen before?"

Kendall shook her head.

"It could be nothing, but I'd rather err on the side of caution and run some tests, if that's all right. You were my first case. I'm lucky I got my pants tied. I totally forgot to grab my coat before they brought you in," the doctor said, by way of an apologized for being dressed in less than his usual full uniform.

"They who?" Kendall had no idea where she was or who the doctor meant.

"The couple in the waiting room." The doctor checked the E-R admittance form on his clip board. "Manny and Martha Keller. They waited, so I assumed they were family. They're not?"

"No," Kendall said.

"Any idea why you fainted?"

Kendall indicated the negative.

"How about where you were or where you are now?"

"I hate to say *No* again, but no."

"You were in front of Maizelle's when you collapsed. Now you're at Biscayne Hospital."

"In Miami!" Kendall couldn't believe it.

Biscayne Hospital closed its doors for the last time in the early 1960's and Maizelle's not so many years afterward. The hospital building had been converted into a walk-in clinic called Dade Health Services.

"Miss–" the doctor prodded.

"It's Mrs.," Kendall absently corrected, as her mind raced. Myriad thoughts so distracted her that she misstated her last name giving the original version of Gordon's family name, the version she and Gordon were about to discuss when her travel began. "Augustein."

The attending wrote it before she could correct the error. Realizing the date had to be some Time in the 'Fifties'; her last name was the least of her worries and made little difference. Jones would have sufficed and meant just as much. No one knew her, or so she thought. For the time being, right or wrong, Augustein it would be.

How she fretted *am I in Miami at a facility that closed its doors nearly three decades ago?* Inattentively, she felt for the carved wedding band she had taken to spinning while thinking. It was missing. Only the pink discoloration, from the rash it caused when it was new, remained.

Having traveled ahead of her full memories, the sparse ones she had in the moment were only of spinning the ring; both in the car on the drive to Terry's and after Tre served them at the Pie Lady II. Had it slipped from her hand? That happened once during the staging of the annual Black and White Ball. Now, when she worked, the ring slept safely in a pocket. Kendall checked her skirt. Save the sample bottle of Carmen perfume she absentmindedly tucked there that morning, they were empty.

"You have a nasty bump, Mrs. Augustein. Is there someone I can call?"

"There's no one."

"You said Mrs. I assumed a husband."

"I guess I'm here alone."

"You guess! You don't know. Do you have a place to go when you're discharged?"

Regrettably, Kendall said she did not.

"Nurse," the doctor called out.

A woman appeared as if by magic.

"Yes, Dr. Spaulding?"

"Get my wife on the phone would you," he requested.

"Yes, doctor."

The nurse disappeared and the doctor continued filling out the ER form.

It ... it can't be Kendall thought.

"Your first name Miss ... er, Mrs. Augustein," the doctor said.

"You go first," Kendall insisted, needing to be certain.

"Why, it's right here on my name tag." He reached for the left side of his chest then chuckled. "Which is on my coat; which is still in my locker; because I didn't grab it. I already said that, didn't I?"

Kendall smiled.

"I hear those coats last much longer if you never wear them." The doctor sat on the edge of the gurney and pulled down his mask. "Okay. I'm Ted Spaulding. I have a wife named Audrey and a daughter named Kendall. That's everyone. Your turn."

Kendall sat up, threw her arms around the doctor's neck and held him tightly. The handsome man in her arms was her own father. Younger, and minus his trademark white hair, but her father nonetheless. She inhaled the scent of his aftershave. Skin Bracer. Ted disentangled himself and made Kendall lay back down.

"I reserve such movements for people I know very well and we've still not been properly introduced. I'm Ted and you're ..." he coaxed.

A person named Kendall, just like your daughter. Well, she chastised herself *I should be. I am your daughter. Think fast! Dad said 'that's everyone' and didn't mention Terry. Use the name he calls you.*

"Candy," she said. It wasn't exactly a lie.

Her father wrote it down. "Short for Candice?" He asked making small-talk until the nurse returned.

"Okay," she answered, not expecting to explain that when her brother was little he mispronounced her name as Candle then later nicked it down to Candy.

"Okay?" Ted asked stunned.

"I mean, yes. It's short for Candice."

"Are you sure I can't call your husband?"

Of course you can, she thought. *He's a little boy living in Boston, but no problem, he'll come get me on his bike.*

"No," she answered.

The nurse reappeared. "Your wife's on the line, Doctor."

"Don't go away," Ted said and exited. He returned a few moments later.

"You're injured, but not badly enough to be admitted," he said. "Unfortunately, you have nowhere to go and no one to call, which means I can't discharge you. My wife will pick you up and take you to our house. I don't normally do this and people consider me a real hard-ass, so don't let it get around," he added as an aside.

Who was he kidding? Her father dragged home countless interns and residents as a matter of course. There was always some lonesome looking stranger at the dinner table or sleeping in the den.

"Time for those tests." Ted handed Kendall a cup. "There's a lav right there." He pointed to a door. "A quick urine sample then back on the gurney."

Fifteen minutes later Audrey Spaulding was looking at the grown woman her daughter would become; a woman with warm blue eyes exactly like Audrey's.

"Is she okay?" Audrey asked, thinking the woman was asleep.

"Yes and no. I'm running some tests."

"She's not one of your wayward interns, Ted. She could be anybody. What do you know about her?" Audrey asked.

"Nothing, except that she's alone and I like her face. She reminds me of someone."

"Your like her face is irrelevant as to whether we can trust her with Kendall." Audrey said.

"It's just overnight and you'll be there," Ted assured.

"A motel would be too," Audrey said annoyed.

"You're right and she is well dressed," Ted said, "but she had no purse and the only thing in her pockets was a tiny bottle."

"This could be a huge mistake."

"So hide the jewels," Ted joked.

"You know very well that our millions are tied up in oil futures," Audrey continued the charade.

"Then it won't take long." Ted kissed her cheek.

"I'm seeing mom on my way out," Audrey said and kissed Ted goodbye.

"Give her my love and tell her I'll be by later," he said.

"Wake up dear." Audrey touched Kendall's arm and she opened her eyes. "You're coming with me. I'm Audrey, the doctor's very understanding wife. I need to visit someone before we leave, so let's get your shoes on."

Kendall did as instructed and accompanied Audrey to Sylvia Baum's room, admitted two days earlier for a hip replacement. The surgery went well, but Audrey was concerned about the recovery. Sylvia wasn't young but her surgeon, Leon Boland, assured everyone that she was a good candidate. A bit uneasy, Audrey left Grown Kendall to wait in a chair in the hall.

"How's your hip today, Mom?" Audrey asked.

"Painful, as expected. Where's Kendall?"

"At a friend's. You know she's too young to visit," Audrey admonished.

"But why didn't you bring her in?" Sylvia pressed.

"Because she isn't here," Audrey said with growing concern.

"But she must be," Sylvia insisted.

"All right, Mom. I'll be right back," Audrey said.

"Okay and send in Kendall," Sylvia said as if their conversation had not just taken place.

Disturbed by Sylvia's obvious confusion, Audrey exited her mother's room muttering, "She's delirious."

Not wanting Sylvia left alone, Audrey pressed Grown Kendall into the service of sitting with her mother while she went to find Leon. Grown Kendall closed the door behind herself still amazed at her presence in the past.

"Hello, Mrs. Baum. I'm Candy Augustein," Kendall said feeling awkward and shy. "Mrs. Spaulding asked me to stay with you 'til she comes back."

"Mrs. Baum, indeed!" Sylvia smiled. "Kendall, Mommala, you're every bit as lovely as I expected." She opened her arms. "Give Gram a hug."

With some of Kendall's memories lagging behind her travel, she totally forgot having spent most of her life afraid of her grandmother. She flew to the bed with memories of Gram's hugs from long ago.

"How did you know?" Kendall asked.

"Same way I know everything," Sylvia answered matter-of-factly.

Audrey said Sylvia knew about certain events before they happened. Kendall sometimes did too. It could be fun, like knowing Terry would be born. Other times it was painful, like with Stuart. An inner voice said he was the one, and he was, but not the one she thought; or in the way she thought. He was the one who destroyed her chances to be someone's mother. He was the one who blanketed her life in an ugly dark cloud. Apparently, Kendall's inner voice could pick Stuart out, but couldn't reveal *everything* it knew about him. Her mind touched on a faint memory of the way they ended, but it was still an incomplete memory. The balance of it would catch up to her later. For the moment all she knew was to think of him as *The incredible shit.*

"Tell me your life, Mommala," Sylvia said.

In Kendall's joy at being with beautiful Gram it seemed foolish to have ever been afraid of her. Kendall knew only how much she loved Gram and did as asked; she told the story of her life – the life she lived after Gram died. Kendall spoke of her work and business, of her brother Terry, for Sylvia as yet unborn, and her friends Lacey and Dana and sweet funny Lindsey, and of course Gordon.

"He loves you very much though sometimes he's afraid to show it."

"I know–" Kendall interrupted herself. "How did you know that?"

"He'll cry for you your Gordon." Sylvia ignored Kendall's question.

"Gordon would never allow himself to do that," Kendall protested.

"Which is exactly why when he does cry, it means he's calling for you. Mommala, when he calls, you must go to him."

"Can I ask the questions I never asked because–" Kendall stopped abruptly.

"Because you were afraid of me," Sylvia finished for her. "Ask. You don't have the luxury of wasting Time."

"Tell me about when you were young. Were you even more beautiful than now? And Grand, was he oh-so-handsome?"

"No one was ever as handsome or funny as my Evan. That's a rare love, but Audrey and Ted have it and now you and Gordon."

"Sometimes he pulls away like I'm a fire that will burn him. He's so hurt, but can't talk about it. How do I help him trust again or at least trust me?"

"He'll find trust when he learns how very much he loves you. It will happen as if in a flash and his tears will call you home. Aja is waiting."

"We don't know anyone named Aja."

"You will."

"How can you know?" Before Sylvia answered, Kendall answered for her. "Same way you always know," Kendall quoted Sylvia back to herself.

"Yes, the same way. Aja told me years ago."

"How could this Aja have known, long ago, that more than twenty-five years from *now* she would be waiting for Gordon and me?"

"Because she's like you." Sylvia gently touched Kendall's left deltoid as if it held the world's magic. "For now, let's talk of more pressing matters."

Kendall asked her questions.

*   *   *   *

Leon Boland assured Audrey that Sylvia was receiving the correct medication.

"But she's delusional. She thinks Kendall is coming to the hospital when she knows that she's too young."

"Its nothing," Leon insisted. "Most likely a side effect from the anesthesia. She'll be her old self in a few days."

They both knew it was a crap answer, but Audrey didn't press the issue. Boland was a wizard of an orthopedic surgeon; unfortunately he was clueless as to what was happening with Sylvia. Audrey would take it up later with Ted. She returned to her mother's room to say goodbye and collect the girl she knew only as Candy Augustein. She was sitting on Sylvia's bed laughing.

"What did I miss?" Audrey asked.

"The story of your father's first day at the bakery. Remember? He told the owner he could bake bread so he gave Dad a job. He returned home covered head to toe in flour."

Audrey smiled at the memory of her father springing through the front door coated in white dust, delighted that he not only got the job but that he enjoyed being a baker. The bonus was the hours. They meant very early mornings, but allowed him to spend afternoons with Little Audrey while Sylvia worked on routines with the orchestra at the dinner theater. As a result, Audrey and her father shared what each considered a very special bond. He eventually bought the bakery and renamed it *Sylvie's*. The best baked goods on the entire west side of Detroit.

"Would you mind waiting outside?" Audrey addressed Grown Kendall.

"Sure." And then to Sylvia, "Thanks for the chat. It was fun."

"Come back soon," Sylvia said.

"I will," Grown Kendall closed the door behind her.

"I told you Kendall would come," Sylvia said, a bit of triumph in her voice.

"That's one of Ted's strays. Her name is Candy."

"That girl's my Kendall," Sylvia protested.

"You're being ridiculous."

"You raised her never to lie to you," Sylvia said. "Ask her who she is and she'll tell you the truth, which is that she *is* Kendall."

"Okay, Mom. We don't have to discuss this now."

"You know I'm right, Audrey. You need only look at her. She has your father's face. Both of you look just like him. You say so yourself."

"Ted will be by later to check on you."

"Ask her, Audrey!" Sylvia insisted.

"Okay, Mom. I will," Audrey said, but had no such intention.

Although Audrey never pressed Ted's new 'stray' regarding Sylvia's accusation, she kept eyeing her noting a remarkable resemblance to Evan Baum. Audrey expected the stranger to give herself away. She didn't. *No*, Audrey was convinced, Sylvia was over-medicated.

Audrey gave a night gown and bath robe to Grown Kendall and sent her to lie down in Little Kendall's room. Kendall loved that room and did much 'pretending' there; some of which came true, like Terry. *Mommy*, she said one day, *I 'tended I had a brother. He teached me things like always to listen to you and Daddy, but that I'm the boss of me and I decide what I do. Is that right?*

Yes, Mommala. That's exactly right, Audrey said. *You are always the boss of you. Your pretend brother 'taught' you a valuable lesson.* She corrected Kendall's grammar then her eyes grew sad. Audrey shed many a tear at her inability to conceive a second child. *I hope you enjoyed your pretend brother, but don't count on a real one. Daddy and I keep trying, but no success.*

Don't worry, Mommy, Kendall reassured Audrey patting her shoulder. *It was only fortend today, but Terry said he'll come and he will. You'll see*, Kendall reported happily.

From that day forward she was like a different child; more confident and not so shy. And all because her pretend brother taught her there were times in life she got to be the boss of her. A total of fourteen months later Kendall's little brother was born. Ted and Audrey let her name him Terry.

*   *   *   *

Ted remained in the ER the whole day and night and never got the chance to see Sylvia. He sent a nurse to ask how she was. The nurse reported that Sylvia was fine and Ted didn't suspect otherwise. He hadn't spoken with Audrey and had no reason to suspect anything was up.

He put a rush on 'Candy's' tests and by the time he left the hospital her results were in. He patted himself on the back for being a damn good diagnostician. Knowing the results meant he really couldn't put her out on the street with nowhere to go. Unfortunately Ted was good only at rescuing the lost pups. Beyond that, he had no answers. He hoped Audrey would have a suggestion. She was in the kitchen when he arrived home.

"Hi, Hon," he greeted. "Well, she's pregnant. Probably somewhere in the first month or so, but pregnant just the same. She's so lean, but what a physical specimen. She hasn't one muscle that doesn't look as though it belongs to an athlete. I wonder if she is an athlete. Until I figure out what to do with her, would you mind if she stays with us or maybe you have an idea."

"I don't mind and at this moment I haven't a clue."

Ted missed Audrey's agitated tone.

Grown Kendall chose that moment to enter the kitchen holding the hand of the little girl who was herself.

"We woke up hungry," the adult version reported.

"You had a rough day. I thought it best to let you sleep. I left a note on the fridge in case you woke up. My note was where I left it." Audrey held it up. "So I pretty much figured you'd be hungry."

"Candy and me voted," Little Kendall said.

"Candy and *I* voted," Audrey corrected.

"Yeah, Candy and I voted," Little Kendall parroted. "We're very hungry and we want pancakes." The child looked at herself as an adult. "Don't we?"

"We sure do," Grown Kendall answered.

"My Mommy makes the best pancakes ever. Better than a restaurant."

"What do we say in this house?" Ted asked. "I flip for flap-jacks. I flip for flap-jacks."

Father and daughter jumped around in their individual circles, laughing the same laugh. It was the way she and Terry and their Dad always got Audrey to make pancakes. Grown Kendall found it difficult to refrain from joining in. Their jumping always made Audrey smile. The smile she was smiling right then. Ted excused himself after their meal.

"Wake me in the event of a hurricane or dinner, which ever comes first."

Little Kendall went to play in the Florida room while Grown Kendall offered to help with the dishes.

"You've been so kind and I'm pretty good in the kitchen. Drying dishes seems the least I can do." What Grown Kendall really wanted was some time alone with Audrey.

"Go see what Kendall's up to."

"If you change your mind ..." her words trailed as she exited.

"Shoo!" Audrey waved her away with a dish towel.

"What do you have?" Grown Kendall asked herself as a child as she entered the Florida room.

"Coloring book. Popeye!" She smiled. "Want to do one?"

"I used to love to color."

"Don't you still like to?" Little Kendall asked.

"Yes. I guess I do," Grown Kendall admitted sitting on the Cuban tile floor beside herself as a child ... and colored ... and laughed; the same laugh.

Audrey finished the breakfast dishes, remembered her mother's words and wondered. *What if Mom's right and it isn't over-medication.* Audrey pushed the thought away as she entered the Florida-Room.

"Kendall, Mommala, would you like some juice?"

"Yes, please," they both answered.

"Kendall is my name." Little Kendall looked confused. "Yours is Candy, isn't it?"

Grown Kendall had been caught; Time for an explanation.

Dumbfounded, Audrey sat on the floor with her daughter and the woman she would become peppering the older with questions as to how she arrived in the past.

Grown Kendall explained to the best of her ability.

"What do I tell Ted?"

"He didn't know so maybe tell him nothing," Grown Kendall suggested. "I get the feeling you knew before you caught me."

"Mother told me. In fact, she said that she was expecting you, but didn't say how she knew to expect you," Audrey said.

"Gram said someone told her when *they* Overlapped," Grown Kendall explained.

"Mother spoke of Overlap when I was little, but I never really understood. I'm still not sure I do," Audrey confessed.

"I think it's that future-me belongs in another Time and only child-me belongs here. By being here as I am now, together with my younger self, I overlap myself and my own Time."

"But, how did you get here?"

Kendall shrugged. "Theory is, Time made it happen and ... I have no other answer. Last I remember my husband and I were talking." Grown Kendall didn't reveal the subject or that their *talking* was more along the lines of arguing. "I had a kind of hot flash and my stomach got all queasy. Next thing I know I'm here with a bump on my head." She touched it and winced.

"Did mother say who it was that told her?" Audrey asked.

"It was an unusual name. Eva ... Ava ... no, Aja. It's kind of pretty."

"I met an Aja at the playground near our house when I was a kid," Audrey confessed. "She was such fun and so smart. We became fast friends. It's because of her that I met Ted. She was the most beautiful child I ever saw, but there was something wrong about her. She seemed too serious and almost sad. Turned out she was a run-away. Mom and Dad let her stay with us. I guess it was about a week. She and I played all day and each night she and Mother had private conversations until very late. One morning she was just gone. Mom said she went home, but that I'd see her again. So far, I never have."

"Can't be the same one," Kendall said almost as a question. "Gram said *this* Aja told her that she'd be waiting for Gordon and me when I return to my own Time. Gordon, that's my husband. If the Aja Gram mentioned and Run-away-Aja are one and the same she'd be very nearly sixty years old in my Time which is 1982. Besides, no one could know where they'd be in the future unless–" Kendall cut herself off.

"Unless what?" Audrey pressed.

"They came from the future."

"You aren't serious!"

"Why not? I'm here from what will be your future." Kendall caressed the cheek of her younger self. "I know what happens to this sweet girl between now and 1982; the people she'll love, the friends she'll make. I also remember events and outcomes that occurred in this Time. If this Aja is like me, which is what Gram said, she won't be sixty-something when I meet her; because she traveled to the past from another Time when you met her. That means your Aja and the one waiting for me could very well be the same person."

The phone rang sending a shiver through both Kendalls.

Together they said, "I don't feel so good."

"Too many pancakes?" Audrey asked of her daughter, reaching out her arms. The child climbed into her mother's lap.

"What's my excuse?" Grown Kendall asked. "I didn't eat too many and I'm feeling *The Big Uneasy*."

Moments later, Ted appeared in the Florida-Room's doorway, his eyes shiny with excitement.

"You'll never guess who that was! Marvin Kanter. You remember his sister and brother-in-law, Betty and Lew Toth? Well they're coming with the kids to visit Marv and June. Lew has his pilot's license and was planning to take his two older kids and Marv for an afternoon in the air. I made no secret of my envy. Color me J-E-A-L-O-U-S," Ted spelled it out. "Unfortunately for Marvin he has an out of town meeting that can't be rescheduled. Too bad! So sad!" Ted pretended to cry. "Fortunately for me," he broke into a broad smile, "Marv said I could go in his place."

"I'm sure it will be fun," Audrey said.

"More than fun!" Ted scooped up Little Kendall from her mother's lap and zoomed all around the house both of them making airplane noises. Audrey laughed after them. Her attention left Ted and their daughter and returned to Grown Kendall, white as a sheet.

"What's wrong with you?"

"He can't go," Grown Kendall said.

"But it sounds amazing and he's been wanting to go."

"No!" Kendall vigorously shook her head.

"Why not?" Audrey pressed.

"I'm not sure I'm supposed to say." Grown Kendall looked away sightlessly.

"Well, I'm sure. Say!" Audrey invoked.

Grown Kendall remained silent. Audrey took her by the shoulders and forced their eyes to meet squarely.

"Say right now, damn it!"

"The plane," tears welled in her eyes, "it crashes. Everyone dies. There are no survivors."

Little Kendall and Ted zoomed back into the Florida room still acting like sputtering planes.

"Spaulding one and two to tower, we're coming in for a landing."

Ted tossed Little Kendall onto the sofa where she bounced happily. Then he fell backward onto the cushion next to her a little out of breath.

"When are Betty and Lew expected?" Audrey did her best to remain calm in the wake of Grown Kendall's revelation.

Little Kendall climbed into her father's lap resting her head against his chest.

"Next month," Ted said.

"Can I go in the plane too, Daddy?" She looked up at her father.

"There's room for only one more, but next time," Ted crossed his heart, "I promise."

He planted a noisy kiss on his daughter's cheek making her laugh then wrapped his arms around her in a big hug and left them there. Little Kendall's hands took hold of them and her head drifted into the natural cradle that formed at his shoulder. Grown Kendall smiled to herself realizing (or was it remembering) the origins of her pleasure in being held by Gordon the exact same way. Kendall thought, perhaps, without realizing it, that her husband possessed other of her father's best traits and actions.

The phone rang again.

"That'll be the hospital calling about rounds." Ted grabbed Kendall under his arm like a football. "Ready partner?"

"Ready, Daddy!" Kendall stiffened, stretching out her arms and legs, and they headed for the kitchen. "Beep, beep! Out of my way! Out of my way!"

"At least there's some Time to figure a way to keep Ted off that plane. Are you sure about this?" Audrey asked out of Ted's ear-shot.

"Betty had baby number three about a year and a half ago? Dad ended up delivering her in the E-R?"

"Yes, she and Lew were still living here then," Audrey said.

"As I said, I know the outcome of events which occur in this Time and I have an excellent memory for crap that means nothing until it means something, like now." Grown Kendall dropped her gaze to her lap then looked squarely into Audrey's eyes. "I'm sure."

*   *   *   *

Ted grabbed the phone from its cradle.

"Myra, where have you been?"

"Sorry to disappoint, Sonny." It was Ted's younger brother, Harry.

"Mortimer! My man! What's up?"

Soon after Harry was born Ted renamed him Mortimer, after the younger brother in the play *Arsenic and Old Lace,* as Theodore was another name from the same play. In the end Theodore ended up too difficult for Harry to pronounce so, as far back as memory, Harry called him Sonny.

Ted and Harry were close from the time they were boys. Since Ted and Audrey moved to Florida the brothers didn't have many chances for in-person visits. Phone was 'the best next', as Harry said as a kid, meaning 'the next best'.

"Sonny, I met a girl. No, a great girl! A great Jewish girl. She has it all. She's just like Audrey, except for the part where she's not married to you, of course."

"Of course," Ted teased. "So what are you going to do about this great girl?"

"I asked her to marry me and live happily ever after."

"And was she fool enough to buy that line?" Ted asked.

"As I said, she's a great girl. Listen old man, how about standing up for the groom?"

"I've been trying to get rid of you for years. I finally got a taker. When's the big day?"

"The soonest we could arrange is four weeks from this Saturday. I can make reservations right in the hotel where we're having the ceremony. You won't even need a car. So will you do it? Will you come?"

To Ted it sounded as if Harry were asking for a favor; the biggest of his life.

"I wouldn't miss it! It's not every day I get to throw away ...," Ted cleared his throat, "... I mean *give* away my baby brother. So, does this great girl have a name?" Ted teased.

"Beverly. Beverly Conner."

"How did such a nice Jewish girl get such a nice Irish name?"

"Bev's biology dad, Joe Simon, was killed in the war. He was pretty tight with his C.O., so when the war ended and John was discharged he came looking for Hanna, Bev's Mom, a half written letter from Joe in hand. John and Hanna became friends. One thing led to another. Hanna and John got married. John adopted Bev and the rest, as they say, is history. John's great! He couldn't love Bev more if she were his by blood. He wanted her to take his name so he converted; says he was never such a great Catholic anyway."

"When did you say the wedding is?"

"Four weeks from Saturday. That's December 17th on my calendar. What? Did you suddenly get a better offer?"

"Marvin Kanter's brother-in-law, Lew, is coming in that weekend."

"You two have something going? Sonny, does Audrey know?"

"Very funny, wise-guy! Lew, offered to take me for a plane ride. I'll just ask for a rain check. The Florida contingent of the Spaulding family will be delighted to come to Boston for your swan song appearance as bachelor of the year."

"Me, Daddy!"

Ted passed the phone.

"Hi Uncle Harry."

"Hi, kid. What's new in the two year old world?"

"Two and a half," Kendall corrected sternly.

"My mistake," Harry apologized.

"Are we really coming to see you?" Kendall asked.

"So your Daddy can give me away," Harry said.

"But I don't want Daddy to give you away!" Kendall's eyes instantly filled with tears as she looked to her father and cried into the receiver. "I want to keep you forever."

"Don't worry, kid. You can't get rid of me that easily. Daddy isn't really giving me away. I'm just getting married. I promise to always be the uncle if you promise to always be the kid."

Kendall promised and her tears disappeared as fast as they arrived. "I like being the kid when you're being the uncle. Bye, Uncle Harry."

"Bye, kid."

Kendall handed the phone back to her father and the brothers said their goodbyes.

"See you in four weeks," Ted said. "I'll call with our flight details. Congratulations. You're a lucky man, Mortimer. I mean that."

Ted returned to the Florida room with Kendall tucked back under his arm yelling a football chant. "Push 'em back, push 'em back!"

"Way back," Kendall finished.

"Was it the hospital?" Audrey asked.

Ted and Kendall fell back onto the sofa. "It was Harry. The old smoothie! He met a girl. Correction, a great, Jewish girl who isn't married to me." Ted winked at Audrey. "The wedding is the same weekend Betty and Lew are in town, so that flight will be postponed. I'll be on another headed for Boston. You ladies look thick as thieves. Are you plotting my dinner?" He grinned arching his eyebrows.

"How's Kelly's sound?"

"Their sign says their chicken is 'delicious'; and I believe them."

"Then we'll go fetch the master's dinner," Audrey said.

"It's good to be the king," Ted confirmed.

Kendall climbed down from the sofa and Ted stretched out. She brushed away an unruly wave of hair from his forehead to make room for a kiss.

"Night-night, Daddy."

"Night-night, baby."

Ted closed his eyes and yawned. Kendall brushed her cheek against his the way he always did when tucking her in at night. His beard marred her skin.

"That's a very scratchy beard, young lady. Maybe you should shave."

"Maybe you should." She smiled rubbing the red mark with her hand.

"Maybe later," he yawned.

"Maybe not." Kendall patted his head.

Ted opened one eye and looked at his daughter. "Definitely not."

Father and daughter laughed the same laugh.

The *women* drove to Kelly's on the corner of 163rd Street and 8th Avenue and pulled into the parking lot under a huge billboard. *Kelly's Chicken. It's not broiled. It's not roasted ... it's Broasted. It's delicious!* They ordered a family bucket, took a number; 12, and sat in a booth. Kendall inhaled the aroma and remembered their disappointment when Kelly's closed in the late 60's.

"I loved this place. Great chicken, but the coleslaw." Kendall made a face. "Yours is better."

"It isn't my coleslaw." It was another of Audrey's tests to confirm this woman really was who she claimed to be.

"That's right. It's Eleanor Markowitz's recipe. The two of you were on the phone nearly two hours while she measured pinches of this and handfuls of that until it was all written down. You tell a story about a day, not so long afterward, when she ran out of time to prepare for a party and called *you* for *her* recipe? Now that's funny!"

Audrey was astonished that the girl who claimed to be her grown daughter knew such intimate details of their lives. Little Kendall stood on the bench seat next to Audrey and touched her mother's shoulder.

"Mommy."

"Yes, honey."

"Will Terry get to go to Uncle Harry's wedding?"

"Terry," Grown Kendall said. It was equal parts question and statement.

"No, Mommala." Audrey took Little Kendall into her lap then turned to the grown woman who was her daughter. "I suppose there's no harm telling you she pretended a brother a few months ago. She keeps asking when he'll come home except that I can't get pregnant again. But then, you'd know that if you are who you say."

"Would I?" Kendall asked a bit smug.

"What's that supposed to mean?" Audrey demanded.

"What's the date?" Kendall solicited.

"November 16," Audrey said.

"And the year," Grown Kendall pressed.

"1955."

"How old are you Kendall?" Grown Kendall wanted every assurance that the details were correct.

"This many." Little Kendall held up three fingers then looked up at Audrey. "Mommy, can you help me make this finger a half."

"Two and a half. You're two and a half." Grown Kendall laughed.

"What's so funny, Candy? Is it funny to be two and a half?" The younger version of herself asked.

"Your brother will be here before you know it," Grown Kendall assured.

"Don't encourage her," Audrey said angrily. "I just said that I can't get pregnant."

"Mom," she said gently. It was the first time Grown Kendall allowed herself to call Audrey that. "You didn't believe me when I was little, but please believe me now. I was three when my brother was born. His name is Terry. Terry Evan Spaulding."

"But that timing would mean–" Audrey stopped herself as she made the calculation.

"It means that you are pregnant," Kendall assured.

"Well," Audrey confessed, "according to Ted, so are you."

Mother and daughter stared at each other as a familiar looking kid behind the counter called out, "Number twelve your order's ready."

They returned home in silence. Audrey pulled into the driveway and turned to her grown daughter. "We still don't know why you're here, but there is a reason. Legend says each Overlap has one," Audrey advised.

Grown Kendall agreed, knowing it to be true.

"Thank God it's not to keep Ted from the plane crash. Can't we warn the others?" Audrey only hoped they could.

"Event," Kendall assured. "They stay in place no matter what we do. Not thinking anyone will believe us?"

"Guess not," Audrey sighed.

"I forgot about Uncle Harry's wedding. My partner, Lacey, and I stayed with him and Aunt Bev when we first moved to Boston."

"What happens if you're still here when we go? We can't leave you behind. You have no money and you're pregnant."

"What if I got a job and earned the money to go with you?"

"What kind of job?" Audrey asked.

"I'm a pretty good bookkeeper and secretary. In High School, you pester me into typing, short hand and bookkeeping classes insisting the skills will come in handy. In all my life they never have," Kendall smiled, "until right this minute."

Audrey was certain the flash of light she saw in her grown daughter's eyes was imagination.

"If I could get a job at the hospital then I could see Gram everyday."

"Ted's been saying he needs office help. I'll talk to him," Audrey offered.

"I think it would be better coming from me," Kendall suggested. "Coming from you it might sound as if you want me to earn my keep. I also noticed a dancing school upstairs from Kelly's. Maybe they'll let me teach. That's what I do, in case you were wondering. I'm a choreographer and a performer. I inherited Gram's voice and style. My partners, Lacey, Dana and I ... we have our own business."

"But you're pregnant," Audrey objected.

"I can't be very far along,"

It sounded to Audrey as if Kendall were quoting Ted.

"I should be fine if I don't over-do. The doctors from my Time encourage expectant mothers to keep active. It's healthier and you get your body back sooner."

"Ted would never agree!"

"So we don't tell him. You take me to the studio tomorrow," Kendall suggested. "I think you'll be impressed. I'm really quite good."

"I'm sure you are," Audrey was unenthusiastic. She had plans for her only child and the life of a dancer was not it.

*   *   *   *

After dinner that night, Audrey and Grown Kendall drove to a record store to purchase a newly released 45, which Kendall had choreographed many times over the years.

They arrived at the James Ferretti Dance Studio first thing the next morning. Ferretti was alone and sitting at a desk in the corner. Audrey and Little Kendall waited in the doorway while Grown Kendall strode over to him. Even in street shoes, the familiar feel of her feet against the good wood of the dance floor bolstered her confidence. The man looked up when she approached.

"I am James Ferretti. I run this school." He remained seated but noted the woman's strong resemblance to the child standing in the doorway. "Would you like to enroll your child for ballet classes?"

"I'm here for myself," Grown Kendall said.

He visibly winced then blurted, "I don't offer adult classes." Ferretti anticipated her quick departure.

"You should," Kendall was undaunted. "This is a beautiful space and it's huge."

"You wish to take class?" Ferretti knew the conversation was leading nowhere.

"No. I want to teach class."

"What makes you think you are qualified?" Ferretti asked.

"What makes you think I am not?" Kendall asked in return.

"Your hair is cut like a boy's. Where is your ballet tradition, your discipline, your preparation? You've not even brought slippers," Ferretti complained.

"Hair slicked back into a bun, ballet slippers and toe shoes are not the only calling cards of a well disciplined dancer with traditional training. There's a whole lot of dance out there besides ballet, Buster," Kendall advised.

"You dare speak to me in such a fashion," he blustered.

"Why not? You speak to me in such a fashion," Kendall was unflustered. "I'm not one of your abused ballerinas waiting to be treated as a doormat. A two minute audition," Kendall requested.

Ferretti assured himself that the split second flash of light he saw in her eyes was imagined, but granted the request.

"Two minutes," he said. "Use the piece on the record player."

"I brought my own audition piece, thank you very much. After that you can test whatever skills you like." Both Kendalls and Audrey walked over to the record player and put the 'new' 45 onto the turntable.

"If you really want to work here, shouldn't you be nicer to him?" Audrey asked.

"That asshole doesn't know it yet, but I'm handing him the future of dance on a silver platter. The question really is: shouldn't he be nicer to me."

Grown Kendall kicked off her shoes and struck an awkwardly balanced pose in the center of the floor. Audrey placed the needle on the spinning record. The music and Grown Kendall both came alive. When she was done both Audrey and James Ferretti were speechless. Ferretti had never seen anyone dance that way to popular music. He imagined the reign on his excitement would minimize the potential value the new dance style had for his studio.

"Your audition was most original, but I run a ballet studio. I have no use for such choreography?"

"*Such choreography* can make this studio profitable. I need work. You have studio time," Kendall said. "Don't even pay me. I'll pay you for studio time only and collect my fee from the students."

"If students were coming they would already be here," Ferretti finally admitted.

"Really?" Kendall asked facetiously.

"I have no time for this," Ferretti blustered some more.

"Man, that's about all you do have." Kendall scanned the room. "Very ... expensive ... studio ... time." By that point, she was in his face and he witnessed another instantaneous flash of light. "This is the opportunity of a lifetime. Do us both a favor and don't be a complete ass. Take it. You can't exactly afford to turn me down."

"But where will you get students?" Ferretti's tone was milder.

"That's my problem," Kendall said. "I pay you a flat fee for Monday through Friday nights, 7:00 to 8:30, and Saturday from 1:30 to 3:00 payable at the end of each class. Deal?" She extended her hand.

After the third flash of light Ferretti was convinced it was something other than imagination. Frankly, his imagination wasn't that good. Could the woman really accomplish what she said? His accountant assured him that an unchanged student situation would force him to close. Myriad thoughts raced through his head.

"Madam," James Ferretti shook Grown Kendall's hand, "I can hardly say no."

"Where will you get the students?" Audrey asked when they were in the parking lot.

"My partner and I started in a studio a lot like that one. I'll just do now what we did then. Girls get tired of only ballet and dancing only with each other. They need good training, which I provide. But what they really want is to dance as pairs, boy and girl pairs, and have some fun. American Bandstand hasn't been a decades-long success for nothing or because dancing isn't killer fun. I sell that kind of fun. Want to watch?"

For Audrey, American Bandstand was a relatively new show, but the woman claiming to be her grown daughter said it was decades old. Decades; more than one; meaning it would run well into the future. Audrey deemed Grown Kendall assertive without being pushy, brash without being offensive and she didn't fool around when she needed to get down to business. Audrey found the entire thing most intriguing so, yes, she most definitely wanted to watch.

They drove to North Miami Senior High and went directly to the principal's office. A very young Sidney Hart was standing behind the secretary's service counter.

"Good morning Mr. Hart." Grown Kendall greeted him as if they had been introduced before, which of course they would be in the future. "I'm Candice Augustein of Hott Jazz and this is my assistant, Audrey Spaulding, and her daughter, Kendall. I'm just in from Boston to introduce a new dance wave. Young people always take great interest in them and this time Broadway's choreographers are extremely excited as well.

"Some of your students have been taking class since they were quite young and anyone able to learn this new dance style has a real shot in New York. My business is to see to it that they get that shot. I'm offering introductory classes at the James Ferretti Studio to scout and teach the local talent pool. I was hoping you'd allow me to speak to your students, to help the process along. I'll need the auditorium stage, a microphone and a record player. I'd also appreciate your calling Principal Jackson at Norland. I'd like to provide this opportunity to as many students as possible."

"I'd like to help, Miss Augustein, but this year's student body is restless, peevish, and unmotivated. They don't listen to my teachers. I doubt they'll listen to you."

"If you make the arrangements, I'll make them listen. I'm a great motivator."

Principal Hart saw a light flash from Grown Kendall's eyes lasting no more than a nano-second. He didn't quite know what to make of it; or her. She was all business and seemed to know him and Tom Jackson, though Hart had no memory of their ever meeting. She seemed to be on the up-and-up and clearly was not taking *'No'* for an answer. Frankly, he didn't want to say no. If she could motivate his students to anything beyond smoking in the parking lot he'd let her. He gave his consent and scheduled an assembly. All students were to report to the Auditorium directly after home room for a brief lecture and a short demonstration. The kids were unruly and noisy, as predicted, but glad for the delay in starting the day's classes.

The trio reached the double doors to the auditorium when Audrey stopped. "Mother reminded me that I raise my daughter never to lie but, back there, you didn't seem to have any trouble. In fact, you laid it on pretty thick with all that talk about choreographers and Broadway. You sure made up a whopper."

Kendall opened her side of the double doors and smiled. "Who said I made it up?" That day Kendall took the high school's stage. Two years later *West Side Story* took New York by storm making its Broadway debut to rave reviews.

"I'm here to talk about dance," Grown Kendall said taking the *mic* in her hand. Boys moaned in disgust. "You're right to moan," she continued, regaining their attention. "In the past dance was all about too-toos and pink toe shoes or blue cellophane grass skirts and sequined bras." Everyone laughed. "You and I are about to change that. This is your music." She pointed to the audience. "Popular music; music that means something to you.

Grown Kendall gave Audrey a nod and she placed the needle on the 45 which spun on the turn-table Mr. Hart so generously provided. You could hear a pin drop when her routine was over.

"Don't be fooled." She gracefully rose from the floor. "This is more difficult than I make it look. It requires training, hard work and commitment. I have no patience for goof-offs. I work with serious students with serious intentions. Broadway intentions. I'll work with you if you'll work with me, and I do mean work. I expect nothing more than your full cooperation. I'll accept nothing less. Ladies, exciting offers such as this are few and far between. Gentlemen, for the first time in dance history you are included in the big excitement. I'll remain to sign up anyone interested in this opportunity." The family threesome left forty minutes later. Two hundred students had gladly paid the three dollar fee in advance.

One of the last to sign-up was Paul Kelly, Jr. A boy Kendall knew would become a dance legend with a career dreams are made of. First shot out of the box he landed a plum roll in the musical drama *Tarmac*. His had become a household name before the show ended the first week of its Broadway run. His audition piece had been choreographed by his roommate – the man who, ten years later, would become his partner. The piece won for that roommate and future partner *Tarmac's* much sought after position as assistant choreographer. Paul and his partner reportedly came out of nowhere with unbelievable raw talent and energy. Word was, some unknown dance teacher inspired them, then promptly dropped off the face of the earth. Disappeared.

Eventually Paul and his partner formed the most dynamic dance ensemble anywhere on the planet. They called themselves *Black and White*. Kendall wondered if her class were the *'nowhere'* from which Paul Kelly and his partner came. She need only have asked them whether they saw a flash of light in her eyes as they stood at opposite sides of the rear of the auditorium listening to her lecture and watching her performance. Beginning that night Kendall Layne Spaulding would literally teach the master. Paul Kelly, Jr. would be her student.

"How did you get those students to listen?" Audrey asked amazed.

"My mother calls it *'gentle persuasion'*," Kendall explained. "Say that you need someone to do what you want. By offering something they want then making it perfectly clear that the only way to get it is to do what you want, they do what you want."

"*I* always say that!" Audrey exclaimed.

"Isn't that what I just said?" Kendall smiled and put an arm around Audrey's shoulder. For the first time Audrey began to believe Sylvia was right. Both Kendalls and Audrey returned to thank Mr. Hart.

"You can only imagine what your cooperation in this venture means," Kendall said.

"I watched your presentation," Sid. Hart confessed. "I never saw anything like it. You are a great motivator. The kids seemed so excited and charged with positive energy. You sure do shake up a room."

"I never thought of it that way, but I suppose you're right. I do shake up a room."

"Will we be seeing your name be in lights?" Mr. Hart asked.

"One day." In the future there would be films and videos for which she designed and staged the choreography. "Thank you again." Kendall extended her hand which he accepted.

"No. For inspiring my students, thank you. I feel it in my bones," he said, "things are going to be different. I phoned Principal Jackson. The staff at Norland is expecting you."

Maybe the light Principal Hart saw in Grown Kendall's eyes was imagination or desire. Maybe it was the future setting the past in stone. In any event, she had made a difference and changed a school by way of changing its students. One day soon Sidney Hart would say: *See those kids, they weren't like that before.* By day's end over 400 students had signed up and Kendall had more than enough money for the flight to Boston.

Each morning Kendall went to the hospital with Ted to organize his office. She set up a bookkeeping system, paid bills, caught up on his correspondence, and made sure he ate a decent lunch. She spent hours with Sylvia sharing the lives by story that they hadn't shared in person. Thank god Ted never noticed that when Kendall left the hospital each day she went to the dance studio instead of to the house, her classes populated by an ever increasing number of students.

Word spread from the fifty kids who took her Monday night class and unexpectedly returned every night afterward, as did the fifty who signed up for Tuesday and Wednesday and so on for the balance of the week. Kids who weren't signed up at all arrived, plus their friends from other high schools as far away as Homestead. The initial money Kendall collected multiplied by more than ten.

James Ferretti attended every class and never paid such close attention to anything in his life. The girl had handed him the future of dance. Even if none of the brat kids had Broadway plans he was determined to be Broadway bound. He pictured himself as the choreographic consultant for new shows. He pictured himself coaching dancers aspiring to fame on the Broadway stage. Once everyone discovered the spark and energy of 'his' version of Hot Jazz they would beat a path to his door fulfilling the picture he had of his new reality.

In *The Book of Life*, things don't always happen as we picture them.

*　　　*　　　*　　　*

The third night, as Audrey signed in students and collected any unpaid fees, she asked, "How are you going to handle so many kids? As huge as the studio is there are simply too many bodies. Even you can't teach this many students at once?"

~ 137 ~

"There are ways of managing limited space even when it seems you have unlimited students."

By the end of that class, however, even Kendall realized one class per day wouldn't cut it. Additional classes would need to be added. She stressed over her own words *'if I don't overdo'* and whether the extra classes would be too much. If she really were pregnant, would she lose her baby because of the added work load?

The class having ended and all students gone, a lone black boy entered the studio as Kendall prepared to leave. He was tall and lean with features that belied a toughness he did not possess.

"Excuse me, Miss," he said politely.

"Can I help you?" Kendall asked.

"I heard you at the assembly. What you said sounded too good to be true so I figured it wasn't. But then I heard the kids at school talk so I came. You probably didn't see me, but I watched your class."

"I saw you. Would you care to take class Mr.–"

"Hardy James." He reluctantly extended his hand, afraid the pretty white woman would refuse to shake hands with a colored boy.

There were no early pictures of Hardy James and the face in front of Kendall was too young to be familiar ... but his name! She turned internal cartwheels at the sound of it as she calmly accepted his hand.

"It's an honor," she said. "Candy Augustein," she introduced herself.

"You saw me? How come you didn't say nothin'?"

"*How come you didn't say anything,*" she gently corrected him.

"Okay. How come you didn't say anything?"

"Because you wouldn't have come in," Kendall said.

"What I mean is ... I'm colored," he was almost apologetic of the fact, "and you let me stay. You don't mind?"

Caught off guard by a word left over from the fifties, a time when *'colored'* meant Negro and pictures of Negros were conspicuously left out of all sorts of history books, Kendall collected herself to use the vocabulary of another time.

"Are you asking if I mind that you stayed or if I mind that you're colored?"

"Both, I guess." He chuckled at how silly she made it sound.

"I never object to an appreciative audience and I teach students, Mr. James."

"Even a colored student?" He doubted her.

"The color of money remains the same no matter who's holding it. Do you have three dollars or is there another issue we need to address?" Kendall asked not wanting him to leave.

"I got three dollars!" Fierce pride erupted in Hardy's voice and reflected on his face.

"But not more than that," Kendall gently pressed.

He hesitated but finally admitted that he could afford only the one class.

"Pay for tomorrow," Kendall said. "I'll handle the rest."

"I don't take no handouts!" Hardy's fierce pride resurfaced.

"*I don't take any handouts* and I wasn't offering one. Consider it a *hand up*. I plan to work your butt off choreographing combinations." She punctuated the last two words by poking her index finger into his chest.

"Ow!" He objected touching the spot. "The other kids, they barely tolerate us in school. Bad enough on the inside. They don't exactly care for coloreds on the outside. I come, they'll stay away." He didn't want to hurt her business.

"These kids want what I'm offing. Want it more than they hate the color of your skin. And in the war between greed and prejudice, Mr. James, greed always wins."

"You believe that?" He asked.

"As long as you have what the public craves, I believe they'll forgive you anything. Your religion. Your name. Even the color of your skin."

"They said you was different," Hardy said.

"*They said you were different*, Mr. James," Kendall corrected his grammar again.

"How come you keep fixin' me and calling me Mr. James?"

"I do it to everyone. You can't make a name for yourself with careless, sloppy grammar and low self-esteem. People think only as much of you as you think of yourself, see only what you show them.

Why show them poor speech to criticize, when you need them to see and praise your talent?"

"You think I have talent, that I could make a name for myself? You think there's opportunity waiting for me?" Hardy asked.

"You, Mr. James, can do anything including make your own opportunity."

"You can't *know* that," he protested.

"What if I said that I did know? What if I said that you were one of the most talented choreographers in the dance world and, one day, producers from film and other media will laud your name? What if I said that one day you and another man from this very class will found New York's most dynamic jazz dance ensemble?"

"I'd say you were crazy," Hardy admitted.

"My lunacy is a well documented fact, Mr. James. The question on the table is would you believe me?"

"You got a crystal ball?" He asked.

"Something like that," Kendall said.

"All those things happen," he said.

"Yes," she said evenly.

"Me and someone from this class," he pressed further.

"Yes, again," she said.

"There aren't any other colored boys in your class ... are there, Miss?" Hardy asked already knowing the answer.

"No, Mr. James. There are not," this time she was apologetic.

"Some white boy becomes my partner," his words were equal parts question and statement.

"Yes," Kendall's voice was as even and flat as before.

"Not this week!" His response was sarcastic, but he asked sheepishly, "You aren't funnin' me ... are you, Miss?"

"Not this week," she echoed his words and escorted him from the studio locking the door behind them.

"Miss ... which boy becomes my partner?"

"Come to class. You'll figure it out," Kendall said with a wink.

"What do we call ourselves," he descended the stairs with her, still not believing, "Black and White?"

"Class will hold many lessons, Mr. James, not all of which involve dance. Tomorrow?" She asked.

In the mili-second it took for Hardy to make up his mind, he noted an unusual light in her eyes. He blew it off as imagination, exactly as he had while standing at the back of the high school auditorium. He reached into his trouser pocket and brought out three crisp one dollar bills folded in half. He handed them to Kendall.

"Yeah," he said. "Tomorrow."

Hardy's entrance the next day caused quite the stir. Murmurs and a single caustic remark from Sandra Scott came from the back of the room. Kendall ignored both and greeted him at the door. As Hardy dropped his belongings in a corner, he spoke with her in hushed tones.

"I told you, Miss," he said.

"And I told you. Greed always overcomes prejudice, the same way *'rock'* always beats *'scissors'*." Kendall then gushed. "Mr. James! I'm relieved you were able to join us. I was afraid your schedule was overbooked." She hooked an arm through his as if he were a foreign dignitary and escorted him to the mirrors at the front of the room. "Class, I'm pleased to introduce Mr. Hardy James, choreographer extraordinaire."

Sandra Scott murmured a racial epithet.

"Miss Scott, if you are dissatisfied with our class structure, I will leave the door open for the duration. Feel free to *exit* at any time. Mr. James," Kendall continued undaunted, "would you honor my class by joining them for the warm-up?" She indicated a space that would force Sandra Scott to make way. She backed up into a boy a few years older than herself then turned to see if he was okay. He was. She smiled. Considering her remark, he didn't smile back.

At mid-class Hardy assigned groups for combinations. His ideas were exciting, the energy level was high, and he utilized intricate foot-work. He paired Sandra Scott with Paul Kelly for the final combination – an adagio. Sandra's execution of the complicated steps was clumsy.

"Miss Scott. Mr. Kelly. Again please." Hardy followed Kendall's lead with formality in class.

"*Again* implies that it's do-able in the first place, which it isn't in the second place. Great choreography, *boy*!" Sandra's intent was to insult Hardy.

"I see." Hardy's slumped posture and failure to rebut gave the impression he'd been undone. Still slumped, he spoke. "Miss Turner, please take Miss Scott's place."

"Hey!" Sandra looked to Kendall. "Make him change it!"

"I'm sorry, Miss Scott. The piece is the intellectual property of Mr. James. Only he can change it and he doesn't seem to be so inclined."

"Miss Turner," Hardy's voice was full of the authority Kendall just gave him. "If you would be so kind as to replace Miss Scott."

Sandra had no choice but to stand down and watch with the others from the side of the room. Amy reluctantly assumed Sandra's place. Hardy laid the needle on the record.

"With the music please," his calm voice did not betray his racing heart, "and on my count." He measured the beat. "Five ... six ... five ... six ... seven ... eight!"

Paul and Amy were flawless. Everyone applauded including a reluctant Sandra Scott.

"Beautiful combination, Mr. James," Kendall said. "Just beautiful." With a nod in Sandra's direction Kendall whispered so that only Hardy could hear. "In the war between greed and prejudice, greed always wins just as rock always beats scissors. *'Believe and it shall be so',*" she quoted. "Be a believer, Mr. James. It's more fun!"

As everyone collected their belongings Paul Kelly advanced on Hardy. "Nice job." He extended his hand. "Not half bad ... you know, for a black boy." His crooked smile said that he didn't buy into the racial issue at school or expressed by Sandra Scott.

"You're not a half bad dancer," Hardy accepted Paul's hand understanding, "you know, for a white boy."

Words said in jest. Shades of the night before; *What do we call ourselves, Black and White?* Hardy glanced at Kendall whose face was impassive, but her quick wink answered his serious, questioning eyes. Paul and Hardy exited like old friends.

Kendall's original plan was for one class each night. Hardy's help meant that, four times a day, *would-be dancers* received innovative choreography and a run for their money. Kendall prayed it also meant a better chance of keeping her pregnancy, assuming it was real. The first of the additional week-day classes began at 4:00 PM. The last one finished at 10:00. Late Saturday of their third week, Kendall called for a last run and then a wrap. No one realized she meant the final wrap until she said, "I leave for Boston in five days."

"So we have our last class in four days." Paul was determined to extend classes for as long as time allowed.

"Yeah," Sandra pouted. "Hardy hasn't completed my solo combination yet."

Amazing, Kendall thought, *how very quickly the war between greed and prejudice ended.*

"The studio has other commitments," Jim Ferretti piped up lying.

"But you could reschedule those commitments couldn't you, Jim, and add a class tomorrow." Paul knew how slow Ferretti's business had been before Kendall arrived. It was why he'd been hanging-out at his grandfather's chicken place downstairs. "We'd be ever so grateful for the favor," Paul stroked Ferretti's ego until it shined. He looked to the others who agreed.

"What about the Blue Laws?" Kendall asked knowing she could persuade a principal and maybe Paul could persuade Ferretti, but there was no persuading the law.

"I'll take care of it," Paul offered.

"How?" Kendall feared he couldn't.

"That's my problem."

Crap! Kendall thought as Paul echoed the very words she used on James Ferretti only three weeks earlier.

"Okay dancers, tomorrow at nine," Kendall said. "Paul will bring our bail money."

Students were lined up when Audrey, Young Kendall and *Candy*, arrived early at 8:30.

"Did you all sleep here? Don't you kids have homes," Candy teased as she unlocked the door. "Has anyone seen Paul?"

No one had. *Great,* she thought, *it's a beautiful day to go to jail.* Audrey signed in students and collected payment as usual. Class started just as Paul entered. He stripped off his street shoes and took a place for the warm-up. Twenty-five minutes later, two uniformed officers climbed the stairs to the second floor.

"Officer Paul Kelly, North Miami Beach Police," he introduced himself.

"Audrey Spaulding."

"You'll have to close the studio Mrs. Spaulding," he said, noting her wedding band. "The Blue Laws are very specific–" He stopped mid-sentence. "That's my kid," he almost whispered pointing at Paul. "Hey, Mack," he called.

His partner stepped inside and they watched Paul, Jr. and his group take center studio. Paul Jr.'s performance was amazing.

"*That's* my kid!" He pointed to his son.

The officers watched the group finish and the next group take their place. "That's *my* kid!" Paul, Sr. sounded every bit the proud parent.

"Say it again. I didn't quite hear you the first two times," Mack said.

"That's my kid," Paul, Sr. teased.

"Shh! The next group is starting," Mack reprimanded.

Officer Kelly and his partner McCoy "Mack" Barnes waited as Paul, Jr. came over.

"Not exactly the gridiron," Paul, Jr. said.

"I thought you were up to no good," his father said, "never home; out till all hours; constantly exhausted; half-in-the-bag. I thought ... drugs. I never thought *this,* that you could *do* this."

"I didn't say; 'cause I was afraid of your reaction ... dance and all," Paul, Jr. said.

"You're really good," Paul, Sr. complimented.

Paul Jr. was surprised by his father's calm reaction rather than the expected objection. *No son of mine is going to be a fairy dancer. What will the guys think? What will my Captain think?* Paul wondered whether his father was putting on a show for his partner or was sincere. If his father was being straight with him, he had everything to gain by being straight in return.

~ 144 ~

"I want to go to New York," he admitted. "This woman can get me there."

"Best get back to your class then," his father suggested.

"And the Blue Laws," Paul, Jr. pressed.

"Nothing in those Laws says you can't throw a *party* on a Sunday."

"Thanks, Dad." Father and son embraced.

The studio being on his father's beat, Paul knew his father and Mack would respond to any complaint. Paul believed his dad would be lenient, as no harm was being done and Kelly's would be extra busy feeding hungry kids when class ended. Being on the scheduled from the minute class was over, Paul would know exactly how busy in another two hours. *Faith*, he told himself, *is a beautiful (and powerful) thing.*

Officer Kelly radioed the station that no laws were broken and that he and Barnes were taking their morning break downstairs at Kelly's with his father as usual. He returned to speak with Audrey.

"Is my kid as good as I think he is?"

"He's sensational." Audrey turned to watch Paul dance. "Candy says he's better than anyone ever imagined."

"Who is this woman?" He asked as Kendall demonstrated a combination.

"A dancer. A dance teacher," Audrey said.

"I'm no philosopher, but she's beyond that. Look at her eyes!" He'd seen a sudden flash of light in them which did not appear for Audrey.

"Is she your sister or something?" Paul, Sr. asked.

"No. She's a friend."

Audrey and Grown Kendall had become true friends.

"Well, she sure looks a lot like you," Paul, Sr. commented.

Without saying so out loud, Audrey acknowledged their remarkable resemblance to each other and to her father, exactly as Sylvia said that first day. The students were just kids, but Audrey admired the respect Kendall gave them, as if they were corporate VPs.

"Will you look at that!" Paul, Sr. pointed. "She's yelling at them and they don't even mind. I want to know how she does *that*!"

"No, no, no!" Kendall clapped stopping the performance. "The combination isn't fan-kick, drop." She demonstrated. "It's fan-kick, body-roll." Another demonstration. "Head back, chin up, lead with your chest. Be molasses ... slow, graceful molasses. Now, from the top."

"How much longer will you be here?" Paul, Sr. asked.

"Just 'til next Thursday," Audrey said.

"Well, Audrey Spaulding, you find yourself needing anything, anything at all, you call Officer Paul Kelly." He extended a hand which she accepted.

"And if I do, will you remember me?"

"Lady," he covered her hand with his, "I got a feeling I'm never going to forget you. You see, that's *my* kid!" He pointed at his son.

Thursday evening was Kendall's last class. Kids came from as far away as Dania and Fort Lauderdale. The studio was packed. DRO – dancing room only.

*   *   *   *

Everyone in the studio said their final goodbye to Kendall and departed. Once they left, and only she and Hardy remained, he gave voice to what he'd been dying to say the entire night.

"I have a present for you, Miss. A piece for you and me to dance. Will you let me show it to you and then ... would you dance it with me?" Hardy explained both parts, demonstrated the lift and drop several times, then put on the music and extended his hand. Kendall accepted it blushing. All the while she'd been in the past she felt the purpose of having been transported back in Time was to be there for others; including Hardy, not the other way around.

Hardy's piece ended in an aerial lift directly overhead, his hand supporting her by her belly. He slowly lowered her until their lips almost touched. The finish was a sharp roll straight toward the floor. He stopped her short by half an inch. It was a beautiful piece. Kendall hugged Hardy tightly, like a proud mother, her eyes shining with joyful tears. She knew that in a performance in the future, she of all the students would be selected to dance Hardy James' signature piece. The piece she just finished dancing with the man who created

~ 146 ~

it. In all of history Hardy James never revealed the origins of the piece or for whom it was drafted. During the applause in that future performance, Kendall would be unable to contain her emotion. Her question that night was why tears streamed down her face. She had her answer. The piece entitled *Mother and Son* had been drafted for her. Her heart sang.

"It's the most wonderful present I'll ever receive, the most beautiful piece I'll ever have the privilege of dancing. This piece, this is what happens when you believe, Mr. James."

"Class is over, Miss. Won't you call me Hardy? You done so much for me. I can never begin to thank you."

"*You did so much*," she corrected. "But it was you. All you."

"No," he objected. "You gave me the first break of my life. No one ever done ... I mean *did* that before. My mother died when I was little. I live with my aunt and she cares for me, but it ain't the same."

Kendall winced at his grammar, but kept silent.

"I have pictures, but I hardly remember her. You've been like I imagined she'da been. Stern but kind and you believe in me."

"It's easy to believe in a sure thing," Kendall said.

"Ain't no sure thing in life," Hardy cautioned.

"Please don't say ain't, Mr. James," she tried to sound stern. "It isn't refined." On impulse, Kendall decided to make Hardy an offer he couldn't refuse. "Would you like a look into my crystal ball? A glimpse at the sure thing? "

He shrugged.

"Take a seat."

Kendall pushed Hardy to the floor by his shoulders then kneeled behind him. The front of her body was pressed against his back, her lips near his ear, one arm around his shoulders, the other hand pointing toward the mirror like a giant paint brush.

"You and Paul arrive in New York on a summer day. You get a newspaper and find an affordable apartment in Soho. The place is tiny but clean. You get night jobs washing dishes in a restaurant and take more classes during the day. You create an audition piece for Paul that lands him a roll in a play. The director and choreographer both flip over your style and creativity. You are hired as the assistant choreographer. The show is a huge hit, nominated for a Tony, and your work is suddenly in great demand. It's the sure thing, Mr. James. Bet on it. Believe in it."

Hardy checked her face in the mirror for any hint of teasing. All he saw was the quickest flash of light in her clear blue eyes.

"I have a present for you as well." Kendall left him sitting in the middle of the studio to retrieve something from her dance bag. "It's payment really, for all your hard work."

Kendall pressed a fat envelope into his hand. It was one thousand dollars in twenty dollar bills.

"I can't take this, Miss," Hardy strenuously objected.

"What? You don't like the color of *my* money," Kendall teased and Hardy smiled remembering that first day. "I want you to have it. You earned it. I couldn't have run class without you."

"Is this a handout," he asked, reflecting on their first meeting, "or another one of your hand-ups?" He extended his hand and Kendall helped him up off the floor.

"Neither." She smiled. "It's me believing. It's my investment in our future. In fact, it's seed money. You'll need it to get to New York and to pay for more classes. Now you have it. Go do great things with it."

"Miss, twice you said *take more classes*. But you didn't say with who?"

"*With whom*," Kendall made her final correction.

"Fine, with whom," Hardy parroted.

"If you do exactly what I said there will be no one to find. The *whom* in question will find you. Promise to learn everything he'll teach you." She chuckled, knowing Bob Fosse was the choreographer so impressed by Paul's audition piece.

"I promise. Miss," he said suddenly excited. "Paul and I are leaving at the end of the school year. This is more than enough for all three of us to go together." He held out the envelope full of money.

"I must be elsewhere, but you don't need me. You'll be great. Both you and Paul will be just great," Kendall assured.

"I ain't never going to see you again, am I, Miss?"

Kendall made a stern face then bugged out her eyes waiting for Hardy to correct his own grammar.

"Will I ever see you again?"

"Life is funny, Mr. James. Some day when you least expect it I'll be right in front of you."

Chapter 12

---------------------------------- ▼ ----------------------------------

Leavin', On A Jet Plane
Miami to Boston – 1955

The Spauldings, et. al., left for Boston. The family was excited about the impending wedding. The woman they all came to accept as Candy Augustein was more than a little apprehensive about what awaited her in Boston.

Harry Spaulding drove to Logan Airport with the intention of greeting his family at the gate. Callahan Tunnel traffic was so backed up that, by the time he finally parked, he ended up waiting for them at the luggage carrousel.

"Uncle Harry! Uncle Harry!" Kendall squealed when she saw him. She wiggled her hand from her mother's and ran into his welcoming arms.

Harry was so thrilled to see his brother and family, with whom he seldom got to spend time that, at first, he barely noticed the woman Audrey introduced as the baby sitter for his niece. They piled into Harry's beat-up '49 Oldsmobile and drove toward Arlington Street in the Back Bay to check into the Ritz. That night the *'Florida Contingent'* would meet the woman who would become Harry's bride and, of course, her family. The wedding would be the next day.

"This is a big step, Mortimer." The brothers strolled side-by-side to the suite and Ted draped an arm around Harry's shoulders. "Are you sure Beverly can stand being married to a used car salesman?"

"No but she is so the wedding is on." Harry blushed. "You're welcome to join us for dinner, Candy."

"I'd love to if it's not an imposition."

"This is John's wing-ding. He said to gather as many family members as I could." Harry wrapped his own arm around Ted's shoulders. "Sonny, here, is about the only blood family I have, except for maybe one cousin out in Michigan. *Mañana Billy.*" Harry and Ted said simultaneously. "He and his family won't get here until, well ... Mañana," Harry said with a chuckle. "As far as I'm concerned, the more the merrier."

"Thanks. Can I rent a car through the hotel?"

"At the desk, but the whole to-do, wedding and all, is right in the hotel."

"The wedding is for family only," Grown Kendall insisted. "I'll entertain myself tomorrow night. Boston is a fun town when you know where to go."

"I never think of Boston as that much fun. Do you know something I should?" Harry asked.

"On our way to get the luggage, people were passing out flyers. I tossed the others but I kept these."

She pulled two folded pieces of paper from her jacket pocket. Harry watched her face as she displayed the first, treating it as she would a rare jewel. There was a curious flash of brightness in her eyes.

"A clown, in full regalia, handed me this. It announces the arrival of Ringling Brother Circus at the Topsfield Fair grounds. Too bad they don't get here until Monday; we'll be gone by then. I don't understand why they aren't coming into Boston. It would mean a far better turn-out."

"Tent fires." The brothers said in unison.

"So many people maimed or killed," Ted said, reflecting on the last patients he treated after an evening at the Circus. "Beyond the parade announcing their arrival, they're ban from the city. In fact, they've been ban nearly everywhere. Only small towns like Topsfield are willing to take the chance. I heard the Circus may have to close. Permanently."

Kendall remembered hearing frightening stories of people burned in horrific fires before the Circus gave up the flammable tarps of the Big Top and came indoors.

"It would be terrible if they closed! I go every year just to see the clowns and the smellephants."

"Smellephants," Harry laughed. "I like that. You're funny."

"My uncle is the funny one," Kendall corrected remembering that Harry called elephants, smellephants, just to make her laugh. "He calls the grown ones smellephants and the babies smellyphants."

Harry caught a second flash of light in Grown Kendall's eyes. He blew it off.

"What's the other flyer?" He asked.

"This is my flyer of choice for tomorrow," she beamed. "A one night appearance by The Benny Goodman Orchestra. It's once-in-a-lifetime for me. I can't miss it. And Wonderland Ballroom is so close even I can to throw a rock there, figuratively speaking of course."

"You swing dance?" Harry asked, making more than polite conversation.

Though he told himself the flashes of light he saw in her eyes were imagined, he was more than a little curious about 'Candy'.

"Don't tell me you don't," Kendall always had so much fun dancing with Uncle Harry, it was difficult to imagine him ever not knowing how.

"Mortimer?" Ted asked. "I assume you mean in a vertical position. Surely you jest."

"I'm afraid Sonny's right. I can barely put one foot in front of the other without tripping over it," Harry admitted.

"I can have you dancing in a day," Kendall offered. "Let it be my way of thanking you for tonight or, better yet, consider it my wedding gift. One size fits all and you can never lose it or break it."

"Sounds perfect and Bev will be so surprised." Harry indicated Kendall's flyers. "Mind if I have a closer look at those?"

"Keep them," she handed them over.

Harry checked his watch. "Um, dinner isn't until 7:00. What would you like to do in the meantime?"

"You mean being that Newbury Street is practically underneath this room," Audrey said. She, Grown Kendall and young Kendall answered together. "Go shopping!"

The group headed back to the elevator and Harry carefully tucked the Circus flyer into the inside pocket of his coat. He quietly disposed of the other in a nearby trash can. Side-by-side again, the brothers walked behind the women.

"You have a sudden interest in the Circus?" Ted asked.

"This baby-sitter is unusual," Harry said avoiding the question and thinking back on the momentary flashes of light he'd seen.

"She's great with Kendall," Ted said, inwardly acknowledging the woman he knew as Candy Augustein was like no other woman he'd ever known, except for Audrey. It surprised him how alike they were. Candy organized his office the way Audrey organized their home. She set up everything so he could lay his hands on anything as needed. Candy, herself, was totally efficient and left everything neat, orderly, and in its place. She even organized his day so that appointments were tight enough not to waste his time, yet left him the flexibility to easily modify as necessary. He considered her a scheduling genius.

Ted and Harry were like night and day. Ted was centered and practical. Harry was spontaneous and innovative, with wild ideas. Harry saw potential and multiple possibilities while others were still struggling even to see the facts. Ted considered the Circus flyer and silently wondered what Harry was going to pull out of his sleeve.

*   *   *   *

Harry arrived at the Ritz the next morning and obtained the hotel manager's permission to use their ballroom. Kendall and Harry worked on the basics for the better part of an hour. He was a quick study. By the end of his lesson Harry could dance with the best of them. They sat to catch their breath.

"You're really good at this," Harry said. "You should teach dance for a living."

"I'll take it under advisement," Kendall laughed to herself.

"Mind if I ask something?"

"Nothing too personal," Kendall warned.

"All I really want is your opinion."

"Don't give up your day job," Kendall suggested.

"There you go being funny again," Harry teased, wagging a finger. "Remember yesterday when you said how you loved the Circus? Well, I was just wondering what it was about the Circus that you love. What I mean is, would you love it less if there wasn't a tent and maybe the midway was separate from the main action?"

In all of Kendall's life she'd never once been inside a Circus tent. She loved the Circus because of the Circus and because of Uncle Harry.

"Like I said, it's the clowns–"

"And the Smellephants," Harry interrupted. "I remember. You know how Ted said the Circus is on the verge of closing," Harry reminded her. "Wouldn't it be a crime if the only reason they went under was because no one was smart enough to save them." Harry leaned in conspiratorially. "Just between us, I love the Circus too. Last night, I kept looking at that flyer and had this stupid idea. What would you think of a Circus in a warehouse? Would you still go?" He asked carefully.

"I don't know about a warehouse," Kendall said skeptically.

"Then, how about … an arena like, say, the Boston Garden?"

Even before she answered Harry was out of his chair pacing excitedly. "You know," he said, "every major city has some big mostly unused building associated with it. Boston has the Garden."

"Miami has Convention Hall," Kendall volunteered.

"Maybe my idea *isn't* so stupid," Harry said.

Kendall could only encourage him. Her Uncle Harry spent ten years working for the Circus. The story of how it began was family legend. He and Aunt Bev honeymooned in New York, stayed in a fancy hotel, conceived her cousin Joshua and saw Broadway shows; not necessarily in that order. Their first morning in the city, Harry rose early, left his new bride to sleep and went in search of adventure.

Andrew Barkley was having little luck booking the Circus in any city let alone a major one. People were afraid. And who could blame them. The last fire killed 75 people, and they were the lucky ones. Barkley grimaced over the child who was burned over fifty percent of her body. Weeks in the hospital, treatments, surgeries, skin grafts, and the doctors still didn't know if she'd make it. She died that morning, making it a particularly bad morning for the Circus. Later, the Sarasota office would call and Barkley would dispense the news everyone had been dreading for nearly a year.

Not so fast! That morning, Harry Spaulding was having a particularly good morning. Ted was right. Harry definitely had something up his sleeve. He knocked on Andrew Barkley's door and stepped inside.

"Excuse me, do you have a moment?" Harry asked and introduced himself.

Barkley looked at his watch. "A moment's about all I have, Mr. Spaulding." The call from Sarasota was due any minute. "What's on your mind?"

"I want to represent the Circus, be the advance-man," Harry announced.

Barkley snorted as he stifled a nervous laugh. From his perspective, Harry's suggestion was ludicrous. "Town officials are terrified of another fire, Mr. Spaulding. No one is coming to the Circus. In fact, they're staying away in droves. There's no Circus for which to be the advance-man."

"I'll book you in every major city in the country and take five hundred thousand dollars a year for the next five years," Harry continued, impervious to the brutal facts.

"Why not a million a year for the next ten years?" Barkley sarcastically suggested.

"Okay," Harry willingly upped the ante, "a million a year for the next ten."

The phone rang.

"Barkley," he said into the receiver, paused to listen then started to explain what no one wanted to hear.

"I can book the circus in every major city," Harry insisted in a voice loud enough to be heard on the other end of the phone.

Barkley listened again and hung up.

"Mr. Spaulding, I've been authorized to write a contract with whatever terms you want. Write your own ticket."

Andrew Barkley and Irving Wallace knew the paper on which Harry's contract would be written would ultimately be worthless. No one could book the Circus.

Just the same, Barkley drew it up and both he and Harry signed on the dotted line. The contract was short and sweet, but most of all they had it notarized making it binding and very legal. Harry and Andrew shook hands and Harry returned to his hotel on 5th Avenue where his new bride was in a luxurious bath filled with scented salts and bubbles up to her newly married chin. Harry briefly explained what he'd done and displayed the signed contract.

"Can you do it?" Beverly asked. Though she recognized Harry's ideas for the brilliance they were, she considered that this time Harry might have bitten off more than he could chew.

"What does nearly every major city have in common?" He quizzed.

"Dirt and lots of people," Beverly guessed.

"There's that," Harry agreed. "They also have some sort of huge mostly unused brick facility not likely to catch on fire. Huh? Huh?" He looked at Bev nodding agreement with his own idea.

"But will people think a building is Circus-y enough?" She played Devil's advocate.

"One way to find out."

Harry left Bev to finish her bath and began making calls. He started with his home town of Boston, took Kendall's suggestion of Miami then Chicago and Dallas. Everyone was delighted to add the Circus to their schedule of events, particularly with Harry's assurance that the Circus, and not their own crews, would be cleaning up after the *'smellephants'*. The word made people chuckle and people liked Harry. What was not to like? He made them laugh. The next morning Harry called Andrew Barkley.

"Mr. Spaulding," Andrew's greeting sounded as disappointed as it did superior. "Giving up already?" Barkley and Wallace wanted very badly for Harry to succeed. Although his efforts were certain to be a shot in the dark, it was most likely the only shot the circus had, making it a shot worth taking.

"The bad news is," Harry started, "I'm looking at the world's biggest long distance phone bill."

"As Circus advance-man that type of expense is your sole responsibility. Check your contract," Andrew suggested.

"The good news," Harry continued as if Barkley hadn't spoken, "is that the Circus is booked in Boston, Miami, New York, Detroit, Los Angeles, Dallas, Denver, Chicago, Atlanta, Tulsa." Harry stopped. "Would you like for me to continue?"

Silence.

"Mr. Barkley? Andrew?"

         *   *   *   *

Grown Kendall helped Little Kendall dress for the wedding, opted for an early dinner in the hotel dining room and, in spite of the rain, never rented that car. Instead, she caught the Green Line just outside the hotel, transferred to the Blue Line at Government Center and exited the 'T' at Wonderland station on the out-bound side; the side furthest from her destination. She ascended the stairs to cross over the tracks and raced down the stairs on the in-bound side, but even with the extra output of energy, her borrowed coat was insufficient against the raw December night. Kendall then made a mad dash the sixty or so yards to Wonderland Ballroom but, even running, she was more than a little wet and half frozen by the time she entered through the double doors. The sounds of Benny Goodman's Orchestra greeted her. The band members looked so impressive in their black tuxedoes that she gawked at them from the entry to the ballroom itself.

Kendall checked her coat and pocketed the ticket. A three person family arrived immediately behind her. The child was wearing a yellow slicker over his winter coat. They stopped at coat-check and headed for seats at the far end of the dance floor.

A sleazy man with greased back hair noted her presence. He eyed Kendall thinking *Long as I have to be here all night, might as well have some fun.* 'Sleaze' approached her asking for a dance. She politely declined. Unprepared for the winter chill, which went right to the bone, he noted that her hands were trembling.

"Come on baby. I'll warm you up," Sleaze said by way of a second crude invitation.

"Please take no for an answer," Kendall suggested and started to walk away.

"One dance ain't gonna kill ya." He grabbed her arm pulling her toward him and breathed Scotch in her face.

No, but your breath might, Kendall stifled the thought. "Let go!" She spat the words still trying to keep her composure.

"Afraid of a real man?"

As if from nowhere, someone extracted her arm from Sleaze.

"The lady said she isn't interested. She is also with me." Pretending to ignoring Sleaze, but knowing he was well within ear-shot, Kendall's savior continued the charade. "Didn't you see us, dear?"

"I must have gotten lost in the music," Kendall played along.

From across the room a woman and child waved and smiled. Kendall did likewise. As they crossed the dance floor, she thanked the stranger.

"I think you just saved my life."

"No thanks necessary," the man paused then teased, "but you can owe me."

"All right then," Kendall agreed with a smile. "I owe you."

She joined the man's party.

"I'm Jack," he started the introductions, "my wife Dorothy and this handsome young man is our son, Gordon."

"Nice to meet all of you. Having a good evening?" She addressed the boy.

"Better than yours," he said. "We voted to send Dad to save you." The boy eyed the man. "What a goon!"

"You're right." Kendall glanced over her shoulder at Sleaze. "He is a goon."

"And doesn't look the type to take no for an answer so easily. Care to really join us?" Jack offered.

"If it's not an imposition," Kendall answered.

"Certainly not," the man named Jack assured.

"You aren't local, are you?" Dorothy entered the conversation.

"How did you know?" Kendall asked.

"Your clothes. They're a little tropical for this climate."

"And I'm afraid my coat didn't make up for it," Kendall admitted.

"Hey, her hands are shaking," Gordon observed.

"Is that the cold or fear?" Dorothy asked.

"Both I think." Kendall rubbed her hands back and forth trying to warm them.

Dorothy took Kendall's hands in hers. "You're frozen stiff. Jack, be a dear and get her something hot."

"What'll it be? Coffee? Tea?" Jack asked.

"Tea, please."

"Sit. Sit." Dorothy motioned to the chair between herself and her son. Jack returned in a flash with the tea. "The knight in shining armor already introduced us," Dorothy said smiling at her husband as he took the seat on the far side of her. "Who did he rescue?"

"Candy Augustein," Kendall casually used the name she'd been using right along.

"What a small world. Our name is Augustein," Jack volunteered. "Well, it was, until Dad shortened it to August."

"You're Dr. Jack August?" Kendall realized who the family probably were.

"One and the same," Jack said.

"My brother, Terry, his specialty is the same as yours; female infertility." Kendall could barely control her excitement. "He's a very big fan."

"Gordon, Dorothy, did you hear that?" Jack breathed on his nails then fake-polished them on the lapel of his suit coat. "I have fans."

"Don't let it go to your head." Dorothy gently poked him with her elbow. "She said you have 'a' fan. Singular."

"Yes, but he's a very big fan." Jack held his arms open then wrapped them around Dorothy in a bear hug. "I don't think I know a Terry Augustein," he said.

"It's Spaulding," Kendall corrected awkwardly.

"No. No Terry Spaulding either I'm afraid," Jack confirmed.

Be a neat trick if you did thought Kendall, *since he isn't born yet.*

"Augustein isn't your family name?" Dorothy asked noticing the absence of a wedding band.

"My husband's family," Kendall said.

"Is he in Boston with you?" Jack asked.

"Oh, he's here." *How twisted is this!* Kendall thought glancing at a six-year old Gordon.

"Doesn't he like the big band sound?" Dorothy asked.

"He loves the music." Kendall noted the young version of her Gordon absently tapping his right foot, keeping time to the rhythm.

"Well, too bad he couldn't join you. The orchestra is in rare form. I wonder if your husband and I are related," Jack said.

"He has no relatives in Boston," Kendall stopped him cold, flashing on the unyielding stony faces of Gordon's Uncle Adam and Aunt Sarah.

The orchestra began playing another song.

"Since your husband isn't here may I have the honor of this dance?" Jack asked.

"If Dorothy doesn't mind, I'd love it."

"The night is young. I'll wear him out on the next one," Dorothy jibed.

"Do you know how your brother's research is progressing?" Jack probed, once on the dance floor.

"He's been relatively successful." Kendall smiled thinking of the baby Audrey said was growing inside her at that very moment.

"What do you mean relatively successful?"

"Fertilization, outside the womb."

"You seem very familiar for a layman."

"Terry and I often talk about his work," Kendall said.

"That could be um ... unhealthy," he suggested.

"How do you mean?" Kendall asked.

"There are people willing to go to great lengths to stop the research your brother and I do. I've had anonymous calls ... with threats."

"You aren't serious!"

"As a heart attack," Jack confirmed. "My own relative success aside," he continued, "my work is on hold until some of the tension blows over. It sounds as if your brother has gone beyond my experiments. Think he'd be interested in my outline and research results?"

"You can't give your research to a stranger," Kendall protested on Jack's behalf, "even if the stranger is *my* brother."

"If he's half the man the glow in your eyes would lead me to believe, he'll do the right thing and give credit where credit is due when he succeeds. Meantime the threats are real. These people will stop at nothing to keep our work from seeing the light of day. I'm just protecting my family. Suggest that Terry do the same."

They finished the rest of their dance in silence.

Dorothy had the next dance and Kendall sat with a young Gordon August, not at all sure what to say.

"It's nice that you enjoy big band music."

"How did you know?" Gordon asked.

"Your right foot speaks volumes."

Gordon looked down at his foot and laughed.

"Would you care to dance?"

"There aren't any other kids." It was almost a complaint.

"How about you and I dance? I'm pretty good."

"I don't know," Gordon hesitated.

"Come on. No one will be grading us," she encouraged.

The orchestra began a Fox Trot and Gordon escorted Kendall to the dance floor. The song and dance ended and Kendall leaned down to give him a hug. The light smell of her perfume and musk from the physical exertion of dance filled his head. He pulled away.

"That isn't what we learned at cotillion. The partners separate like this." Gordon stepped back a few paces. "The lady curtsies." Gordon waited for Kendall to do her part. "And the man bows."

Kendall watched the top of Gordon's head dip and the dreadful skanky man who accosted her earlier swooped by and whisked her onto the dance floor.

"Let go!" She protested as he muscled her around.

They were on the opposite side of the room from Gordon, when he made a real move. "Come on, baby." He breathed Scotch in her face again.

"Gordon! ... Gordon! ... Gordon!" Out of habit Kendall called for her husband 'til she realized that, as a child, there was nothing he could do.

"Dad was right," Gordon said to no one in particular. "That guy didn't take no for an answer." He ran for the manager.

"I never said I'd dance with you." Kendall squirmed, but the man's grip tightened.

"I see something I want, I ask once. Then, baby, I just take. And I want you big-time." Sleaze wrapped himself around her like a Boa-constrictor and forced his tongue into Kendall's mouth. She physically protested, but couldn't get the leverage necessary for any of the moves her friend, Andrea, taught her.

Sleaze became intoxicated by the feel of Kendall's body pressed into his. Over confident and considering his size an advantage, he expected size alone to guarantee control. He relaxed his grip just a bit. Just enough. Without thinking or a moment's hesitation, Kendall executed a flawless take-down, surprising everyone including herself. The last time she used the move was on Gordon. His stunned look at the time matched that of the guy on the floor in the moment. The bouncer arrived in time to see the man hit the ground, his arm pulled up behind him and his face pressed into the wooden floor. In short order, the bouncer ejected the man from the ballroom making it clear he should not return. Not that night. Not any night.

"I got a great memory for faces, low-life," the bouncer said picking the guy up from the floor. "And I ain't gonna forget yours." He hustled toward the door and tossed the man out like so much trash. "Be smart. Don't come back."

The bouncer reported to the manager that the matter was handled then interrupted Jack and Dorothy fussing over Kendall.

"Those were some pretty fancy moves, lady, but you were lucky. He didn't have a weapon. Next time he might. Anyone treats you like that in the Ballroom you ask for Dick Catalano ... *hasta pronto!* Remember, I can't do nothin' *after* it's too late. Catch my drift? Low-life like that don't need much reason or time to hurt you. Capisce?"

The balance of the evening proceeded without incident.

"I'm so glad we met," Jack said when it was time to leave. "Even if the initial reason was a bit ah ... out of the ordinary."

"Me too." Kendall extended her hand to Jack with Gordon half asleep on his shoulder.

"Please look us up the next time you're in town," Dorothy said as she and Kendall exchanged hugs.

"I'd love that," Kendall answered even knowing it would never happen; she would eventually return to her own Time.

She swept the lock of hair from Gordon's forehead then kissed his cheek. He came awake long enough to kiss hers as well. Each silently felt the same body jolt they experienced in Kendall's own Time, young Gordon's future. One day the sleepy child in his father's arms would be the man she loved. Her husband. Her Gordon.

"Bye-bye." She touched his cheek with the back of her hand.

Her voice, touch and scent pulled Gordon sufficiently from his dreamy slumber to answer. "You smell good." His eyes closed.

"I'll bet he says that to all the girls," Kendall said.

"Can we drop you somewhere?" Jack offered.

"The 'T' stops right in front of my hotel," Kendall said.

"If you're sure," Jack said.

The foursome exited the Ballroom through double doors which banged shut behind them. A set of high beams came to life nearly blinding them. Even through the glare Jack made out the driver's face. Dick Catalano appeared as if by magic.

"You folks need a walk to your car?" He offered.

"We're fine," Jack assured, "but it seems our *'friend'* appears to be a bit hard of hearing." Jack indicated the man's vehicle with his head.

"Wait here."

Dick and Sleaze had words. Loud words which roused Gordon.

"You're either dumber than you look or you don't hear so good. I recommended you get lost," they heard Dick say.

"Get outta my face!" Sleaze spat the words and tried to grab Dick in order to punch him.

Dick got in the first blow and the man's lip started to bleed. Dick reached into the car, grabbed the guy by the lapels and pulled him part way out his open window.

"I already told you, asshole, I got a great memory for faces and, now, I ain't likely to ever forget yours. Get lost and don't come back," Dick repeated.

Sleaze exited the parking lot, turned left onto 1A and sped off.

Dick returned to the group in time to hear Jack say, "It isn't safe for you to travel alone by 'T' at this hour."

"You're better off together, Miss," Dick agreed. "I got a bad feeling."

"I hate to say it out loud, but I think you're right," Kendall agreed.

"I never wrote down your address to send the information we discussed." Jack tried to sound nonchalant. "How about we stop by my office to pick it up then drop you at your hotel."

"I don't know," Kendall hesitated accepting Jack's work.

"Everyone into the car! It's freezing and we're getting soaked standing here discussing it."

"Can we drop you somewhere, young man?" Jack offered to Dick.

"I got it covered. The manager always gives me a ride."

Their car exited the parking lot, also turning left onto 1A south, then west onto Route 16 toward the Tobin Bridge. Sleaze was nowhere in sight until they rounded the Chelsea curve. Making no attempt to curtail their progress, Jack told himself that the guy had to live somewhere and behind them didn't necessarily mean following them. By the time Jack pulled up in front of his Harvard Street office, even with Sleaze's car M-I-A, he continued to feel uneasy. Dorothy insisted on remaining in the car with Gordon rather than waking him to go inside. Jack locked the doors making a joke of it.

"Can't have you two running off to Zanzibar without me."

Once inside Jack retrieved a manila envelope from a supply cabinet and placed his outline and research notebook inside. Next he typed a quick note to Terry as well as a letter transferring ownership of his research material.

"It's missing all the usual; *'party of the first part'* lingo but you've witnessed my signature so it's legal. Everything in this envelope officially belongs to Dr. Terry Evan Spaulding. Now that he's the caretaker of it, suggest that he be extra careful."

When Jack and Kendall returned to the car, Dorothy and Gordon were fast asleep. Kendall climbed in back, pulled Gordon toward her so that his head was on her lap then covered him with the slicker he refused to wear when they left the ballroom. Gordon snuggled down and made himself comfortable.

As they headed onto Storrow Drive east, it was apparent that Sleaze wasn't M-I-A after all. He was behind them again; his high beams almost blinded Jack who said nothing until he rammed their rear bumper. Again. And yet again. Kendall turned around.

"Over a stupid dance," she said.

"I doubt it was the dance. I suspect you were an attractive distraction while he kept track of me and why he stuck around. Hold on," Jack warned as he saw the car behind them speed up. Its driver continued his twisted game of actual bumper cars though Dorothy and Gordon slept through it. The car eventually dropped back and Jack drew a sigh.

"Are you okay back there?" He asked checking the rearview mirror.

Before Kendall could answer, Sleaze's car changed lanes and sped up again. The fear reflected in Jack's eyes made her look out the rear window. Whatever had been covering Sleaze's front license plate flew off exposing the number. 52B-351. Sleaze pulled his car even with theirs and rammed them.

As usual, parts of Storrow Drive were flooded from the heavy rain. Patches of shallow puddles froze into black ice. Both of Jack's right side tires hit one and his car lost all traction. Between the intermittent skidding and hydroplaning their car went airborne then crashed to earth flipping over and over and over and ...

Sounds of breaking glass and crunching metal surrounded the car's occupants. Try as Kendall might to keep hold of Gordon, she lost her grip when the car hit terra-ferma. Gordon awoke for the briefest of moments reaching for her, then his head and left arm smacked the rear driver's-side window; hard. The impact knocked him unconscious, broke his arm and splintered the window glass into a spider web pattern, the pieces held together by nothing but luck. The car spun a one-eighty on its roof and came to rest with its passenger side pressed against the guard rail in the median. The front portion of the roof had caved in on both front seat passengers. Jack's legs were pinned under the dash and his chest had rammed the steering column, making every breath a struggle, but he was painfully aware. Dorothy, as her son, had been knocked unconscious. A trickle of blood also ran from her mouth.

"Are you okay?" He managed under labored breath.

"Gordon's hurt, but I'm fine. This window glass is shattered, but it's opening okay. If I can get it to roll all the way down, I mean up, without falling into a million pieces, I think we can all get out of here."

Kendall might have had no idea but, from the size of things and even without medical tests, Jack knew his own and Dorothy's internal injuries were extensive. Their chances for survival, even should they escape the wreck, were slim. Recognizing a faint odor, Jack wanted only one thing in that moment.

"Take Gordon first," he instructed gasping for a suck of oxygen, "then come back for us."

Kendall crawled backward through the rear window into the street. She pulled a motionless Gordon with her then carried him to the side of the road. She stripped out of her thin jacket, shaped it under his head to hold it elevated and motionless and covered him with his slicker. She headed back to the car. In her absence Jack got his own window down, groped around for and located the envelope containing his life's work – work that would ultimately cost him his life; that of his wife; maybe even that of his child.

"Take this," Jack offered the envelope struggling to speak.

"But it's your life's work," she said.

"Exactly," Jack confirmed. "Take it, for your brother. Leave it," Jack meant the envelope, "and who ever hired that man at Goodman wins. Don't allow it! Neither Dorothy nor I will survive this. You said you owe me and I'm holding you to it," Jack struggled again for air. "I'm calling in my marker. Don't let us die for nothing," he insisted, in obvious and excruciating pain.

"There must be *something* I can do." Kendall looked at the crushed vehicle hoping that somehow this moment wasn't the event she knew it to be, but finally admitted to herself that it was.

"Look after my son and get away from the car. *NOW!*" Jack ordered.

Kendall accepted the envelope, clutched it to her chest and walked away. She turned back for a last look at the parents the Gordon of her own Time so missed; that he so mourned. She would miss and mourn them as well; because now she had met them. She knew first hand the kind of wonderful people they were; because she had spent time with them ... even if it was just the one night. Kendall returned to Gordon, picked him up and cradled him in her arms. Gazing into his peaceful face, she knew the events of the last hour ensured that, once he awoke, he would know no peace. Kendall looked back to Jack and Dorothy wishing their accident wasn't the unchangeable experience that haunted her husband; knowing that it was and that nothing, not even Overlap, could alter what was about to happen. She held Gordon tightly to her, shielded him with her body and tucked her head. Seconds later the ground shook; the car became a fiery ball engulfed by flames.

Tears spilled down Kendall's cheeks as she looked into the face of the child her Gordon once was. "Poor baby," she said. "Guess you're nobody's baby now. But someday, you'll be my baby. Body and soul, you *will* be mine."

Had Gordon been conscious and awake, he'd have witnessed the instantaneous flash of light in her eyes.

Some sleepless soul; the back of whose home faced Storrow Drive, must have felt or heard the explosion. Metropolitan Police and the Boston Fire Department arrived within moments.

Officer Dennis Sullivan, first on the scene, found Kendall repeating an endless loop of words that made no sense to him. Her mind was mostly elsewhere; centered on the last things she saw and Jack's final words. A scramble of the snippets and scenes kept insinuating themselves on her mind and escaped her lips. *That - man - died - at - 52 - for - B - Goodman - 35 - 1 - nothing.* Sullivan jotted it into his case notebook exactly as he understood it. *That man died at 52 for Bea Goodman. 35 won nothing.*

"Miss? Miss?"

Sullivan tried to get Kendall to communicate something beyond the gibberish he'd written. She barely acknowledged or heard him. Sullivan finally took her by the shoulders and shook her back to the reality that two people were dead. Her subsequent responses provided little help and changed nothing.

I'll try again tomorrow Sullivan thought.

Kendall refused to relinquish Gordon even while Emergency Rescue examined him. At last, allowing the ambulance driver to take him, she whispered in his ear.

"Dream of me. Wait for me. Remember me."

The last of the fire extinguished, a waiting ambulance took the charred remains of Jack and Dorothy August to Boston Memorial's morgue, another took Gordon and Kendall to its ER. Gordon was admitted and Kendall was pronounced sound enough to be released. She returned to her hotel. Sullivan handed-off his notes to the second on-scene officer who returned to the Lower Basin District. Sullivan was grateful for his Second's offer to write up the report and went to speak with the next-of-kin.

Upon his arrival at the Ritz the next day, Officer Dennis Sullivan discovered that his witness was gone.

Chapter 13

-------------------------------- ▼ --------------------------------

The Plot
Weston, MA – 1955

Adam August sat alone in his den nervously sipping a bourbon. It was well after two in the morning and Sarah and the kids went to bed hours earlier. The phone rang. It was Rogers calling to report.

"Yes," was all Adam said.

"Ya two packages were delivahed." Rogers' Boston accent was thick.

"You idiot. There were three."

"Ya paid for the two big ones. The little one was going to be a bonus if it was convenient," Rogers corrected Adam.

"And," Adam demanded.

"It wudn't convenient. They hooked up with a girl. Some lookah, that one. I tried to persuade hur differently, but she wouldn't give me so much as a dance. The bitch! She left with them."

"You left witnesses!"

"I beg your pahden, but 'witness' implies that someone who stuck around maybe saw somethin', which they didn't. It was ovah too fast so no one saw nothin'. Maybe that girl pulled the kid from the wreck, but he's unconscious and she's from out-of-state. And she ain't exactly a witness, if she ain't exactly around.

"What if she pursues it from out of state?" Adam asked.

"Also not a problem. Eithah the girl or the cop got there facts wrong," Rogers supplied. "Meantime, that don't leave nobody to ask nutin' anyone can confirm."

"How do you know what they saw or said?" Adam panicked.

"I got my sources," Rogers confirmed. "So relax! The rest of your ordaah was delivahed. I mean, I feel bad about the dead broad and all, on accountah she didn't have nothin' to do with this. But all that screwin' around with unnatural baby makin' is ovah and ya bruthah's outah the pitchah ... permanently."

"How did you know he was my brother?" Adam was surprised to learn he hadn't been cloak and dagger enough.

"It is always in my best interest to know everything about everything that involves me. But don't lose no sleep," Rogers comforted, "same price you *off* family, friends or strangahs."

"You're sure the girl can't I-D you?"

"Ain't no one can I-D me," Rogers was emphatic. The line went dead.

Adam returned the phone to its cradle, turned off the lights and went to bed. A few hours later the door bell rang. Officer Dennis Sullivan delivered the grizzly news about Jack and Dorothy and that an injured Gordon was taken to Boston Memorial. Adam was appropriately shocked and appropriately upset.

"The fire means the coroner will need dental records to make positive I-Ds. He'll need the name of the family dentist."

"Fire!" Rogers hadn't gone into detail. "You said accident."

"Between you, me and the wall," Sullivan shook his head, "that was no accident. The car had to have rolled three, maybe four times. It's just lucky the woman passenger got your nephew out. Apparently right afterward the gas tank exploded."

"Was this woman the cause?" Adam hoped he could divert attention from outside forces and focus blame on the girl; the cause of the additional grief he knew lie ahead. "Who is she?"

"An out-of-towner. I'm no doctor, but she was most likely in some degree of shock. She was speaking gibberish when I arrived. The only info of value were her verbal I-Ds of your brother and sister-in-law and the circumstances of their acquaintance."

Rogers was right Adam thought.

"Apparently she met them at Wonderland Ballroom and they were giving her a ride back to her hotel."

"You mean to say they gave a ride to a stranger!"

"That is how it looks, sir."

"It isn't something my brother's family was likely to do."

Actually, it was exactly what they would do.

"Well, as I said, all we can confirm is that they met last night and your brother and his family were giving her a lift. You can check with the desk Sergeant tomorrow to see if anything new has developed. Everything we know will be in the report. Sir," Sullivan hesitated, "I still need a contact for those dental records. It's just a formality."

Adam gave the officer the name of the family dentist, thanked him and shut the door. He woke Sarah to inform her of the evening's events, but delayed breaking the rest of the news. He and Sarah were already arguing like Siamese Fighting Fish. How would he explain promising to be Gordon's guardian ... in case.

Fuck! Adam thought. *There wasn't supposed to be any damn woman passenger and there wasn't supposed to be any 'in case'.* Adam counted on Rogers delivering all three packages. Maybe Gordon wouldn't make it, except Adam didn't have that kind of luck. Perhaps with his brother out of the way his luck would turn, the way a worm does when assaulted.

Before Adam left for the Dorchester impound he told Sarah to make funeral arrangements for Jack and Dorothy; he would be unavailable. Adam was on the road by five to identify what was left of his brother's car. During the drive from Weston, he centered his thoughts on his new life outside of Jack's shadow with money from *'The Voice'* who wanted Jack's research stopped. Upon arrival at the hospital, Adam was directed to a Dr. Landers to learn the extent of Gordon's injuries.

"He has a broken arm and a concussion and is still unconscious," Landers said. "He's young, so the bones should heal just fine, but we've no way of knowing the permanent damage, if any, from the concussion. All we can do is wait and hope for the best."

Adam was certain his idea of the best and that of Dr. Landers were nowhere close to being the same.

Chapter 14

-------------------------------- ▼ ---------------------------------

You Can't Go Home Again
Miami – 1955

The Spaulding family, et. al., returned from Boston the Sunday afternoon following the wedding. The woman they all knew as Candy was lost in thoughts she felt better kept to herself. Ted checked in with Myra at the hospital. There was one message. Marvin Kanter called to say Lewis Toth's plane went down. There were no survivors. Every detail was exactly as Kendall explained them to Audrey. The funeral service was set for ten o'clock Monday morning, Parkway Memorial Chapel. Marv thought that if Ted were back in time he might wish to attend. Myra rearrange Ted's schedule to make it happen.

Of course he would tell Audrey the shocking news, but was certain she would opt-out of the service preferring to go to the Shiva house instead. To his surprise Audrey not only said she would go but that their daughter should accompany them. Candy also insisted upon attending. "The Toths live so far away," she said. "It's unlikely their friends will be able to come on such short notice. It's wrong for a poorly timed tragedy to leave them alone in death." Though her heart broke for the Toths, her thoughts were with Jack and Dorothy ... and Gordon.

The memorial service for the Toths was mercifully brief, but Ted knew that all funerals did a number on Audrey. He was surprised, in the face of one so tragic, that she was dry eyed. She held their daughter's hand throughout and wore an unexplained expression of gratitude. When Little Kendall asked about the two small coffins,

Audrey explained that they were small because the people inside were children. Even at just barely three, Kendall instantly understood that anyone could die, not just someone who was old or sick. She touched her mother's belly.

"Is Terry okay inside you, Mommy?" She asked.

"I'm sure he is, baby," Audrey said.

"Audrey, I thought we settled all of this imaginary brother stuff." Ted was visibly concerned that Audrey was now playing along.

"Terry is not *magicanary*, Daddy," Little Kendall insisted. "He's real!" She looked at her mother for support. "Isn't he, Mommy?"

"Audrey," Ted prompted.

"I'm pregnant," she confirmed. "I got my results back this morning."

"Results? When on earth were you tested? Why didn't you tell me?"

"Wynn Sandler checked me out just before we left for Boston," Audrey said. "I saw no sense getting your hopes up if it was just my flakey cycle being flakey.

"I'm so pleased, Audrey. I love you very much."

"Ted Spaulding you're going to make me cry," Audrey said.

"We're at a very sad funeral," Ted said. "I doubt anyone will notice." They smiled at each other. "Do you think the baby will be a sister for Kendall?" He asked.

"No!" Kendall answered her father's question looking up at him exasperated. "For the last time, Daddy, our baby is a brother and his name is Terry!" She made her point by poking her finger in his side punctuating the last two words.

"Ow! Okay, okay! It's a brother." Ted gave in still smiling.

"Named Terry," Audrey added, also smiling.

"That's right!" Little Kendall finished. "Now stop smiling. This is a very sad funeral."

At the conclusion of the service, the three women currently in his life dropped Ted at the hospital and returned home. After changing out of their funeral attire and Little Kendall went outside to play, Audrey spoke to Grown Kendall.

"I don't like the way you look at Ted when you think I'm not looking," Audrey said.

"What ever do you mean?" Kendall knew exactly what Audrey meant.

"As if you haven't seen him in a very long time. Haven't you seen him in a very long time?" Audrey pressed.

Kendall didn't answer.

"He didn't die in the plane with the Toths, but I get the feeling I'm going to lose him anyway."

Again, Kendall didn't respond.

"At least tell me how long I have," Audrey persisted. "One year? Two? Twenty? I want to know."

"Knowing won't change the events. They stay in place no matter what you do. I learned that in Boston."

"How so?" Audrey waited then persisted. "Won't you tell me?"

"You know how I went off on my own the night of Uncle Harry's wedding."

Audrey nodded.

"With the 'T' nearly right outside the hotel, I opted against renting that car and took the trolley to Wonderland." She mechanically recounted the people and events of that night. "But for all the *hoo-doo* with that awful man at the beginning, it was really a wonderful evening," she concluded without emotion. "When it was time to leave, the guy was in the parking lot just hanging around. The family I was with offered a lift back to the hotel. What with the guy, the rain, it being freezing cold, and that it was pretty late ... long story short, I accepted the ride." Kendall sighed heavily. "The man followed us, rammed our car from behind."

"Surely not deliberately," Audrey didn't want to believe it.

"Several times," Kendall confirmed. "If we hadn't hydroplaned over a puddle he would have run us completely off the road. When that didn't work he side-swiped our car making it skid on a patch of black ice and go up ... and over ... and over ... and," Kendall's voice trailed off. "The car landed upside-down. The front part of the roof caved in on the man and woman."

"Dear god! Where were you?" Audrey prodded.

"In back with their child. The father told me to get his son out of the car first, which I did by pulling myself and the boy through a window I got to open. I returned to the car but the father knew there was no escape for himself and his wife. He ordered me to move away." Kendall shook her head still unresolved that her words were true. "I went back to where I lay the boy, picked him up and held him in my arms. I heard the man say *Dorothy! Dorothy! Sweetheart, please wake up.* I don't know if she came around or not. The last thing he said was *I love you.*

"Just like the Toth's plane, I knew about this car. There was no escape for the parents. There was an explosion. Much as I wanted to help them, I couldn't. Shit! I was right there and it changed nothing."

"Maybe nothing changed but your being there is the one thing that *did* help them."

"How? They're dead! Very helpful."

"You saved their son," Audrey said gently. "Had you not been there he surely would have died with them."

"My husband has a file, this thick, on that accident," Kendall's index finger and thumb indicated an inch and a half, "every awful detail. The police report says the child was thrown clear of the car through an open rear window. My pulling him out was just an alternate outcome of the same variety. With Overlap, what's important isn't *'how'* it happens only *'that'* it happens."

"That may be true, but it can't ever have been that he was thrown out a window," Audrey said.

"But–" Kendall stated to object.

"You forget that I was in Boston too and I know exactly how cold it was and that it was raining cats and dogs that night. You just said some of those cats and dogs froze into black ice. Given all that, no right-minded parent opens a rear window they can't close from the front seat? The window was never already open."

Kendall didn't respond.

"Well, did you open it or didn't you?" Audrey insisted on an answer.

"Guilty," Kendall admitted. "That and getting the boy out were the outcomes of the accident, which was the event."

"Suppose you're wrong. Suppose getting the boy out was a second event and the reason you traveled ... to be there to set the event in stone. If not for you the boy would have remained in the car. If not for you it simply couldn't have gone any other way," Audrey concluded matter-of-factly.

"But the police report," Kendall objected.

"Who can know what happened with that. But it likely wasn't the first time one was either written incorrectly or rewritten just to close a case. You left town with us and you'll eventually return to your own Time. Disappear."

"I guess," Kendall shrugged.

"And except for the car that caused the accident, my money says there wasn't anyone to corroborate what you just told me."

"No. There wasn't," Kendall confirmed then took a beat. "There's more and it's worse." She looked at Audrey. "The boy I pulled from the wreck, the boy I held in my arms while his parents died, he isn't just their son. He's my husband. I saved the life of my own husband."

"Seriously!" Audrey was flabbergasted.

"The boy was Gordon August and the people trapped in the front seat were his parents, Jack and Dorothy. Lovely people. I hardly knew them and I miss them. I can only imagine how Gordon's felt all these years."

"Why didn't you say something?" Audrey asked.

"What good would it have done? In Overlap as in life, born is born and dead is dead. Nothing I said or did after could bring them back."

Audrey nodded. "What happens to Gordon?" Her parental concern surfaced.

"He'll go live with his aunt and uncle."

"At least he'll be with family," Audrey said relieved.

"It's no blessing. Adam and Sarah are nothing to be grateful for."

"Kendall! That's a terrible thing to say."

"Be sure to tell me that again *after* you meet them. Fact is; you think even less of them than I do and that's saying something." Kendall paused. "You called me Kendall just now. Does that mean you believe all of this and that I am who I say?"

"I suppose it does." This time, Audrey took a beat. "Even if it can't change events I want to know about Ted."

"You know, it's forbidden to tell this unless you specifically ask." Kendall warned summoning up her courage to voice the unspeakable.

"Perhaps that's why I specifically asked," Audrey said.

Kendall nodded, thinking about what she told Hardy – all about the sure thing. But none of it was news. Hardy and Paul already planned to go to New York, even before their chat and, once they arrived, certainly would need to buy a paper to find a place to live and jobs. No doubt, Soho would be the only place the boys could afford, even with Kendall's 'investment'. Hardy already choreographed so many pieces for Paul, what was the one more Bob Fosse would see once he and Paul were roommates. Kendall understood that each step was an event that would happen; already happened ... with or without her. What she was about to tell Audrey, on the other hand, perhaps it was an outcome not all of which was set in stone; perhaps once Audrey knew all she could change it in some small way. Kendall took a beat.

"The hospital calls Dad to cover for Mick Sawyer on my thirteenth birthday. While he's in the E-R a nut pulls a gun. He shoots my father – three bullets in the chest. One goes straight through. One punctures a lung. And one lodges ... in his heart."

"Oh, my god!" Tears immediately sprung to Audrey's eyes. "Does he ... does he die?" Audrey almost couldn't bring herself to ask.

"No, but Dad never fully regains his health. His work is restricted and the on-going medical bills nearly wipe us out financially. You get a job as a secretary, and I–" Kendall stopped.

"You what? I need to hear the rest," Audrey pressed.

"I don't go to medical school. I know it's what you want, but it doesn't happen. The shooting changes everything and all things considered, Dad wishes that somehow the gunman had either missed or that he'd been a better shot."

For just a moment, Audrey thought she saw the quickest flash of light in the eyes of the woman her daughter would become. Unlike when Audrey was a child, seeing the same flash in the eyes of the little girl named Aja, she did not convince herself it was imagination.

"Is the man who shoots Ted ever caught?" Audrey asked.

Kendall shook her head. "Gets away clean."

"That gives us only ten good years," Audrey said.

"Spend them correctly," Kendall suggested, "and they can be enough.

"I'm going up to the Rehab around four to visit Gram," Kendall said. "Don't wait dinner. She said we need to talk."

"I'll leave something in the fridge," Audrey said.

"Thanks." Kendall hugged Audrey.

It was, in fact, so close a hug that Audrey was taken aback.

"That's the kind of hug you get when you're being left behind," Audrey accused. "Is it time?"

"No," Kendall protested, though she'd already begun to hear a distant whistle. "What with everything; including the funeral, I'm wiped. I just need a nap. Wake me if I'm not up by three?"

"Sure," Audrey assured and went to the kitchen to start dinner.

Kendall caught the 4 o'clock bus. She and Gram had their talk, spoke of everything that happened in Boston, and cried and laughed and cried some more. But Audrey's gut was correct. Grown Kendall did not return. When the moment arrived, the moment she feared nearly her entire life, Gram held her tightly, expressed her love then did as promised so many years before.

*   *   *   *

"Whoa. I don't feel so good." Kendall's hand went to her forehead. Once again she began to experience a hot flash and queasy feeling. New, this time, was the faint sound of a man's voice. "Do you hear that?"

Sylvia heard nothing.

"Sounds like chanting," Kendall said as the voice grew steadily louder.

"Time for you to go home, Mommala," Sylvia said.

"But I'm not ready," Kendall objected.

"Remember I said you must leave when Gordon calls," Sylvia reminded. "He's calling."

"Gordon, but–," Kendall finally recognized her husband's voice as the one repeating lines of poetry.

"Your mission is complete. You trained those young dancers; helped your Uncle Harry; saved your Gordon. There's nothing left to do."

"One more outcome needs to be unlived," Kendall objected.

"It's no longer necessary," Sylvia said smiling.

"But I don't want to go yet."

"I know," Sylvia said.

"I wish we had more time, Gram. I love you so much. I always did. Never forget I said that. It's so very important you remember I said that." Kendall buried her tear streaked face in her grandmother's shoulder wetting Sylvia's blouse.

"I'll remember," Gram assured. "I love you, baby. Grand and I, we both love you." Sylvia looked for the flash of light in Kendall's eyes, the one she prayed would not be there, the absence of which would confirm that down the road she would be strong enough to change the outcome of a moment. Better never to see the light Officer Paul Kelly saw that Sunday in James Ferretti's dance studio; the light Ferretti himself saw; the light Sidney Hart and Harry Spaulding and Hardy James and Paul Kelly, Jr. each saw; because their lives had been changed.

Better to change my own life Sylvia thought.

For Kendall, Gordon's voice and the sound of mechanical beep both came through clearly. She tried to block them out, but her hands were as ineffective in that moment as they had been on Beacon Street the day she traveled to the past. The beep which blipped behind Gordon's chant became a squeal. Kendall heard Gordon cry out.

"Gram, it's awful!"

"There's only one way make it stop, Mommala. Go to him; go to your Gordon," Sylvia said. "I love you."

"I love *you*," Kendall said as she had so many times in dreams.

"Quick kisses," Gram instructed.

Kendall leaned in and kissed Gram's cheek. Fresh tears spilled down her cheeks. Sylvia returned the kiss, grasped Kendall by the shoulders and took a last look for the dreaded flash of light that never appeared. In its place, came an undeniable crack sound and Sylvia immediately knew what happened. After decades of wishing for the opportunity to change the outcome of an event, the moment of change was upon her and Sylvia discovered that some wishes do come true.

"This is the moment you've been dreading," Sylvia said with pride. "When I push you all the way home because I love you."

Astonished at hearing Gram's frightening words again, Kendall tensed just enough for Sylvia to achieve the leverage necessary to give her a good hard shove. As Kendall stumbled backward, unusual layers of color became visible and surrounded her. She slipped through the holes in Time and they closed behind her.

Sylvia's heart simultaneously soared and broke as she prayed that every long ago promise was true. When Aja appeared at the Rehab, in the moments before Kendall's arrival, she was a few inches taller, a few years older, a few years wiser, and reconfirmed that, if Sylvia only continued to believe, the promised future was afait accompli. Aja assured that in her own Time, it had already happened.

Sylvia swore that, when Grown Kendall's Overlap was complete, she would guard against uttering the fateful words to her tiny granddaughter, the saying of which Aja confirmed was an event. And although nothing could change the event itself, nothing said the event could not be moved to a more appropriate Time. The thought that the child who was everything in the world to Sylvia would grow up afraid of her was simply more than she could bear and forbid the words from changing her life. To that end she promised to say them only to the adult traveler her granddaughter would become. With the mercy of Time and the aid of its travelers, Sylvia was given the tools to change her own life.

She reached into her blouse pocket for the fresh linen hanky she always carried. There, too, was the school picture Aja left behind so Gram could always remember her, along with the small plastic card that Audrey would one day give to Gordon. Sylvia wiped her tears, held Aja's picture in one hand and the card in the other. She recited and repeated the printed words as if they were a mantra.

*　　*　　*　　*

That night, as Audrey prepared Little Kendall for bed after her bath, she noted a manila envelope casually left on the night table. On top of it was an unfinished, unsigned, hand written note from Grown Kendall. Perched atop the note, like a paper-weight, was a small glass bottle of perfume. Audrey picked it up and examined the half empty vessel. On the bottom were tiny raised glass letters. *Carmen Parfum 1978.* Audrey pocketed it and read the note.

Dear Mom,

This will be more than a little difficult to digest, but try. I took the leftover class money and bought stock in Terry's name. It doesn't look like much but, whatever you do, <u>don't sell it</u>. It's his ticket to college and medical school. He must become a doctor. It's Terry made it possible for me to be pregnant now after a slime, named Stewart Cosgrove, made it virtually impossible. It's too much to explain, just know that it's true.

It's what you still want but there won't be enough money for two of us in medical school. I inherited your clever gene, but Terry's the real brains of this outfit, so I choose for him to go. I'm a choreographer and a dancer and I have a good life that makes me happy. Please believe that.

The other things in the envelope are also for Terry; my early birthday present before he turns fifteen. Use your own clever gene and you'll know the proper time to turn them over to him. There's an outline of Dr. August's work; his notes on the research and experiments he conducted just before his death and a letter legally transferring ownership of the information to my brother ... to Terry Evan Spaulding. You and dad allowed me to give him Grand's Hebrew name, Eliahu. He almost busted his buttons the day Terry was born. Don't make any big plans for the afternoon of June 26. Time already made plans for you.

By the way, Candy is short for <u>Candle</u>. (You'll understand in about two years.) The note abruptly ended.

Audrey emptied the envelope's contents. There was a letter to Terry from a Dr. Jack August, a letter of transfer, an outline and a notebook which Audrey understood was his research. She unfolded the stock certificate. On the face was the name *Terry Evan Spaulding*. Completely unbelievable. In anticipation of the future Audrey now believed would happen, she returned everything to the envelope and refastened the metal clip. *The future* Audrey mused. Ted being shot was most assuredly an event she could not change. But perhaps not every part of the outcome Grown Kendall knew was carved in stone. Her words echoed in Audrey's head. *Dad wishes that somehow the gunman had either missed or that he'd been a better shot.* For the gunman to be a better shot meant that Ted would die. For him to somehow miss, Audrey had ten years to consider it. Meantime, she had two choices – deny the evidence or believe.

Next day, Audrey went to the bank and acquired a safe deposit box. In it she placed the envelope she would turn over to her as yet unborn son when he was nearly fifteen. Their collective futures would be built on the outcome of three gun shots, the research of a man Audrey would never meet and shares of The Haloid Company.

In 1961 The Haloid Company changed its name to Xerox Corporation. Terry Evan Spaulding would go to medical school.

Chapter 15

----------------------------- ▼ -----------------------------

The Office
Mass. Ave. – Lacey, 1982

The phone on Lacey's desk rang. She answered it before the first ring finished.

"This is Lacey."

"It's Gordon. She's the same. Gruenwald detects unusual brain activity, sporadic or something. It's almost as if she doesn't want to come around," his voice broke. "It doesn't seem possible, but she may not last the night. Someone will need to say a few words at the service. Even if I found them, I couldn't say them. Will you? She loved you so. Please … call Lindsey."

There was a click and the line went dead. Lacey held the receiver forgetting to return it to the cradle. Thoughts washed over her. Flash backs really; bits and pieces of a life that would soon be over, that would be over too soon. She thought of how different all of their lives would become without Kendall in it. Without her to talk to, plan with, laugh and cry with. For Lacey it would never again be just the two of them. No husbands, no kids … just friends. Though Lacey's husband, Bruce, and their daughters, Mia and Paige, were her world, Kendall was Lacey's heart. No pun intended.

She recalled a long ago conversation with Kendall, repeated more times than Lacey could count. *Gram says it will never be your job to cry for me. Only my husband can. Gram's always right about these things. No matter how bad or how sad, never cry. Swear and promise!*

Husbands! In the days of Kendall's request they didn't even have boyfriends. Just the same, Lacey promised. Now the future husband of whom Kendall's Gram spoke asked her to say 'a few words'. But which words would allow Lacey to make good on the commitment she was just sucked into and still keep her long ago promise never to cry for her friend? There weren't any words which would not leave tears in their wake. One simply could not speak of Kendall in the ultimate past tense and not cry. *'Cause and effect'*; Kendall said meaning tears on her behalf from anyone but her future husband, any and all of which would have an effect that would not be to the good for any of them.

Lacey decided a eulogy would never do, but perhaps something about her life – that she filled everyone else's lives with joy and was leaving behind people who loved her; that her life was totally remarkable from beginning to end, and that it was over before it really got started. How could it be that she truly wouldn't be rushing through the door all breathless and 20 minutes late only to rush back out again still 20 minutes behind schedule. Kendall teased about one day etching the sentiment on her head stone. *HERE LIES KENDALL LAYNE SPAULDING – LATE, AS USUAL.* In subsequent years, Kendall changed her mind and there would be no headstone or earthly remains buried beneath it. She wished to be cremated and have her ashes scattered under the bright lights of Broadway. Still, Lacey felt Kendall's vibe as if it were very nearly a presence in the room. As if Kendall were still connected to this life rather than slipping away to whatever after-life existed in the beyond.

If Kendall really were slipping away, Lacey imagined she would sense it, feel it happening, know it in her soul. Either her connection to her dearest friend on earth was failing or somehow Kendall would not really *'go gentle into that good night'*. Instead, she would *'Rage. Rage against the dying of the light'*. Lacey only wished she knew and, more than that, she wished she knew the unspoken details of Kendall's life, powerful details. Details even Lindsey didn't know. Neither she nor Lindsey ever asked and Kendall never fessed-up why she wore fear like a suit of armor or suddenly dropped out of a conversation to glance over her shoulder. Was she looking for someone or maybe the other way 'round? And the nightmares – impossible as they were to ignore, Lacey knew better than to pursue them, ask about them. She always let them slide. Knowing Kendall at all was always enough, until she needed to find 'a few words' for the friend she'd held so dear for decades, yet hardly knew at all. Lacey always expected Kendall would reveal all when she was good and ready. Given their current situation, that they were about to lose her, the moment of being good and ready would never arrive.

Lacey finally replaced the receiver in its cradle then slid her hands forward and back over the arm-rests of the soft leather chair Kendall had delivered on their first day in business. Lacey had drooled over it. The business couldn't afford it. Somehow Kendall found a way to make it happen. Lacey leaned back allowing her memory to relive the day they decided to be partners as well as friends and turn the Hot Jazz movement into a business called Hott Jazz.

"You keep the business in order," Kendall teased, "and I'll be the one in terrific shape."

"You're all heart," Mock sarcasm laced Lacey voice anticipating Kendall's comeback.

"I think that'd be you ... all Hart. Get it? Oh, I'm so funny!"

"I got it but, seriously, you're not *that* funny."

"But I'm a little bit funny. Right," Kendall piped.

"Yeah," Lacey said, "a very little bit."

They met in Home Room on a scorching hot day in late August of 1968. Kendall was a little shy, but ready from the first to be friends. The first day of high school can been rough on anyone, but Kendall and Lacey found each other, and hardly even noticed.

"I'm Lacey Hart," she said.

"Say you're kidding," Kendall said.

Lacey shook her head.

"Must be tough around Valentine's Day."

"Yeah," Lacey agreed, "and, my dad's the principal."

"I know I shouldn't laugh, but come on," Kendall said around her mirth. "Lacey Hart; her father's the principal ... now that's comedy!"

Lacey was all too familiar with that drill. Her father was in charge of every kid on campus and her name drew more than a fair share of ribbing, but Kendall's off-handed humor completely diffused any potentially damaged feelings.

"Kendall Spaulding," she introduced herself. "Some people call me Kenny. Those people wishing to be my friends call me Kendall. What's your first period?"

Lacey shrugged, then checked the assignment slip she was handed.

"I got boys' gym, again. The office Bozos in Junior High assumed the 'F' in the block marked sex on my school records represented 'Frequently' rather than 'Female' and assigned me to the boys' locker room three years running. Showing up was funny that first time. After that, not so much. Some coach always informs me that I'm female and, duh, I already know that. Say, maybe your dad can fix this," Kendall suggested.

Try as he might, somehow Principal Hart couldn't correct Kendall's records so that they remained corrected and; because they were so screwed up, she received a draft notice which she promptly ignored. Failure to report caused M-Ps to collect her. They, too, informed her that she was female and ineligible for the draft. *Ya think!!!*

From day one, Kendall and Lacey were peas in a pod. They did everything together including that which was strictly against the rules, like pledging a High School sorority. Those days saw them getting each other into one embarrassing situation after another with quotes from Oliver Hardy. *'Here's another fine mess you've gotten me into.'* They'd have done anything to be included in the sisterhood and once inducted most of what they got into were lifelong bonding experiences which carried them forward once they were enmeshed in the business world. *That was just yesterday. Wasn't it?* Lacey thought. *Didn't we just do those things? Didn't we just laugh? Now, only Gordon can cry while we remember the future dust that was once Kendall – my heart; my friend; my confidant; a woman who loved me; someone who never did anything half way; someone without whom the world is a smaller, darker, and far dirtier place. Let us pray.*

Lacey had just found her few words.

She tried attending to her current 'Gomer's pile' of work, but it was useless. She was still holding out for the chance, no matter how small, that Kendall would recover. *Hope is an odd commodity* Lacey thought. *Perhaps with enough hope I won't need to grieve without crying; because there will be no need to grieve in the first place.* "Spaulding, it would be just like you to scare the shit out of everyone and, when all is said and done, be perfectly fine. If you know what's good for you," Lacey spoke aloud into the ether, hoping no one but the ether heard her, "you better just be scaring the shit out of everyone."

She depressed the intercom button on her telephone.

Dana popped her head in through the slightly opened door with her ready, cheery smile that always made everyone glad she was around, especially in times like these.

"Get you something?" Dana asked.

"A great big mug of very weak tea and if you can somehow manage to get Spaulding back in her office I'd be forever grateful," Lacey said.

"Back in a flash with the first. Pray is all I can do about the second and I'm already on it."

Lacey nodded as Dana closed the door.

During the two years Dana worked as Lacey's assistant she became great friends with the women at the helm of Hott Jazz. It was Ms. Hart and Ms. Spaulding in front of others at the office, for the sake of protocol, but their friendship was irreverent to the max, especially when sweating side-by-side at the gym or in the studio.

Dana loved them, worried for them, prayed for them. At twenty-three and only two years out of school, she carved out a career for herself at Hott Jazz. Her business degree having done nothing to land her a job, she was discouraged she'd find a job at all. Five months later, she spotted Lacey's ad.

WANTED: SECRETARY, ET.AL, AND ALL. GOOD SKILLS, GOOD GRAMMAR, PLEASANT VOICE, NEAT APPEARANCE, HARD WORK, WORSE HOURS, NO RESUMES, CALLS ONLY.

There was a phone number.

Dana had no desire to be anyone's secretary; et.al. or any other kind. Still, she was intrigued by the oddity of the ad. In desperation for financial support, she set up an interview.

Lacey knew that someone like Dana; with skills, voice, and appearance that were done deals would respond to her ad; because she wasn't afraid of hard work or bad hours. Lacey also knew that, for the most part, resumes were embellishments which landed just this side of lies. Add into the mix that a worthwhile and recent graduate, a jewel with no experience or bad habits needing to be weeded out, wouldn't have a resume let alone one worth reading.

As advertised, Dana discovered her job carried a ton to learn; another ton to do; and a third ton of responsibility. After two years at Hott Jazz, she came to understand the meaning of *et. al. and all* – the prospect of making partner. As Dana considered the unreasonable workload and impending grief currently sitting on her shoulders as quarter partner, she knew she would never forgive nor forget that Lacey and Kendall took a chance on a very green kid … with lots of drive but no resume.

Chapter 16

---------------------------------- ▼ ----------------------------------

Is It Death
Boston – 1982

My time is too precious to waste it,
> my tears to plentiful to keep

My life is too dear not to live it,
> before I am gone please weep.

Gordon hung up the phone blinking back tears, which once he let them go would be unstoppable. He lingered at the hallway phone, his hand still on the receiver, thinking over the memories he and Kendall made. His Kendall. His wife. How warm and loved he felt since she entered his life and re-taught him how to do better in the world than just exist in it and to laugh at himself every now and then. Even with her still unconscious, and as foolish as it seemed, he felt the need to thank her for all that she did and all that she was.

Before Kendall, success and failure were Gordon's learning tools. Success meant stepping up to the next challenge. Failure simply meant trying again. Each was of equal value ... until failure meant there was no do-over. In the past, in life as well as in court, he'd been a gracious loser the few times it came to that. In the present, he couldn't be, wouldn't be. Not this time. He waited nearly his entire life just to find Kendall and already lost her once. He could not survive losing her again. Those foolish days, which now seemed a lifetime ago, were his fault. Kendall had loved him. He'd been afraid to allow himself to feel it. Today he feared never feeling it again.

He returned to her room, dragged the overstuffed chair; where he slept most of the previous three nights, over to her bed and sat beside her only hoping she regained consciousness. If only she would.

"Thank you for the time we had," Gordon said gazing at her. "If it had been a million years it wouldn't have been nearly enough. I'd have always wanted more."

Lying peacefully in her repose, Gordon preferred to think of Kendall as she was that fateful day in front of Terry's office; animated, feisty, determined. But the words were adjectives that created past tense memories – final memories with no adjunct; memories destined to cause only pain, just like before, just like with his parents. All thoughts of a future without Kendall in it were frightening beyond reasons Gordon could explain, especially to himself. Add to that an odd sensation of guilt he could not shake over an unspoken debt he knew he owed to her, but could not remember why or even what it was. Whatever the debt, he'd gladly repay it a thousand times over if only he could have her back.

Gordon examined the palm side of Kendall's hand inspecting the lines, the meaning of which she said they held the untold story of her life – the long life as predicted by the life line on her hand. The line taunted him.

"Liar!" Gordon cursed the line and its tiny break describing the nightmare he was currently living; a life abruptly cut off only part way through. His unchecked tears rolled down his cheeks and dropped to Kendall's palm. The salty liquid traced its way down her lifeline to the break. There, his tears disappeared into her hand.

Kendall once took a stab at explaining auras – the colors of life; and the way they mixed and blended together when an aura found its counterpart and how, for Kendall, that counterpart was Gordon. For him, the true meaning of the colors remained elusive. Whatever significance they once held or ever had, all too soon the meaning would be irrelevant. Soon enough, life would have no meaning or color. His heart broke.

There was nothing to say and no one to hear him had he found adequate words. Gordon's god hadn't heard from him in decades, not since he stopped believing communication with a higher power would do any good. With the death of his parents Gordon felt abandoned by everyone including his god. It was then he stopped praying for that which he knew would never arrive.

Gordon absently reached for the card Audrey gave to him during the last visit she and Ted made to Boston. He nervously sprung the thin card between his fingers and palm. Exactly as prayer had been useless, he was certain of the uselessness of reciting the words Audrey demanded he memorize. In deference to her; and because she liked him from the second they met, welcomed him into the family with open arms; per her request, Gordon bowed his head and repeated the poem as if it were a mantra. He leaned in, whispering into Kendall's ear, and begged her to open her eyes.

"Sweetheart, please come back to me."

Vanishing tears, a wife who won't regain consciousness and dies from nothing. It felt senseless. Hopeless. His head spun and he gave a low aching moan for Kendall's precious life slipping away in front of him. He loved her more than words could express, would always love her, felt as if he'd done so his entire life. Or, at least that part he could remember. He took her motionless hand in his, ran his thumb across the tops of the long delicate fingers and began to cry the tears he promised himself he would not; tears he promised Audrey that he would. At once, the monitor flat lined. Without realizing he'd done it, Gordon snapped the card in two and dropped the broken pieces to the bed.

"No!" He screamed. "Kendall!" He called to her.

A glow formed around her made from the exact colors she claimed made up the layers of her aura and her closed eyes flooded with tears. Gordon supposed it was her spirit being lifted away and the final tears of her life. Her hand twitched. *Her body releasing energy in death* he thought and brought the hand to his lips. All that was left to do was gaze at the woman he loved. A woman more than beautiful; she was lovely. Gordon caressed her face as his mind grabbed at a memory, something his once father said: *'The dead can't cry'*. No sooner did he acknowledge the fact than the monitor beeped back to life. Kendall's eyes fluttered open.

"I thought I'd lost you," he sighed with tremendous relief. "When Terry said you were gone. I thought he meant dead ... brain dead," Gordon admitted. The man who hadn't spoken to his god in decades silently thanked whichever god was in charge of Kendall's life. "But, how can one be gone but not dead?" Gordon asked.

"My arm. My mark," she shoved up the sleeve of the hospital gown revealing what was, for her, a newly closed circle.

"It's a birthmark," Gordon said almost as a question.

"It's a before-birthmark," Kendall corrected, "which now acknowledges my mission is complete, I fulfilled Time's purpose for me."

"What are you saying?"

"That everything you ever heard about Overlap is true."

"You think you're a–" Gordon couldn't voice the word. His wife was alive, but she'd obviously lost her mind.

"Lightening won't strike you dead if you say it. I'm a Reweaver."

"I'm calling Gruenwald," Gordon protested.

"Who won't believe me," Kendall advised. "Overlap is considered myth by nearly everyone. Gruenwald is among them. Please don't you be as well."

"Why didn't you tell me?" Gordon asked unable to accept what he was hearing. Had it all been a ruse? Had he been deceived by the woman he loved.

"You wanted me to say that on top of every other thing you had to deal with as my husband that one day I would travel thru Time. You would have believed me? You would have married me?"

"Should I have married you?" Four days of worry quickly felt like betrayal. "Do you even love me?"

"More than my life. I risked–" she couldn't finish.

"What? What did you risk?" Gordon demanded.

"Everything! For you. For us. Whatever you think happened in the past, I now know it isn't real."

"Like what?" Gordon pressed.

"Like that your parents died."

"They did," he insisted.

"Trust me ... they didn't," Kendall insisted.

"Then how are they dead if they didn't die?" Gordon demanded.
"Someone killed them."
Gordon shook his head hard refusing to believe it.
"It's true," Kendall assured and shared her new found knowledge.

"I heard you cry and my Gram insisted I was ready to return to my
own Time … to you. My memory and heart said I needed to unlive
one more outcome. Gram insisted it wasn't necessary and then I was
back here."
Kendall and Gordon slipped into each other's arms lost in old
memories and silent tears.
Kendall's memories were actually Second Memories; those of a
stranger, a nice lady who stayed with her family and shared stories
with her in private. The lady made the details so vivid they were very
nearly snap shots or may as well have been. Kendall finally
remembered those story parts which were warnings to be wary of
Stuart. Her too young age and the passage of time eroded the warning
and left behind only the memory of his name and comfort in the
familiar. Now she twice remembered the details of the conversations
with herself where she both gave and received information of events to
come and their eventual outcomes including Terry and his absolute
need of her during his measles. But the stories weren't simply stories;
they were a recounting of her own past, the one which lay in the future
for the young child which was herself and would one day be her
reality.
She gave a sigh and suddenly knew two different versions of that
part of her life at the same time. The first version, her Prior Memory,
contained a fear of Gram; the other, Kendall's Second Memory, said
she was never afraid. The Prior Memory reminded Kendall that
shortly after the lady left, Gram proudly proclaimed to the just barely
three year old version of herself *'One day I'm going to push you all
the way home; because I love you'*. As the first version slipped into
quiet oblivion, the second version confirmed that Sylvia never said the
fearsome words to her as a child. Somehow, Gram knew to make her
statement in the exact moment that a grown Kendall, as an adult
traveler, returned home. Her presence in the past created the perfect

opportunity for Gram to unlive the outcome and the harm the statement inflicted on her tiny granddaughter.

Kendall sighed again and other Second Memories took their proper places – memories of Sylvia's new and slightly odd behavior after the strange lady left; nervousness mixed with caution, yet fearlessness. The original pushing conversation was the outcome and the actual pushing – an outcome which tore a hole in Time. At last Kendall understood why Gram said unliving the outcome was no longer necessary; she planned all along to move the event to its proper place in Time. Kendall wondered how she knew.

Other Second Memories crystallized filling in the blanks of the lingering questions of Kendall's life. Why, at nearly fifteen, had Terry so suddenly chosen a career in medicine? Her own note to Audrey specified that she be the one to choose the perfect day for Terry to receive Jack August's research – a day early enough in the school year for him to get serious with his studies and select preparatory courses which would lead to pre-med in college. It was Jack's notes that sparked Terry's initial interest in medicine with the hopes of helping their father. Once learning Ted's only hope of leading any sort of a normal life was a transplant, which he absolutely refused, Terry lost all interest in heart surgery.

As with Gram's words and the P-I-D (which nearly ruined her future), a transplant for Ted would have amounted to an unchangeable event. For some reason, he remained steadfast in his unwillingness to be a patient. Kendall wondered if, in this life, her father needed to be any sort of patient; willing or otherwise. She also wondered if Time, as people say, had taken care of everything. Continuing to consider the alternate outcomes she now recalled, she would soon get her answer.

Audrey shared Kendall's letter with Terry; which is what made him so adamant she ditch Stewart the second she met him, in the hope of preventing *The incredible shit* from worming his way into her life at all and prevent the damage he knew Stewart would leave in his wake. Ugly as it was, the horrendous P-I-D infection was an unchangeable event designed to provide Terry with his life's mission; to continue the work Jack August started, that his sister might have the DNA child she so wanted. Terry's switch from heart surgery to female infertility appeared to be the single changeable outcome and, hopefully, the only outcome in *need* of changing. Kendall's unbridled desire for a biological child galvanized Terry's zeal to be a part of another man's work. Jack, and Terry by extension, created the opportunity for Kendall and Gordon to have their dream baby.

Of course there was the matter of Terry's name. Curiously, Ted caved on that point allowing a name he said sounded like a nick-name belonging to a girl. Audrey taking up Kendall's cause in the quest for a brother named *Terry* suddenly made all the sense in the world. Everything; including Jack's letter and research and the stock certificate, was addressed to or in the name of Terry Evan Spaulding. With any other name there was no way Terry could own them or use them. And so it was that the original version of Kendall's life became a far and distant Prior Memory. In the end, Kendall appreciated why no one but her husband could cry for her. Tears for her, at any Time, would always call her. Only Gordon's tears had the capacity to call her from the appropriate place, at the appropriate Time, for the one who was waiting. The one called Aja.

*   *   *   *

At long last, Gordon allowed himself to find his heart; because it was finally time to do so. His tears had prevented yet another loss and he could finally and properly mourn his parents and the life he lost when he lost them. He could also rejoice in those who loved him in his current life. He ultimately understood Audrey's gift of prayer and what he'd been carrying around so cavalierly, so casually in his pocket. It was Time's guarantee that he would not lose Kendall a second time.

The words Gordon believed were written for him by Sylvia echoed in his head; the lines emblazoned on the card, the breaking of which formed a doorway from the past into the present and closed a hole in time.

A daughter will tell a mother her life while a husband cries for a dying wife.
Overlapping a life which is her own, every tear can bring her home.
Spoken words and force from hearts will move the intermingled parts
Broken pieces open space for a love to take its proper place
Eight & done brings Aja alone. She's waiting mother. Please come home.

The brittle plastic prison looked like a credit card. Unlike a real credit card, it possessed an ability which no amount of money could acquire. Seemingly possessed of knowledge beyond her ken, the moment Audrey presented the card she said *'One day, you'll need it.'* She then insisted Gordon carry it and memorize the poem. He deemed the sentimental lines too girly and promptly tossed the card into his sock drawer ignoring Audrey's request. Still, Audrey was adamant, which she never was before, which left Gordon feeling a little guilty and wondering why she wouldn't say why she was so adamant. Two days after relinquishing the card, Audrey asked to see it and hear Gordon's recitation. Sweet, gentle Audrey, who loved him dearly, just about ripped off his head.

"Look at my face," she insisted. "Do I look like I'm joking?"

Gordon attempted to probe but she held up a hand.

"My mother asked that you carry it and learn the lines. Just do it, then tuck it in your wallet and don't lose it. The card is invaluable."

Gordon didn't particularly want to carry another piece of plastic, but it was easier than upsetting Audrey. She liked him from the moment they met. He liked her in return and if carrying the card and learning the lines made her feel better, well, what the heck. Of late, Gordon picked up the habit of playing with the card and reciting the lines when he was upset. His own comfort in the familiar made him reach for it at Kendall's bedside; exactly the way it was supposed to happen. In the end, Gordon recognized the valuable nature of Sylvia's invaluable gift.

When Kendall first collapsed Terry said *'If you know any prayers I'd say them.'* The cards printed lines were much like a prayer. Gordon wondered if it was just something Terry said or if he knew about the card. Until that moment, it hadn't struck Gordon that Audrey hadn't said her Mother wanted Kendall's husband to carry the card. It struck Gordon that Audrey said he carry the card meaning that somehow Sylvia knew all about him and intended the card specifically and exclusively for him. But how, when she died before he even met Kendall? Illogical and impossible as it all was, every bit as much as Gordon believed in the law, he believed that Audrey, Terry and Sylvia had a hand in the fact that Kendall was back and alive. Perhaps they even managed to see to it through him.

This time wouldn't be at all like last time. This time Gordon did not lose the one he loved. There was no way to thank Sylvia for asking that he cry for her granddaughter, at least not in person, though he was certain he'd figure out a way when it actually mattered, like when Aja arrived ... in *'eight and done'*.

Gram was right Kendall though. *'He'll cry for you, your Gordon.'* Her eyes locked with his and he experienced a sudden flash of a night long ago as vividly as if it happened that day.

"You've heard Benny Goodman perform live," he said. It wasn't a question. "It's not just a screwed-up dream. I do remember you. It's how you know what happened in my life. You're not just *some* Reweaver, you're the witness, the one for whom I've been searching. I had you all along and never knew. It's why I had to marry you. If you weren't in my life– " he started, but couldn't finish. "Without you–," he started once again. "If you didn't love me–," his thoughts trailed. That was the whole of it – without Kendall in his life, if she hadn't loved him. Kendall told the story of the night Gordon's parents died and of pulling him to safety.

*   *   *   *

"How much do you remember about that night?" She asked.

"Only a fraction more than is in the Police report," Gordon said. "The witness, I mean you, disappeared, leaving no one to ask anything."

"What about the responding officer. He was young then and could still be on the force or in the area."

"Killed in the line of duty," Gordon countered.

"Officer Sullivan is ... dead," Kendall could hardly say the word.

"Who's Sullivan? The guy's name was Henderson."

"Parts of the Overlap are still a bit blurry, but I'm certain it was Sullivan. Danny ... Donny ... something like that."

"Well, someone named Robert Henderson signed the report. Whatever's going on; it's waited this long, it can wait another day. Your family's outside."

"And who are you if not my family," Kendall said.

Gordon sighed with relief for the first time in four days. Terry entered alone and gave Gordon a nod.

"Hey, Candy-cane." He smiled. "This is yours."

He returned her wedding band.

"You had it? Why'd you take it off?"

"You didn't need it where you were going and it fell off once before. We dared not take a chance it would happen again only to lose your ring somewhere in Time?"

Kendall nodded.

"There's news I haven't told the others yet."

Terry and Kendall finished each other's sentences, telling each other that she was slightly pregnant.

"We're pregnant," Gordon said stunned.

"We are," Kendall confirmed with a smile.

"How did you know?" Terry asked Kendall.

"Don't pretend with me, Terry Evan Spaulding. You have all of your Second Memories."

"Are you saying Terry's a ..."

"Reweaver," Terry was loath to admit it.

"Does this thing run in families?" Gordon asked.

"Apparently, yes," Terry said revealing his mark for the first time.

"I thought we told each other everything," Gordon practically accused Terry.

"That was need to know and–"

"I didn't need to know," Gordon interrupted.

"Pretty much," Terry confirmed.

"How come you never told *me*?" Kendall asked.

"You didn't exactly need to know either. Plus, I was five. You think I knew then what really happened. I thought it was a pleasant little fever dream from the measles; where I got to play big brother to my big sister for a few hours. By the time I did figure it out I discovered there were reasons not to say. Better to leave it as a happy 'coincidence' of nearly matching birth marks."

"But we don't believe in coincidence," Kendall said.

"We don't believe any longer," Terry corrected. "We accepted the marks as birth marks and even after I learned what they really were I thought it best to leave them at that."

"And, you weren't around long enough for anyone but me to see you."

Terry nodded. "Funny how that worked out. So, we both went home."

"The place we were needed," Kendall added.

"Well, now this is home and we need you here, so no leaving again," he said sternly and began disconnecting Kendall from the machines that monitored her vitals the past four days.

"You're my kid brother, not my boss," Kendall teased.

Terry checked the mark on her arm. "Well, it appears your traveling days are behind you and being that you're pregnant," he bent down aligning his face with hers, "you'll take orders and like it, Candy-cane. I plan to be a doting uncle like Uncle Harry and no one, including you, is putting a kink in those plans. Capisce? If we're right, you'll be our greatest success so far."

"What's this 'we' stuff? You planning to be pregnant with me?"

"You know very well that 'We' is Jack August and me."

"My father, but–" Gordon's head spun.

"Your father's research and the generosity of Candice Augustein made this future," Terry explained.

"You have my dad's research?"

"Apparently, it's what he wanted. Someone," Terry indicated Kendall, "led him to believe that, in time, there would be credit where credit was due. That's my other news. I'm to be published in *The North East Corridor Medical Journal*. Jack will be named as co-researcher."

"You'd do that?" Gordon asked on his father's behalf.

"Too late for 'do'," Terry smiled. "It's already done. Magazine goes to press tomorrow."

"I don't know what to do to thank you, for myself … for my parents."

"That's already done as well," Terry smiled, "you're turning me into an uncle."

Gordon silently nodded his heart overflowing. "Everything for a reason," he finally said.

"Exactly. Look hard enough, wait long enough, you'll see them. It's why Mother never corrected me when I started calling this one Candle and then Candy." Terry jerked a thumb in his sister's direction. "She was going to need the name. My own Overlap was to be Kendall's big brother, suggest she make her own life decisions and show her the way out of her shell. A shy performer is something of an oxymoron.

"And to be a performer was my destiny," Kendall said.

Terry placed a hand on Kendall's shoulder. "Nothing is certain, but I believe it was." He smiled. "Then I followed your example and was never in a shell in the first place. I needed to have stage presence and a personality that would garner grant money to continue Jack's research. Jack bequeathed his research, never anticipating his own son would need it to have a child with the ever impossible and slightly annoying Kendall Layne Spaulding," he teased. "Then you saved Gordon and helped me decide to go into medicine. See? A nice little circle of events. It really is everything for a reason, even if you don't exactly see the reason in the moment.

"Even if you don't exactly like the reason," Gordon added.

"I'm afraid so," Terry confirmed; a degree of resolution in his voice unable to offer more comfort than that, explaining that everything was as it was supposed to be and everything became what it was for a reason they could not see just yet.

Those facts sat uncomfortably as Kendall thought of their father. Was it truly necessary he take bullets meant for her? She needed to know what Terry thought.

"What possible reason could there have been for Dad to be shot?"

"Maybe you should ask the slime who shot him."

"What do you mean?"

"What do you mean, what do I mean? He looked at his sister. "Oh, still don't have *all* your Second Memories. They'll come," Terry assured. "Anyway, the guy's cooling his heels at Raiford. Maybe him being caught closed a hole in time."

"I guess anything's possible." Kendall paused. "How is Dad?" She asked, still not realizing the difference her final travel-conversation with Audrey had made.

"Exhausted like the rest of us." Terry smirked and walked to the door. "Dad," he called into the hall then spoke over his shoulder to his sister. "You're gonna just love this."

Ted Spaulding entered. His trade-mark white hair was the same as before and the strain of the last few days was clearly etched on his face, but something was different. An old sparkle was in his eyes and he wasn't relying on anyone or anything for support. Somehow he was whole.

"Dad!" Kendall could hardly believe her eyes.

"How's my girl?" He gently sat on the edge of her bed.

"You're here."

"Of course I'm here. Don't think I'd follow the example set by Mortimer, Bev, the cousins and those partners of yours. The great big softies all went home to sleep. Can you believe it," he teased. "I must say, I question their devotion."

"You look wonderful and terrible all at the same time," Kendall said.

"A fine how-do-you-do." Ted looked at Gordon. "I spend four nights on that awful sofa in the waiting room and Sleeping Beauty here has the nerve to critique my appearance." Ted leaned in and abraded Kendall's cheek with his beard as he did when she was little then kissed the pink mark it left behind. "That's a very scratchy beard young lady. Maybe you should shave."

Kendall put a hand to her cheek and answered as she did when she was little. "Maybe you should."

"Maybe later," Ted suggested.

"Maybe not," Kendall said.

"Definitely not," Ted completed their routine; his conversation light, the concern on his face was anything but.

"I'd say you look terrible, but that'd be a lie," Ted confessed. "You're beautiful as always."

Kendall sat bolt upright, wires and tubes still attached to almost everywhere, threw her arms around her father's neck and breathed in remnants of his aftershave. Skin Bracer.

"Oh, Dad!" Tears slid down her cheeks.

Unlike that far distant day in the past, when Ted revived her in Miami, he did not release himself from her embrace, he held her closer.

"This family," he eyed Gordon, "best hugs in the world. Mom's been waiting very impatiently, so I promised to be brief. I'll be back later."

Ted disentangled himself, made Kendall lie back down and started for the door. He suddenly stopped in his tracks.

"Something wrong, Dad?" She asked.

"I just had the funniest feeling you and I did that before. Silly, huh?" He shrugged and smiled. Terry and Gordon followed him out of the room.

"Sweetheart," Audrey entered, smiling brightly. "Terry said you're going to be better than fine. Actually, he said you're pregnant. My first grandchild. It's wonderful news." She sat on the bed where Ted had just been. "I knew that if you had faith in Terry's work you and Gordon would have the baby you both want so badly."

"It's okay." Kendall rested her hand on top of Audrey's. "I remember the Overlap – what Jack gave to Terry, what I left behind to pay his way into learning how to use it."

Audrey nodded.

"How is Dad ... like Dad?" Kendall asked.

Audrey told the story which caused the past to take a slightly different path.

"Paul Kelly, Sr. was rushed to the hospital with appendicitis. There wasn't time to prep an O-R so your father performed his appendectomy right in the E-R. The appendix was all tied off and Ted was about to snip it when it burst in his hand. Paul knew that it might just as easily have burst inside him and considering the ramifications of peritonitis ... well, it could have been fatal. Paul, Sr. felt he owed your father his life.

"As thanks, he got his Captain to offer me a part time secretarial job when Terry started kindergarten and we all became close friends. By the time you kids were twelve and nine I was working at the station full time.

"The day you turned thirteen, the station received a shipment of experimental bullet-proof vests made from some revolutionary new material. I told Paul how fascinated your father was by all that product development stuff and that he would love to try one on; blah, blah, blah. I laid it on so thick I was almost embarrassed. But, the stakes were too high not to use what I learned from you. Like daughter; like mother," Audrey added.

They chuckled.

"Paul, Sr. called the house before he left work that night wanting Ted to stop by the station, but he already left for the hospital to cover for Matt Sawyer just as you said. The Station being right up the street from the hospital, I suggested Paul bring the vest by the E-R." Audrey looked at her daughter. "He did it. Paul unwittingly changed our future by giving the vest its first test-drive. But, if I hadn't insisted you say what lie ahead, your father–" Audrey's voice trailed off.

"Every event happened exactly as you said. The single difference was that Ted was wearing the vest when the woman in the car accident was brought in and had no time to remove it before gowning-up. That timing left Paul stuck in the E-R waiting to take the vest back to the station house. Almost immediately after the woman was stabilized and taken to surgery, the nut you warned me about came in waving the gun and started screaming at the top of his lungs. *'Candy. I want Candy.'* He was already high on something and Ted felt certain the Candy he wanted was heroin. Then the guy just started shooting. If not for the vest–" Audrey didn't finish.

"Paul identified himself as an officer and the man fired a couple rounds at him; which only added to the charges which ranged from grand larceny to possession of a stolen vehicle, attempted murder, assaulting a police officer, assault and battery with a dangerous weapon, resisting arrest. The list seemed endless. Paul being there meant the gunman was caught and contributed to him being sentenced to life without parole. Turned out the guy was a professional criminal with outstanding warrants in Massachusetts. That he was caught is the only thing different from what you said."

"Think that change was enough to close a hole in Time?" Kendall asked.

"Yes," Audrey said. "I decided that if I couldn't change the event you diagramed the least I could do was attempt to change its outcome. The man still burst into the E-R brandishing the gun and still shot the same three rounds at your father, but the vest ... that wonderful vest, it changed our futures by changing the outcome. Maybe that's all Time is anyway," Audrey mused, "events and outcomes. I loved Ted practically my entire life. I couldn't allow some arbitrary outcome to destroy him. I could hardly imagine the life you described. I'm not strong enough to have lived it."

"Trust me, mom," Kendall took Audrey's hand, "you are."

Audrey shrugged. "I'm sorry you remember a past different than everyone else knows, but I just had to try. I had to. And your father, you saw for yourself ... you spared him."

"You did that," Kendall corrected, "by figuring out a way to get Paul, Sr. to help make the fate that could be so the future ended up what it should be. You're the smartest woman I ever met. I love you more than anything, more than everything."

Kendall sat up. Mother and daughter held each other close. Audrey made Kendall lie back down.

"This is yours," Audrey said pulling something from her purse. It was the perfume bottle Kendall left on the night stand.

"You kept it all these years?"

"As a reminder of how I couldn't lose sight of the tragedies life held if I stopped paying attention. See the raised letters."

"I never noticed them," Kendall said.

"But I did, and whenever I lapsed into doubt, all I had to do was look at them. The only way something marked 1978 could have gotten to 1955 was Overlap, which meant the myth was reality and my daughter would grow up to be the Reweaver you claimed you were.

"Mom, what did you mean by *'a past different than everyone else knows'*, sounds as if you're not including yourself."

"There's something I never told a soul," Audrey reached into her purse again. "Mother left this for me." It was a photograph Kendall had never seen – Gram, Audrey as a child and Audrey as an adult.

"How? When?" Kendall could hardly comprehend it.

"Remember the last medical convention Dad and I went on before he was shot?"

"You got 'Q' fever. Dad wouldn't let Terry and me in your room. Gram came to Florida to take care of us."

"The following year everyone thought I had a relapse. They often happen with 'Q' fever so it was a natural assumption."

Kendall sighed lightly, gaining a memory. "But it wasn't a relapse."

"I see your Second Memories are catching up with you. Well, I remember everything everyone else remembers," Audrey said, "that is, up to the time of the supposed relapse. I also remember Ted being shot without the vest and our lives being in the toilet. The icing on that cake was that you became afraid of Gram. I suppose Time took pity on me." Audrey pushed up her sleeve revealing a Red Tattoo Kendall didn't remember ever seeing.

"My guess is the marking process simulated the relapse symptoms. I Overlapped home with Gram and Grand and me as a kid. Gram and I had one of her famous one-on-ones; just the two of us in the den behind the closed door. I warned her to watch what she said to you as a child that had anything remotely to do with Overlap. Turned out, she'd already been warned once. She asked only if it were really true. She raised me the way I raised you; never to lie, so when I reconfirmed what she already knew, she promised," Audrey pulled her sleeve back down, "I sighed with relief which allowed my Second Memory of the new outcome to take its rightful place. When I returned to my own Time, everything followed my unlived moment in the past and you were no longer scared of Gram. Once the Paul, Sr. change happened, everything sort of snowballed from there."

"But, how sad Gram never heard me say how much I loved her until the final moments of my own Overlap."

"Sweetheart, sigh deeply. I swear. There's nothing to fear in your Second Memories. Let them flood in. You're postponing knowing everything good."

Kendall did and sweeter memories of Gram, absent all fear, took their rightful place – Second Memories of telling Gram how loved she was and singing in her kitchen using vegetable microphones. Kendall smiled. Audrey was too emotional to say much more.

"You need your rest." Audrey started to leave, but Kendall took her hand and stopped her.

"Mom, I once knew a girl named Avra and always liked the name. If the baby's a girl, that will be her English name, but I want her to carry your Hebrew name. I want my baby to be named for the smartest woman I ever met. Audrey Joan, how do you feel about Avra Jade?"

"It's lovely. Avra Jade August. A - J - A"

Mother and mother-to-be looked at each other speaking in unison. "It spells Aja."

"It couldn't believe it's the same one," Kendall said.

"Maybe it can't be, except that it is. Mother's note insisted she received the card I gave to Gordon from the same Aja I met when I was young. I didn't believe her, but I gave him the card anyway."

"There's a card?"

Audrey checked the room knowing the broken pieces would be there. They fell from Kendall's bed to the floor when she sat up and hugged her father. Audrey handed them over.

"Where did you get this?" Kendall asked.

"A lawyer named Smith Garbett. He called just before we left Miami the last time Dad and I came to Boston. Said he'd been holding something for me since1955. Imagine. Gram took care of everything, even left instructions for when Mr. Garbett was to give it to me. Considering his age when he showed up, I suspect Gram was his very first client and he thought her a crackpot." Audrey pulled a yellowing envelope from her purse. "My instructions were to give the card to Gordon and coerce him into memorizing the words on the card."

"And you did it." It wasn't a question.

"Yes," Audrey admitted, "and so did he."

"Bossy much?" Kendall teased.

"Apparently bossy just enough. He was at your bedside the entire time, repeating the lines like a prayer. When he broke the card somehow you came home."

"The somehow is Gram pushed me. She said it then did it."

"But Mom promised, not a peep. She went back on her word?" Audrey was stunned.

Kendall's Second Memories all in place, she knew. "Gram saying was an unchangeable event. Her promise had to revolve around saying anything to me as a child."

Audrey nodded.

Kendall put the two halves of the card together and read the words. They were the ones she heard Gordon repeating.

"The manila envelope from Mom contained a tiny jewelry box, a letter, the picture I just showed you and the little card," Audrey said. "The letter retold the story of how the girl I met so long ago gave Mom the card the second time she Overlapped, which was to Biscayne's Rehab, and that Mom's wedding band was to bypass you and me and go directly to her, to Aja. You visited Mom everyday. Maybe you and Aja crossed paths."

"Do you remember what she looked like?"

"She left a photograph with Gram, so I wouldn't have to. I wanted, so badly, to show you this when we were here last, but I didn't dare." Audrey took the picture from her purse. "This is her, our Aja. Don't you think she looks like Gordon?"

"She looks exactly like Gordon's mother. She was quite beautiful. Oh, and she has Gram's hair. All Auburn waves." Kendall paused. "I did see this child. She was exiting Gram's room at the Rehab that last day and said something as I went in." Kendall struggled to remember. "*Your Grandmother's wonderful. See you soon.* She gave me a quirky smile then left." Kendall looked from the picture to her mother. "This is my child, the one I'm carrying. And this amazing girl did all of this for us. She made this future possible."

"One person cannot make a future," Audrey corrected, "that takes a family – our Aja; you and Terry; Gram and Grand; Daddy and me; Gordon; his parents, and both Paul Kellys. Mommala," Audrey started to change the subject, but hesitated voicing the unthinkable, "I've wondered this for the longest time, but there was no one to ask. Do you suppose the man who shot at Ted was really looking for you as Candy Augustein? I mean, rather than the heroin kind of candy? Could he be the man from the Ballroom looking for the only witness to his crime?" Audrey's question hung in the air.

*   *   *   *

"I didn't see him," Audrey said, "but Dad said a black fellow stopped by this morning asking after you; nearly desperate to see you. When Dad said how bad everyone else thought it was and that we had nothing concrete about your condition, the man was devastated. His assistants kept rescheduling appointments so he could stay and wait for news on you. Any idea who he is."

Kendall shrugged.

Terry entered at that precise moment followed by a tall elegant black man; his tie was askew, his collar open. His suit was clearly expensive, but rumpled; as if maybe he'd slept in his clothes exactly as Kendall's family had. The worried look on his face transformed into love and relief when he saw Kendall and that she was all right. The man was Hardy James.

Audrey left them to speak in private.

"I was in from New York visiting my son at B.U. My wife, Angela, and I had to rush him here," Hardy said. "Bee sting. Tony's allergic. With him discharged, we were ready to get back to life and the business of family. They wheeled you past us on a stretcher on our way out and your words popped into my head. 'Life is funny, Mr. James. Some day, when you least expect it, I'll be right in front of you.' The sound of your voice saying 'Believe and it shall be so' wouldn't let go of me. I'm guessing you say that a lot." He smiled. "I believed but forgive me; I had to see with my own eyes.

"Not to be all full of myself, but anyone wanting an appointment would just have to wait until I did see for myself. I see now that I should have just believed, the way you said. I hoped for so long to run

~ 208 ~

into you again. When it never happened, I finally put the idea of finding you or thanking you out of my head."

"Thanks aren't necessary. I didn't do anything. Not being in my own Time, I couldn't."

"Except that you did everything – respected me, pushed me, backed me up, gave me a chance I wouldn't have had otherwise. You nurtured me like I was your child. Cared in a way no one else did. I think I loved you from the moment we shook hands. You took my three dollars as if my money was as good as anyone else's."

"Because it was ... wasn't it."

"Other people didn't think so. Only you." Hardy shook his head, loathing the memory of those old days with their painful ways. "And that last day, when you held me and painted my future in words ... I thought my heart would burst. I never forgot you," Hardy paused embarrassed, then stepped closer to the bed. "You knew that I loved you. Didn't you, Miss? The way I wished I could have loved my real mother."

"Yes, Mr. James." Joyful tears slid down Kendall's cheeks. "I knew."

"When I was most afraid of failing, your lessons are what held me up, kept me from leaving New York. You believed in me, even though I thought you had no reason. You were why I *had* to succeed, so that if I saw you again ... *when* I saw you again I'd have proved you were right to believe. Guess you didn't really have a crystal ball, did you, Miss?" He took hold of her hand and squeezed gently. "You believed because you already knew."

"Yes, Mr. James. I already knew. The sure thing," Kendall squeezed Hardy's hand in return. "But you were just a boy and so scared about the future. For those wonderful weeks in the past, Time turned you into *my* boy and my boy's future had fame in it. In that part of your life my role was to make sure you got the future Time intended."

"Time did this?" He questioned. "Is that how you look the same now as you did then?"

Kendall explained the way Overlap worked. Hardy accepted what she said and understood that whatever else she might have done while she was in the past she also assured his future.

"In this part of my life, though I'm the one who's older, another woman gave birth to me and yet another woman raised me, would you mind terribly if I continue to think of myself as … your boy."

"Mr. James," Kendall said, "you're going to make me cry."

"Class is *long* over, Miss. Won't you please call me Hardy?"

"It would be my great pleasure," Kendall slipped him a wink, "Mr. James."

Chapter 17

-------------------------------- ▼ --------------------------------

Dennis Sullivan
Lower Basin District – 1982

The next day Kendall was released with a clean bill of health. Gordon was helping her dress when she asked a similar question to the one Audrey asked of her.

"Do you suppose the man who tried to kill my father is the same one who killed your parents?"

Gordon didn't answer.

"It's probably a long shot but we need to start somewhere," Kendall pressed the issue.

"The Lower Basin District dispatched the responding officer," Gordon said. "If you're up to it we can see if your Officer Sullivan is real."

"*My* Officer Sullivan! Are you doubting Overlap and the word of a pregnant woman?"

"I'm in trouble no matter how I answer that."

"I suppose you are, but you needn't be such a lawyer about it." Kendall messed up Gordon's perfectly groomed hair. "It's okay to be just a rumpled husband."

Gordon took her in his arms, held her close and spoke into her ear. "Promise never to leave me again and I'll be as rumpled as you like, as often as you like."

They arrived at the Lower Basin District and spoke with Desk Sergeant Cameron Foley; a man with pale skin and jet black hair, who looked far younger than his forty years.

"Did an Officer Sullivan ever work out of this station?" Kendall asked, still trying to remember the officer's name on her own. "First name was Danny or Donny."

"No Danny or Donny that I recall, but there was a Denny. Lieutenant. Retired last month."

"Danny ... Donny ... Denny." Kendall displayed a victorious grin and shrugged. "I was close."

"Can we get a home phone?" Kendall asked the Sergeant.

"It's completely against policy. Best I can do is ask that he call you."

Gordon slipped his business card through the opening at the bottom of the glass partition.

"My office or service will know where to reach me any time; day or night. It's urgent that we speak with Lieutenant Sullivan."

"Did I hear someone take my name in vain?" The booming voice came from a tall, slender, gray haired man in his middle sixties. He sauntered up the stairs with a smile. "I'm Lieutenant Sullivan. Call me Denny."

"Gordon. Kendall." Gordon made brief introductions.

"How can I help you?" His eyes lingered on Kendall. "You look awfully familiar. Don't I know you?"

"Doubtful," Kendall evaded, unwilling to explain having not aged since that horrible night in 1955.

"I know I've seen you before," he wagged a finger, thinking. "I'm sure it'll come to me."

Kendall hoped it would not.

"We need information," Gordon said, "and you're probably the only person in the world who can help us."

"Hey, Cam," Denny addressed the Sergeant, "anyone in the Cap's office?"

"Nah! He's at lunch." Foley buzzed them in.

Once inside, Gordon shared the date and few details they had. Sullivan instantly remembered the incident "Messy business organized crime," he said, "but everything I had should be in the report."

"What makes you think it was Organized Crime?" Gordon couldn't believe it.

"I was a cop for forty-five years, son. I don't need to think; I *know*. But for one busted piece of tail light, the scene was clean," Denny shook his head. "That was a hit if ever there was one. All we got on the second car was that it was a brand new '56 Fairlane that we never found. Guy either drove it directly out of state or straight to a chop-shop." Denny shook his head again. "Two people ended up dead and their kid ..." Denny scowled berating himself. "I lost track of him and the only witness. I tried for years to locate her, just to clarify her initial statement. Appears she dropped off the planet."

Gordon and Kendall exchanged looks.

"There's no statement in the report," Gordon said.

"Should'a been. It was in my notebook."

"Notebook," Gordon and Kendall said in unison.

"Incident notebooks. I wrote everything in them including the witness statement but, like I said, it was useless giberish. Guess that's why Bob left it out."

"Bob?" Kendall asked.

"Henderson," Sullivan confided.

"And he signed the report," Gordon said.

"Yeah, I forgot he did that. Man, did the Captain ream us! We were lucky neither of us got a reprimand. I was first on-scene, making it my responsibility to file the report. Then as now my hand writing is a chicken scratch of hieroglyphics. With Bob needing to write up the last call he was on before arriving himself, he offered to do mine while I notified next-of-kin. We'd each had a long night, Bob's wife was pregnant at the time and we both just wanted to get home when we were supposed to for a change.

"Unfortunately, Bob signed both reports and turned them in before we realized the screw-up. Not that it figures into anything, but Bob was the best friend I ever had. We beat the crap out of each other as kids; did High School and the Academy together; joined the force together. We were each other's best-man. I named my first kid after him. Sad, he was killed in the line of duty about sixteen years back.

His case is nearly as cold as the one you're checking. We never caught that guy either."

Bad as Gordon felt about the death of an officer his eyes brightened with expectation.

"Would you, maybe, still have that incident notebook?"

"As I said, the case is cold, but we considered it suspicious so it's still open. My son inherited all my open cases when I retired. Full of piss and vinegar, that one, and the energy to chase ghosts."

Denny checked on the whereabouts of his son. Out on a call.

"I don't think Bobby will mind my rummaging through his desk."

"It would be great to have something more to go on," Gordon said.

"Something more implies that you have something else," Denny maintained his end of the conversation as they exited the Captain's office. "Care to share what you have on this homicide?" They entered the squad room. Denny sat at his son's deck and pulled a bundle of yellowed note pads from the back of the bottom drawer and started flipping pages.

"It's only a theory, but we think this *homicide*," the word caught in Gordon's throat, "is connected to an attack in Florida. If the same man committed both crimes, he's been in stir for the past sixteen years. It's why no one could find him."

"Do-ers almost never leave their own back yard, let alone their home state. It'd require a contract and permission. The families don't give permission except for special circumstances like contracts or maybe that one hit is somehow connected to another."

"Once again in English this time," Kendall said as her mind raced.

"If that guy is this guy, your attack in Florida was a contract hit and somehow connected to the incident on Storrow."

For all of her teen and adult life Kendall wondered what the gunman's cry of *'Candy. I want Candy'* meant and why he chose her father's E-R in which to scream it. She now realized that if the man had seen a copy of the police report, then he really wasn't interested in heroin, exactly as Audrey alluded. He wanted the Augustein kind of Candy. The kind of 'Candy' who gave no permanent address or phone number, just a work place – a place to find her; a place to find her father in her stead; a place to shoot her father in her stead, in frustration at his inability to find her. It seemed so obvious now. The sequence of events began when Kendall accepted the ride from Jack and Dorothy and ended when the gunman shot at her father. It was just one more outcome that tore one more hole in Time. If not for Overlap allowing Kendall to provide Audrey with the opportunity to alter that bad outcome, all of their lives would have been ruined. Kendall's Overlap mission was to save Gordon. By *accidentally* preparing Audrey for what was to come she gave her mother ten years to hone her clever gene and put herself in a position to exchange a bad outcome for a better one. With Audrey's correctly timed cleverness, the rest would hopefully be that Gordon finally learned the truth about his parents' death.

"Couldn't you be mistaken?" Kendall asked, still hoping Sullivan was.

"I could be," he agreed, "but I'm not. No offense, but that accident was deliberate. Helpless people were trapped inside a caved-in metal cage with no way out. Their last moments must have been horrible." Denny shuddered at the memory. "I heard the Doc was okay – led a good life; had a nice family, a pretty wife and a son." Sullivan's thoughts drifted to his own son risking his life every day. "Take my advice, you two. Don't go this on your own. Accept the help of professionals. Capisce?"

"What did you just say?" Kendall asked, as if her memory had been zapped by a cattle prod.

"Capisce. It's the only Italian I know besides pizza and spaghetti," he offered a distracted version of the Sullivan brand of humor. "Success!" He declared half way through the third notebook.

'Capisce? Capisce?' Hadn't Terry said that? And someone else on a night not so long ago for Kendall. She began to tremble.

"Gee, lady, sit down." Denny gave up the chair at the desk. "Are you okay?"

"What?" Gordon looked at his wife; half worried, half expectant.

"Just putting two and two together." She looked up at her husband. "How long ago did you start poking into things?"

"When I was sixteen. I'm thirty-two, so–" They all did the math. "Sixteen years ago." Three little words created a silence so heavy it was almost a presence.

"Suppose the man who shot at my father was looking for someone else," Kendall said, knowing the day she turned thirteen – the day her father was shot; was the same year Gordon was sixteen. "As Denny said, if this man is that man, he couldn't go to Florida without a reason, like an unhappy kid stirring up the past. My dad had nothing to do with your family, where as I–" she stopped herself and eyed Denny hoping he didn't catch her slip. "Who knew what you were doing?"

Gordon distinctly remembered telling the one person he thought would want him to succeed and what their reaction was. *Let it go. The only witness disappeared. There's little risk of finding her.* How right and how wrong that advice had been. At the time, Gordon thought it an attempt to spare him disappointment should he fail. Now he saw the truth. He kept it to himself.

"I requested copies of the incident and accident reports and tried to reach Officer Henderson the same night as the day I received them. He was out on patrol. I left a message then paced a rut in the floor of my room. I remember waiting for a call that never came. I fell asleep waiting. Next thing I knew it was the next day."

"Do you recall the date?" Kendall asked.

"Not an exact date," Gordon said.

Kendall asked Denny when his friend was killed.

"May 16," Sullivan said.

"The night before that awful man shot at my father," Kendall mumbled mostly to herself.

"Did I miss something? This sounds as if you're saying you believe Bob's death was deliberate and that he died in my place." Denny looked from Gordon to Kendall. "Why in my place? Why me in the first place?"

"Police records are public," Kendall said. "Anyone can look at them. Ask for copies of them. See the witness contact information on them. See Bob Henderson's name at the bottom of them. Gordon did. Maybe this guy did as well. Only those still on the force in '55 knew it was you who spoke to the witness; because Bob's name was on the report. Maybe this guy thought that, even without the witness, the responding officer, Bob, would eventually link the car wreck to the guy who caused it. Except it wasn't Bob who was there; it was you. That's why you in the first place, that's why Bob in your place."

Denny refused to believe her.

"Can I see that notebook?" Kendall asked.

Denny flipped to the pertinent page. "That's the witness' statement," he said handing over the book.

Kendall read her own words: *That man died at 52 for Bea Goodman. 35 won nothing* and tried to remember the moments before the car rolled.

"It was worthless then and equally worthless now," Denny said. "First off, the Doc was in his thirties and second, the wife's name wasn't Bea. It was–"

"Dorothy," Gordon interrupted, providing the correct information in a voice devoid of all emotion.

"Right," Denny agreed.

"Let's not be hasty," Kendall continued. "Couldn't something be buried in the statement?"

"Like what?" Both men asked in unison.

"I don't know. You said the witness was in shock, so maybe a clue or the facts only they're scrambled or something." Kendall had a brief flash of memory. "What about a license plate? What did they look like in '55?"

"We store old accident and incident reports upstairs. We could check some."

They followed Denny up to the attic and flipped through the oldest books. 1956. Close enough would need to be good enough.

"Looks like six digits," Denny said. "Wait. Here's one with a letter followed by five digits. Another is five digits followed by a letter and a few with a letter stuck in the middle."

"So what you're saying is; it could be anything." All air suddenly escaped Gordon's balloon.

Kendall touched his shoulder offering calm in Gordon's tornado of emotion.

"Individual pieces are easier to deal with than the whole," Kendall said. "What if we break down what we have the way I do when I teach my dancers?"

They returned to the squad room and wrote each word in the witness statement onto separate pieces of paper. Kendall took a seat and began shuffling them around trying to make sense and memory of them. Denny and Gordon watched over her shoulders.

"Who's been sitting in my chair?" Robert Sullivan entered the squad room.

Kendall stiffened, feeling awkward.

"Relax," Denny leaned in with a whisper, "his bark is worse than his bite. Bobby," he greeted his son, "meet Gordon and Kendall."

Hand shakes were exchanged.

"Say, you're Kendall Spaulding." Bob recognized her face immediately, surprised to see the very person from whom he'd been expecting a call. "Dad, this is the woman whose Company I want to perform at the Policeman's Ball. I was beginning to think you were avoiding me," he teased her. "Have you been lost or something?"

"*Or something*," she said, exchanging a look with Gordon.

"I hope you don't mind. I went through your desk," Dennis said. "They need information on that Storrow hit from '55."

"The desk was yours and, technically, the notebook still is." Robert Sullivan pulled more chairs over to the desk and joined them.

"We're back to looking at the witness statement." Denny brought Bob up to speed. "It's just barely possible a license plate has been in there all this time. Fifty-two, for, thirty-five, and one are probable plate numbers. We're hoping the other words are parts of a disjointed thought."

Bob called in the number they put together. The response was slow in coming. It was 'No'. Neither 524-351 nor any combination of those numbers was ever registered to a '56 Ford Fairlane.

"It isn't here." Gordon was crestfallen.

"But, it must be," Kendall vehemently refused to resign herself to failure. "Nothing can bring back your parents, but you'll never know a moment's peace until you know what happened that night. I won't bring our child into the world with this hanging over our heads."

"You're the kid." Denny eyed Gordon. "I didn't make the connection."

"Yeah," Gordon admitted. "I'm the kid, with no memory of the accident or anything that led up to it."

"Someone was trying to scare the doctor into stopping his research," Kendall offered additional threads. "His life was being threatened."

"It was!" The three men interrupted.

"Maybe *whoever* thought Jack didn't scare so easily," Kendall continued unfazed, "or didn't know they were successful, or just didn't care how many ways they stopped him."

"Wasn't he some kind of women's doctor?" Denny asked.

"Obstetrics and Gynecology," Gordon supplied.

"What was he researching anyone would want to stop? How to have better sex," Denny said, half-serious.

"His specialty was infertility," Kendall offered. "He was working on alternatives."

"I prefer the natural way myself. Five kids." Denny grinned proudly. "But if that's all there is then that's all there is. Right?"

"People thought differently in the '50s. Considered it tampering with the natural order. Jack discontinued his own research but others, like my brother, picked up where guys like Jack August left off and kept the work alive. Had they not he and Dorothy certainly would have died for nothing." An echo of Jack's voice pulled at Kendall.

"What if "for" really isn't a number, but F-O-R just as you wrote it? As in *died for nothing*." She pulled out three of the pieces of paper. "

"That's all well and good," Denny said, "but it still leaves us with a scramble that makes no sense."

"Now pull out the numbers," Kendall recommended. "What do we have?"

Bob swept the numbers aside.

"No, no," she said. "Keep everything in order."

"But there are only five numbers," Gordon reminded her, "and all the plates in the books upstairs had six."

"Hold on. What's left?" She asked.

"That man at Bea Goodman," Robert said.

"Suppose Bea isn't a name," Kendall said. "Suppose it's the letter from the plate." Kendall arranged the numbers and letter in their original order. "Oh my god! 52B-351!" She sprang to her feet.

"But who's that man at Goodman?" Denny asked.

"He owned this plate," Kendall said.

"He did?" Gordon asked, feeling a bit confused. The strain of the past few days caught up with him. He fell back into his chair exhausted and hating that he was correct. His dream was a memory which once more took his mind elsewhere to relive another moment in another time. *"What a goon,"* he mumbled then returned to the present flashing on a particular part of that memory. He took Kendall by the shoulders. It was as if they were the only people in the room.

"You're sure?" Gordon asked.

"And so are you," she said.

"I was a child, an unreliable witness, and no judge on earth would believe you."

"There is someone else," Kendall suggested.

"Who would remember our little fracas?" Gordon asked.

"A young man paid to have a good memory."

Angry words spoken on a long ago night crystallized.

"The bouncer," Gordon said.

"All we have to do is find him," Kendall said.

"Where do we begin?" Gordon asked.

"The Ballroom," Kendall suggested as almost a question. "We can only hope the current bookkeeper is a pack rat who kept their old payroll records."

"You want to, maybe, clue us in on what just happened," Denny said as he and Robert sat confused.

Kendall wrote down the new plate number and offered it to Robert. "Please run it. It's a match."

Denny gave his son a nod. Encouraged by his new found memory, Gordon tagged along to await the results.

"There's more going on here than meets the eye," Denny said.

Kendall neither confirmed nor denied.

"Holding back only makes it more difficult for us to help."

"You wouldn't help at all if we told you everything."

Silence reigned as Denny squinted his eyes into tiny slits. Suddenly, he opened them wide and leaned forward in his chair.

"I don't know how you did it but you're the witness."

Kendall remained silent.

"Go ahead," Denny defied her, "tell me I'm wrong."

"It's too much to explain," Kendall protested.

"Lady, I'm retired." Denny leaned back in his chair. "I've got nothing else to do and no place else to go. Take all the time you need."

Chapter 18

-------------------------------- ▼ --------------------------------

The Plot Thickens
Weston, MA – 1966

"It's gonna cost double. I need permission for Flaahrida."

"Whatever! Just don't leave any witnesses this time."

"The witness ain't my fault! You didn't make no provision for abortin' in case there was someone else inna mix. If that bitch hadn't been inna caah inna first place, the kid wouldn'a made it in the second place and there wouldn't be no need to worry about no witness."

"Okay! Okay! Just fix it. I can't allow anyone to find the girl or speak to the officer."

"Got names?"

"It's all in the report."

The line went dead.

It was a set-up. Officer Robert Henderson was in a cruiser at the bottom of the Leverett up-ramp waiting for the light to turn green. A call came in from Tuffy's Bar; a brawl in the alley. "Without help ASAP," the caller said, "someone's gonna get killed." Bob pealed off to the right with his lights flashing and headed for North Station. And, when help arrived the 'someone' who got killed was Bob Henderson.

All was quiet at Tuffy's, but a clang of garbage cans drew Bob into the alley behind the strip of businesses. He called for back-up, drew his weapon and went to investigate. A lone man in a trench coat with a Fedora pulled down over his face was leaning against a building.

"What took ya so long?" The man lit a cigarette and took a long drag. "I was gettin' tired ah waitin'."

"What do you want?" Bob asked.

"What only you can give."

Bob knew the guy meant his life and stalled trying to keep the man talking until back-up arrived.

"You an' that girl know too much." The man took another drag. "Too bad for hur; she saw too much. Too bad for you; you know what she saw." It sounded like dialog from a bad 'B' movie.

"What girl? No girl told me anything."

"Bob, Bob, Bob." The man shook his head. "You shouldn't lie. It ain't nice. Now, what did she tell you?"

"I don't know who you mean," Bob protested.

"That fiery wreck on Storrow, 'bout ten years back. Except the kid wasn't thrown out a window. That bitch pulled him out. Now, I will ask you nicely one last time ... what did she say?"

"There was a screw-up. I wasn't the first on-scene; means it wasn't my case, I didn't hear anything she said," Bob protested.

Bob's friend Denny couldn't let that one go. A decade later, he was still hunting for the witness. But Bob couldn't give up his God-son's father without a fight. He hoped to protect Denny without getting himself killed in the process, but if one of them had to die Bob chose himself. Denny had a wife and a bunch of kids. Bob had only a young name-sake who looked up to him.

The man stepped out his cigarette and clapped as if applauding a performance. "That was very convincing. Still, I ain't buyin'. Time's up. Say good-night, Gracie."

"What?" Bob did not understand the request.

"Don't nobody watch Burns and Allen? They aah a God damned riot," the man said. "So, say good-night, Gracie."

Officer Robert Zachary Henderson was shot in cold blood. A 'quiet' 45 put three bullets into his chest before he could even react. Back-up arrived moments later and found him in a pool of his own blood and died at the scene. He was buried with full honors. Bob's parents were long dead and he never remarried after his wife, Sally, died in childbirth. His current family consisted of his fellow officers, his oldest friend in the world; Dennis Sullivan, who was also one of his pall bearers and gave the eulogy, and his God-son ... Robert Zachary Sullivan. The future *Officer* Robert Zachary Sullivan.

Chapter 19

-------------------------------- ▼ --------------------------------

Honey-Do
Medford – 1982

With the help of Wonderland Ballroom's old employee records and the Department of Motor Vehicles, Robert Sullivan tracked down one-time bouncer Dick Catalano. He lived in the Medford neighborhood where he grew up.

Dick and his wife, Marie, were doing chores when a cruiser pulled up in front of their house. Kendall waited in the car while Robert, Dennis and Gordon walked to the front door and rang the bell. Dick answered wiping his wet hands on a dish towel.

"Officer?" Dick asked perplexed, noting the two civilians behind him.

"Are you Richard Catalano?" Robert asked.

"Yeah, is there a problem?"

"We're investigating a car accident and thought you might be able to help us."

"I haven't witnessed any accidents. Are you sure you have the right Richard Catalano?" Dick asked.

"We do if you were ever a bouncer at Wonderland."

"I was, about a million years ago. Come in out of the cold and let's see if I can help you."

Dick led them into the family room where Marie joined them.

"Can I get you fellas anything?" She asked sitting on the arm of the chair where Dick was, as a matter of habit. As a matter of his own habit, Dick took her hand.

"Nothing thanks," Bob spoke for their group. "Mr. Catalano–"

"Dick, please."

"Dick, we were given to understand that you have a remarkable memory. Do you remember the night Benny Goodman appeared at the Ballroom?"

"Sure, but it's ancient history.

"Anything unusual happen that night?" Bob asked trying not to lead his best and only witness.

"Unusual? You mean like that the orchestra wasn't the only excitement."

"Is that so?" Dennis asked.

"Yeah, a guy caused problems for this woman. She was some little fire-cracker. The man was at least half-again her size, but she flipped him around like a wet rag then nailed the ass-wipe to the floor like a bug."

"Dick, really!" Marie admonished his choice of words and blushed.

"'Scuse my language, honey," he patted his wife's hand. "When there's so much testosterone in one room, my mouth sometimes forgets you aren't one of the guys." He smiled warmly at her. "But my head and my heart, they always know.

"Anyway," Dick turned back to their visitors, "I tossed him out on his ear and told him never to come back. I thought that would be the end of it, ya know, that he'd go home and sleep it off like a good boy. At closing, I followed the woman and her people outside, just in case. Good thing. The guy'd been waiting in the parking lot, still drunk as a skunk. We had a few choice words. He tried to punch my lights out; but I was younger, faster and sober. He had an unfortunate encounter with my fist, cut his lip on my school ring then drove off."

"We were dating then. How come you never said?" Marie asked. "It was very brave."

"More like stupid, honey." Dick looked at his wife. "Back then I had more muscles than brains and wasn't smart enough to be afraid."

"Does your memory live up to its reputation?" Bob continued.

"They test him regularly over at M-I-T," Marie said proudly.

"Do you think you could I-D the man or the woman?"

"If you had pictures from then, sure," Dick assured.

Denny shared the part of the story which pertained to the accident while Gordon exited to get Kendall and test Dick's memory or discover they wasted their time.

"Dick, this is my wife Kendall," Gordon said.

"Ma'am, have you been outside all this time? You must be frozen sti–" he stopped mid-word. "This is her." He looked from Robert to Denny. "She's the one from the Ballroom. That's not possible?"

"It is," Kendall said.

"I suppose Time Overlapped you," Dick's sarcastic tone said he thought it was a prank.

"You're familiar with Overlap?" Kendall quizzed.

"That Old Wives Tale is my Uncle Fred's department. He tells a story from when Dad's family lived in Michigan but it's mostly about a girl – an odd kid with a funny name. His claims is that she got Uncle Fred and his friends to do stuff they didn't really want to do. It was as if she knew too much, like the kids we used to call 'bookworm'. He says that one day she was just there and a week later, she just wasn't. The last day anyone saw her, she confessed to Uncle Fred that she was a Reweaver. I'd say he made it up, but somehow … I don't think so." Dick tried to remember more but failed. Suddenly his eyes lit up. "Aja. Uncle Fred said the kid's name was Aja. Do you know her?"

Kendall touched her belly. "Not yet."

"What's that mean?"

"How much time do you have?" She asked.

Chapter 20

-------------------------------- ▼ --------------------------------

Starke, Florida – 1982

Gordon, Kendall, Dick Catalano and Lieutenant Dennis Sullivan (retired) flew to Jacksonville, Florida, where they picked up their rental car. Two and a half hours of silence later the group arrived at Raiford State Prison; current home of Johnny *'Little Boy'* Rogers. Suffolk County DA, Luthor Stone, arranged through Warden Thompson for Gordon to speak with Little Boy, but only after both he and Dick Mugg-shot I-D'd him.

"It was twenty-six years ago," Gordon said as they drove through the outermost gates. "He will have aged. I won't recognize him."

"Our man may be small-time," Denny said, "but he was a very busy boy; Mugg-shots up the ying-yang. I pulled some strings so you'll be looking at a '55 Mugg-book. You and Dick must each individually identify the same man otherwise we're in the same boat as before."

"Before we go in, win, lose or draw you can't begin to imagine how much we appreciate this, what this means to us," Kendall said, by way of thanking Denny and Dick on behalf of herself and Gordon.

"Can't Kendall do it," Gordon protested.

"To most people Overlap is theoretical far-fetchedness in the extreme," she answered Denny. "To convince a judge and jury it must be you. You and Dick corroborate each other's story. It will be fine. Just keep telling yourself: *I was there. I remember him.*"

The group exited their vehicle and entered the prison. A guard escorted them to an interview room. Dick and Gordon took turns being sequestered. The escort remained while each man searched the

Mugg-book on the table. Dick went first, he wasn't long. Gordon followed; trying desperately to reclaim an instant from his past for himself if not for his unborn child. All the while he recited his new mantra: *"I was there. I can do this. I was there. I can do this."*

"I wish I *could* do it," Kendall told Denny, "but Gordon needs to for closure. Rogers wanted all of us dead. Perhaps he still does and can somehow still manage to make it happen. You did say he's assaulted a few guards and made several attempts at escape."

"Must have figured he had nothing to lose. Lucky for us, the furthest he's gotten from his cell is Solitary," Denny assured her. "He's dangerous but stupid."

"And a sociopath."

"There is that," Denny agreed, "but this is maximum security and the guy's staring down a couple life sentences. He's going nowhere on his own."

Kendall checked her watch. "Gordon's been gone too long."

"I'm sure he's doing fine." Denny patted her shoulder. "He's doing just fine."

As if on cue, Gordon swung open the door. He was a mess. His hair was matted and his brow sweaty, but it was no longer a *worried* brow.

"I did it. I remembered. We picked the same man."

Gordon contacted his office and gave his partner, Gary Mendelson, final instructions for the nearly completed paperwork on his desk. Gordon had the rare pleasure of informing Johnny that the state of Massachusetts would be extraditing him on two counts of manslaughter, two counts of attempted murder and one count of murdering a police officer. He would travel in two days. Gordon's next call was to his uncle.

*   *   *   *

Johnny's lawyer, Arturo Jaconetti – '*The Fat Man*', arrived the next day. Jaconetti had unsuccessfully defended Johnny in '66. To the average listener their conversation, as all others before it, sounded like so much small talk. In reality, Johnny ordered up an escape, a vehicle, some new clothes, a ticket for South America, a passport, and a weapon ... with a silencer.

"I hear a lot's changed since I been inside -- caahs, clothes and rock-and-roll's loudaah then evaah," Johnny said. "Myself, I like a classic caah, a tailahed suit an' a Ahgentine Tango played real quiet." Johnny's time at Raiford had done nothing to diminish his thick accent or improve his grammar neither of which phased Jaconetti. The Fat Man just nodded.

"So, they got me landin' at Logan." Johnny said.

The nod.

"I heard airlines got somethin' called Business Class."

"I'll check into it," The Fat Man assured.

"I got a sunburn once onna top floor ah Logan's paahkin' garage," Johnny said.

"I remember," The Fat Man said.

"How about some aaht for my new diggs?"

"I'll do my best," the Fat man promised.

"Sure, sure. You do that." Johnny said.

The two men embraced knowing they would not see each other again. Jaconetti left, liquidated Johnny's assets, and transferred everything to a numbered Swiss account. The account number, a 45 with a silencer, a passport, and ticket to Rio de Janeiro were left in the glove box of a nondescript car on the roof-top level of Logan Airport's long-term parking garage. A new suit, shirt and tie were laid out in the trunk. Jaconetti arranged for two thugs to stage an escape so John Anthony Rogers could disappear forever.

*   *   *   *

"You fuckin' son-of-a-bitch. I been inna joint twenty-six yee-aahs just waitin' for this moment," Johnny screamed at Adam. "You set me up, had that cop waiting inna E-aah." Johnny pointed his gun at Adam and cocked the trigger.

"I didn't," Adam pleaded for his life. "I thought you got away. You said no one could I-D you and I believed it. If you'd been caught I assumed you'd name me for a reduced sentence."

"You lyin' sack-a-shit! You're the only one knew about the cop an' they got me on chaahges. There ain't no one else could'a told 'em."

"It's conspiracy just for hiring you. I'm an accessory. It was in my best interest to involve no outsiders. It's true. I swear."

Angry as Johnny was he knew that Adam was correct about the law but he didn't care. He wanted every part of the fiasco behind him. This time there would be *no* witnesses.

"Just so you know," Johnny said, "the Catini family don't make no deals with no Feds. Now, say Good-night, Gracie."

Little Boy fired three bullets into Adam's chest. He was dead before he hit the floor. Rogers exited the library in search of Adam's wife.

Weston Police found Adam in the library and Sarah at the top of the stairs. When the Medical Examiner arrived he pronounced John Anthony Rogers dead at the scene. The investigating officer removed an old Smith and Wesson 38 Special, with a four inch nickel plated barrel and wooden grips from Sarah's hand. A single bullet had been fired. Sarah Cohen August was advised of her rights and taken into custody. She used her one phone call to contact Gordon.

"What in Hell happened?" Gordon demanded.

"Where do I start?" Sarah asked.

"Try the beginning," Gordon said impatiently. With Adam and Little Boy dead, Gordon's victory was a brief and now quite hollow.

"The very beginning?" Sarah asked.

"That would be nice," Gordon said unyielding; clueless as to how far back the very beginning was.

"Okay," Sarah sighed, "the very beginning. The night your parents died, I went to bed early but was unable to sleep. The phone rang rather late and Adam and I each picked up on the same ring. Adam spoke first and never knew that I was on the extension to hear about packages; two big ones, one little one. At first I didn't understand. Once I did it was too late to hang up. I was afraid one of them would hear the click, so I kept listening. Adam came to bed after that call. I had no idea his hate for Jack ran so deep or that he would go to such lengths.

"I was still staring at the ceiling when the doorbell rang. Adam answered. It was the Police. They left and Adam came back upstairs to say what happened. In that moment I had a new fear; one day Adam's *caller* would show up and hurt all of *us*. I called the Police for advice. Off the record, the officer said: *'Get a gun and learn to use it.'* Every morning after you kids and Adam left the house I drove to Blue Hills. An Officer Henderson was giving a morning class at the firing range. 'Care and use of a fire arm'."

"Not Robert Henderson!"

Sarah nodded. Event and outcome. Bob Henderson was inadvertently more involved in Gordon's life than he imagined.

"Bob was a good teacher and I was a motivated student. I stayed in practice all these years just in case. Adam never even knew I had the gun. Tonight he got another of those calls and, some twenty minutes later, the caller did show up. He and Adam went into the library. Even from behind that heavy door I heard the yelling then something heavy hit the floor. I called the police, got my gun and waited at the top of the stairs. I should have gotten out of the house. I'm not altogether sure why I didn't. That man came out of the library alone, saw me and ordered me to come down. I was too afraid to move, more afraid not to. I took my chance and aimed. He said: *'You're kidding me with that little gun, Gracie.'* He never even raised his weapon. Guess he didn't think I'd shoot. Until the second I pulled the trigger, frankly, I wasn't sure I'd shoot. The police found him were he landed ... in a heap at the bottom of the stairs."

"You had to know what Adam was. Why on earth did you marry him?" Gordon demanded as if it still mattered.

"In the beginning, he was fun and I loved him," Sarah said. "He wouldn't commit so I got pregnant. I thought we'd get married and he'd discover how much he loved me. We got married all right," Sarah shook her head. "Things went from bad to worse when I got pregnant the second time then only marginally better because Peter was a boy.

"I had been planning to divorce Adam when your parents died, take my children and leave, maybe leave Boston. Susan and Peter might be alive today if I had. Then the unthinkable happened ... and Adam was your guardian. If I left, I'd have had to leave you behind.

If not for you we could have gotten away. Because of you we had to stay. *We had to*! God knows what he would have done to you without us there. And I ... I just couldn't keep myself from blaming you; hating you. It's why I've insisted on spending holidays and yahrzeit together. I didn't know how else to make it up."

"Why didn't you tell me?"

"Tell you when? Tell you what? That your uncle hired a hit-man to kill your family. That he had his brother killed. By the time you were an adult it was too late. And what was my proof? That Adam and some *'voice'* talked about packages? What if I spoke up and they never found the guy? Imagine what Adam would have done to me when he was willing to have his own blood killed. I did the only thing I could. I bought a gun, learned to use it and prayed I never had to." Sarah shuddered reliving the moment she shot Johnny. "Can you ever forgive me?"

Gordon silently digested Sarah's revelation. Even after the events in Florida and meeting Johnny face-to-face, a small part of Gordon refused to believe Adam planned the deaths of his entire family and that his own survival had been a fly in the ointment.

"Why would Adam do it?" Gordon needed to know what had been more valuable than his parents' lives.

"Adam was motivated by exactly two things. Hate and money. He had limitless quantities of the former. No quantity of the later was ever satisfactory.

"Adam used to try manipulating Jack into discussing his work, into revealing something, but he never said a word beyond that one day everyone could read about it in *The North East Corridor Medical Journal*. That must have meant Jack would eventually be published, possibly become famous. To Adam's view it was all the more reason to hate him." Sarah paused. "Everything your parents left, including insurance, was in a trust for you yet, suddenly, Adam was rolling in money. It came from somewhere and it was too much all at once to have come from selling real estate," Sarah said.

"That's it. Jealousy and money." Gordon couldn't believe that was all there was to it.

"People have killed for less," Sarah reminded him.

Gordon remembered once voicing that his uncle hated their family. Jack assured Gordon that Uncle Adam loved them very much. Jack sounded as if he believed it. Gordon wanted to believe as well. Once he was living in Adam's house, it was clear his father simply hadn't seen Adam for the cold, cruel bastard he was. By the time Jack finally did, it was too late. In the months just prior to their deaths, Dorothy and Jack shared heated words regarding the creation of their wills and were under the false impression Gordon was asleep and did not hear them.

"You don't still want him to be Gordon's guardian!" Dorothy protested. "Adam's a beast."

"What I want is irrelevant," Jack said. "Our parents are gone. You have no siblings. Who do we nominate in Adam's place?"

Dorothy was silent.

"Fabulous," Jack said sarcastically, realizing Dorothy had been correct about Adam from the start. "Adam it is."

Gordon's life with Adam and Sarah had been a painful misery, but Sarah was likely the only thing standing between him and an almost certain death. Given her circumstances, Sarah had done her best and she was only human. She and Gordon forgave each other.

John Rogers was a convicted felon serving 'Life' in Florida. He escaped during extradition to stand trial on additional felony charges in another state. Given that his were the only finger prints on the weapon found near his body which; ballistics showed, was used to commit a homicide in the home where he was found, there was overwhelming evidence that Sarah August had fired in self defense. The charges against her were dropped.

Chapter 21

------------------------------ ▼ ------------------------------

The Return
Miami – 1996

Signs of life are passages through time
A means of getting there from here
Of seeing life's smiles and tears
Watching grass grow and trees sway
Life's little nuances and segues.

Avra arrived at Dr. Spector's office, no more wanting to be there a second time than the first. His greeting was pleasant enough but it was obvious he believed Overlap would prove to be a hoax. He ushered her through to his inner office again, where she remained standing. He plopped into the leather chair behind his desk and eagerly rubbed his hands together.

"Now," he said almost giddy, "I'm dying to see your proof?"

"I don't have it," she said.

"What a surprise!" Spector's voice was smug.

Avra reached for the long chain she still wore and stripped it from her neck. The wedding band, which once belonged to her great-grandmother, was no longer there. At fourteen, it found a new home on the middle finger of her right hand.

"What I do have is this." Avra displayed the item which assumed the ring's place on the necklace. It was half of a bright new silver dollar sliced top to bottom. The year on her half read *96*.

"Many people have such sentimental items," he said, "myself included."

"It was left for you at the front desk of Biscayne Hospital Rehab. Came with a note: *From an admirer.*"

"But, how–," he stammered.

"I'm the one who left it and why I don't have my proof; you have it. Your half is the other half of my half."

Avra removed the token from her chain, placed it on the desk and slid it toward Spector. His expression said he did not believe her but pulled out his key chain anyway. A considerably tarnished half-coin hung from it.

"These halves could fit together with a million others just like them," Spector vehemently protested.

"If there *were* a million others just like them. Check the side," she instructed.

"As I said, like a million others." He was loath to accept the item as proof of anything.

"Yes, minted *after* 1964. You got yours in '55, before the Treasury instituted silver on top and bottom surfaces only," Avra confirmed.

Spector examined his own half.

"How did I miss that?" He asked of no one in particular, having prided himself on always logging even the smallest detail. "Guess I was too young and busy being flattered to notice the copper center. Still, the coin means very little."

"So you say now. I assure you, these halves go only with each other. Turn them over," she instructed.

Engraved at the top of the coin was the name Milton split in half. *Mil–ton.* At the bottom was the name Avra, also split in half. *Av–ra.* Spector's half that read *'ton'* and *'ra'*

"My wife denied it from the start but I always assumed this etching was our names. Well, I was half right," he mumbled mostly to himself. "I never even noticed Sandra until I got this. It's mostly the reason I asked her out."

"Then you kept asking her out and she didn't go to New York to be a dancer."

"How did you know that?"

"It was simple really, being that I inherited Mother and Grammy's clever gene." Aja indicated the photo on his desk. "The frame is engraved *Tony and Sandy* and you're standing right in front of the Rehab. I just seized the opportunity."

"Which opportunity?"

"To be in the right place at the right Time – a kid on her way into the Rehab when you and Sandy were standing outside of it. A kid who agreed to take your photo because no one else was around on the day you proposed."

"That was ... you?"

"That was me."

"And here I meant about Sandy wanting to become a dancer. How do you know *that*?" Spector's continued.

"Unlike most men, most women, especially dancers share their hopes and dreams when they're alone with their friends ... in cars ... on their way to class. My mother was one of the friends in Sandy's car. There is also printing on her sweat shirt and the bag at her feet." Avra indicated the photo again. "Both read Hott Jazz."

"It was a dance movement back then."

"Hot with one 'T' was the dance movement," Avra corrected. "Hott with two 'T's is Mother's dance company. Old habits die hard; even in the past, even for Reweavers including my mom. She has bags and shirts printed for all of her serious students. Sandy got a bag and a shirt. Not a stretch to say *she* was a serious student. She ever say which teacher inspired her?"

"Didn't have to. I was there. I was some years older than the other kids, but there was local area buzz about these dance classes so I went. Turns out I'm no dancer so it was just the one class, but it's where I met Sandy the first time. The mouth on her." Spector shook his head in dismay. "I thought she was a bigot. The woman running the class put a stop to it, but she couldn't be your mother. That woman had to be around thirty then. Today, she'd be older than I am. If I remember correctly, her name was Candy *Something-or-other*. Audrey said your mother's name is Kendall."

"That's because Mother's name is Kendall. But when Uncle Terry was little he mispronounced it as Candle. Candle morphed into Candy which is the name mother used when she traveled to 1955 and taught the class you took. 1955 was the year you got your coin, the year I shoved you in Sandy's direction to discover she wasn't a bigot after all and both of you realized you couldn't live without each other. Do you want more? Do you need more?"

It was clear Spector neither wanted nor needed anything else.

"Shall we begin?" Avra asked.

Milton Spector nodded.

Avra's saga finished where it began. It was a tale of people who opened their homes to relations 'unknown' to them. Such welcome can be viewed only as comfort ... the comfort strangers. Everything else and everything in between was the story of family and love so strong it altered the outcome of events ... and closed the holes in time.

Chapter 22

------------------------------ ▼ ------------------------------

Epilogue

"Destiny is not a matter of chance;
it is a matter of choice."
– William Jennings Bryant

Avra told of the way things came to be what they currently were; confirming that everyone was living the outcome Time always intended. As enlightening as it was, Spector wished to understand how Avra could possibly know what an entity such as Time wanted. She revealed the mark on her arm; said that its circle was newly closed; that the letter 'T' had once been at its center; and that there was only one way The Red Tattoo ever changed – Time was satisfied. The altered outcome was life as it was always meant to be; all for a reason perhaps none of them would ever figured out ... or much like even if they did. Avra recommended he consult his original notes to confirm it was true.

Spector's 'education' consisted of leaning how and why, in a past now set in stone, he and Sandra Scott seemed continually to be thrown together. Once upon a time, he worked at a Rehab. The woman who conducted Sandy's dance class had a part-time job at the hospital to which the Rehab was attached. Every day after the woman's job ended she visited a *friend* at the Rehab and the unreliable bus, destined to make her late more often than not, was her only means of getting to Jim Ferretti's studio, which meant class would be abbreviated more often than not. So hungry was Sandy for dance knowledge that she refused to allow it and provided an alternative to the unacceptable bus. Each day, she swung by the Rehab and picked up the woman.

As sure as any other reason Sandy was at the Rehab she was there to be in proper proximity for Milton Spector to even notice her then notice, too, that she had a kind heart and wasn't really the bigot he first thought. Sandy arrived at the Rehab each day with a friend in tow, Hardy James, who she picked up every day as well. Spector soon discovered Sandy's true heart had nothing to do with the hurtful and hateful words she uttered the first day he laid eyes on her and that it isn't just the monkeys who play *'monkey see, monkey do'*. Sandy's parents taught her the ugly words she said to Hardy. With guidance from a woman named *Candy* and Hardy's friendship she unlearned them. Sandy's desire to dance and her actions which originally sprung from greed became an act of friendship so great, it would last a lifetime. The daily rides she gave to her teacher and classmate created a scenario where Sandy became her own little circle of events.

Jim Ferretti's story ran thus, he knew in advance that his landlord would force him to pay out his lease whether he used the studio or not. It was the reason Ferretti never even tried to terminate it. Instead, he decided to 'fix' his landlord by withholding the keys until the lease ran out. Good thing. Upon arrival in New York, Ferretti was summarily denied entré into the Big Apple's dancing school community. Turned out he only knew a good thing when he saw it. Evaluations of him as a dance teacher were that "he sucked" and as a dancer he sucked worse. He returned to Miami more humble than when he left and hired Sandra Scott who not only excelled at dance but possessed the ability to pass along the dance knowledge she gained from her teacher; the person who became her life-long friend. Hardy James.

Four times a year Sandy traveled to New York and crashed on his sofa. She took class with him and Paul then brought her new-found knowledge back to her students. In one of the very earliest New York classes, she met and became friends with a sexy, graceful, talented, and beautiful black woman, Angelica Winthrop. Angela. Hardy teased Sandy saying she owed him an introduction for all the free sofa time, lumpy though it was. For Hardy and Angela, it was love at first sight. They were married within the year.

That same year Sandra Scott and Milton Spector also said *'I do'*, each knowing that true and honest love doesn't come along so often one can simply walk away from it. That was a lesson Avra's father learned the hard way. He sent Kendall away then had to track her down like a bloodhound and beg her back into his life.

Avra further clarified the purpose of Ferretti flopping on Broadway; why he bombed, big time, then she shined a Proscenium light on why Sandy didn't end up in New York professionally either, though that had been her dream. Both Sandra Scott and James Ferretti were meant to be in Miami; Ferretti to continue operating his studio there, Sandy to teach in it. It had all worked out. Everyone ended up where they belonged – Ferretti, Sandy, Spector, and Avra's own mother.

Ordinarily, the day Audrey took Grown Kendall to audition for Ferretti, she would have left her young daughter at home. Except both of her usual day-time sitters were booked. Audrey had no choice but to bring her child along. Young Kendall stood quietly beside her mother with eyes as big as saucers each time she watched the grown version of herself dance. Somewhere in the middle of the performance at North Miami Senior High Little Kendall said, *'Mommy, that looks fun. I want to do that when I grow up.'* There was nothing for Audrey to do but encourage her daughter's choice. After all, her pretend brother had already 'visited' and said that, beyond listening to her parents, she was the boss of her; that she was the one to decide what she did. And Audrey knew that in the future that was yet to be, her tiny daughter's choice was afait acompli. It had already happened.

Within three months of Ferretti's arrival in Manhattan he was back in Miami and hired Sandra Scott. Sandy's very first position was that of teacher to *The Babies*, Ferretti's youngest students, one of whom was a three year old Kendall Layne Spaulding – the child who became the woman who would one day teach Ferretti, Sandy and Hardy everything they knew about dance, the value of friendship and kindness toward others. Sandy's other purpose in Miami was to turn Milton Spector into a father … twice.

Neither Hardy nor Angela knew their own fathers and had no connection whatsoever to them. When their own child was born, they named him after the only father in their lives … Sandy's husband. They named their son Milton Candide James – Candide being the moniker of the eternal optimist from the operetta of the same name. It was also the closest masculine name to Candy; the woman who encouraged Hardy to be optimistic about his future, gave him the first break of his life then disappeared from it.

*   *   *   *

In a former life, Hardy James worked relentlessly hard, often to the exclusion of all else including his son, for statuettes that sat mostly ignored from the minute they were awarded. For the most part, they gathered dust on a shelf in his office. In Hardy's former life, earning them seemed to be a let down. His son felt an equal part of that let down and sought regular council from Uncle Tony.

How do I deal with being the product of a life that always has something missing from it? He complained. *Shit! Is it me? Am I not enough of a son because I chose a life outside the dance world? At this rate, I'll never know how being a family should feel.*

That was then. This was now, as it is said, and, the fact was, Young Tony's professional choice was never an issue for his father; not in either life. In the previous incarnation of Hardy James' life, his angst over the awards revolved around the *visibility* they provided; that someone from his past might *see* him and *contact* him to say they were *proud* of him. Without the approval of that someone, Hardy's life was something less than complete making his awards instantly meaningless.

The tiny difference in this life was that Hardy's son had no need to question himself or seek Uncle Tony's council ... at his office ... on the day Avra Jade August first entered Milton Spector's life. In this life, Young Tony didn't see Avra as a kindred spirit; because in this life he didn't see her at all. Being at Uncle Tony's had been an outcome that was able to be changed and so it was. Avra keeping her interaction with him fairly nonexistent meant that no events occurred on the heels of it. Young Tony was absent from Uncle Tony's office because in this life, in the days following his near brush with death (by bee sting) his father's life miraculously became complete. In this life, far from the award obsessed Hardy of old was a comfortable and relaxed man; a man not only glad his son carried Milton Spector's first

~ 242 ~

name and nick-name but a man who was thrilled to give them top billing. 'My Two Tonys'. In this life, the statuettes Hardy earned for being a Broadway choreographer were important only because he shared having earned them with family and friends; among whom was Kendall, and he never failed to say so in his acceptance speeches. In this life the statuettes of the same name took second fiddle to the living breathing variety. In this life, Hardy glibly called the seven earlier ones 'fancy paperweights' and referred to the later ones; those earned after Kendall reentered his life, as 'My Lesser Two Tonys'.

*   *   *   *

Last but not least was Gordon's promise to himself; find a way to thank Sylvia for returning his Kendall to him whole. The night of the day before Avra's first trip through Time he went to her room; held his daughter close; and asked for the biggest favor of his life. Avra could hardly believe that her father knew what lie ahead. He would not say how he knew, just requested that she give Sylvia a message from him, "Thank you for my life with my wife and child. I love them more than anything … more than everything. I wanted to be sure you knew, I cried."

*   *   *   *

At the conclusion of Milton Spector and Avra's second meeting, he did as she suggested; he listened to his tape then read and reread his original notes which were identical to his new notes, only not. 'Only not' would present a problem. Even as a respected member of the medical community, no one would believe the notes, the tape, or him; the same way he initially did not believe Audrey and then Avra.

That was then. This is now, he kept saying; by way of "mea culpa". Now he was a believer, but there were few like him – believers who were not also travelers. For the Time being, the newly converted Milton Spector would save the tape and both sets of notes for another day, a day they *would* be believed. It was a day, no doubt, far into the future … or well into the past.

Breinigsville, PA USA
20 January 2010
231030BV00001B/7/P

9 780982 577806